INVINCIBLE

ELIZABETH SAFLEUR

Elizabeth SaFleur LLC
PO Box 6395
Charlottesville, VA 22906
Elizabeth@ElizabethSaFleur.com
www.ElizabethSaFleur.com

Edited by Patricia A. Knight
Cover design by Shanoff Designs

ISBN:978-1-949076-11-0

People say a broken heart can kill, but it's really the secrets that take you down.
~Alexander Rockingham, II

PROLOGUE

June 8, 1981

Alice Wynter took two steps forward and spat, "No." Her eyes, a cold, muddy brown, blazed with fiery hatred directed entirely at him. The two guards who'd thrown him off the Wynter estate flanked either side of her, their faces as still and cold as the marble statues that stood in the gardens behind the closed iron gate.

Alexander curled his fists around the bars. "I just want to see him. One last time. Then, I'll go." He wasn't a man who begged, but for a chance to talk to Charles one last time he'd get on his knees and crawl over broken glass. Charles had hours, perhaps minutes, left to live.

Her eyes narrowed slightly. "And allow you to corrupt my son further? Never."

He should have known she would not reconsider. The woman lacked any semblance of human compassion. He wondered if she felt any emotion at all. "I just want to say good-bye." His forehead fell to one of the railings and his voice cracked, but at least he could say the words. His hands slipped on the rails, leaving a blood trail from palms that'd been scraped raw by the pavement when the guard threw him outside. The serrated skin burned, but he couldn't give a fuck. "Please," he said again.

"I forbid it."

He lifted his head to receive more visual daggers from the woman who called herself Charles' mother. *Mother.* What woman would do this to her son? "We don't have much time. He's dying." For God's sake, just a hundred feet behind her in his childhood bedroom, Charles lay alone. She'd left him with medical personnel who cared about paychecks and IVs not getting infected. Couldn't she see? Charles needed someone who loved him there.

She strode forward so only ten feet separated them. Her lips thinned to a sharp line, and her eyes glowed with revulsion. "And why does my son have no time, Alexander Rockingham? Because of you." She raised her arm and pointed a finger at him. "You're worse than the devil. You're an abomination, an affront to God almighty. Get out of my sight and never come back, or I'll ensure your life is a living hell."

Her hatred didn't matter to him. He'd apologize. Hell, he'd agree with her. He'd say anything to get back inside to see Charles, but his throat clogged and he couldn't breathe. He had to keep trying. "At least let me talk to Rebecca."

"She doesn't want to see you. She told you to leave. Now do it."

For long minutes, the drone of katydids in the trees swaying in the warm early summer air was the only sound between them. He wrestled with what he could say, what he could do to just get her to unlock this gate and allow him inside. Fuck, he needed to be with *Charles*. He'd *promised* he wouldn't let him die like this.

His eyes caught movement just behind the guards. "Rebecca," he called out. "Please, I need to talk to you." Her eyes frantically darted back and forth between him, Alice and the guards. She shook her head violently and then grimaced, rolling her lips between her teeth as if choking back words or tears. He would never know which as she stepped backward, turned, and fled up the front steps to disappear inside. How could Rebecca have told him to leave? How could she have simply watched through the window as those guards had wrestled him down the stone steps of the entrance, manhandled him down the drive and thrown him onto the road. The gate had locked with a loud clank as he'd picked himself up from the asphalt.

How could this be happening?

He leveled his gaze once more on Charles' mother—though the woman didn't deserve the title—and leaned closer to the gate, his face between two rails. He couldn't allow a love that had consumed his life to end like this. He dug deep into his soul and reached for the last shred of self-preservation he could muster. "One day, Alice Peyton Wynter ... "

Hearing him speak her full name, she lifted her chin sharply. No one dared address her that way, did they? She'd left him no choice. He was not surrendering to the likes of her.

"One day," he repeated. "I will walk through these gates as owner of this place." He glanced up at the two W's engraved in oval plates at the gate top. "And, I'll do it with a sledgehammer in my hands to erase anything or anyone bearing the name of Wynter."

"Over my dead body." Alice made a show of folding her arms over her chest. The guards widened their legs as if readying themselves for an altercation. "If he tries to step one foot on this estate, shoot him," she said without even glancing their way. "And aim for the heart."

"Yes, ma'am." One of the guards pulled a Glock out of the back of his pants and let it dangle along his leg.

They didn't need to shoot him. He was already half dead. If he couldn't get inside to comfort Charles in his last moments of life, if he'd been tossed aside by Rebecca, he'd lost every reason to live.

He peered up the drive, his eyes finding the window on the second floor on the far right hand corner of the mansion. "Charles," he whispered. "I'll be back, no matter how long it takes. I promise." His gut roiled with the truth. Charles likely had hours left—and he would not be there. Charles would slip from this earth without him, something he'd promised him months ago he wouldn't let happen.

He gazed at Alice Wynter, who'd turned and headed back to the house. The two guards still faced him. "I promise, I will be back," he called to her back. "Even if I have to walk over your grave to do it."

1

Club Accendos, Washington, D.C. ~ Present day

Alexander got three steps down the hallway when his nephew barreled around the corner, breathless and agitated.

"Ryan?"

"She's dead."

His spine snapped ramrod straight. "Say that again. Slower."

"Alice Wynter passed away last night."

He drank in every word, every syllable of that statement and let it knock around inside his chest. Jubilant relief should have followed. Instead, familiar anger, like a snaking trail of lava, moved inside as if erupting anew.

He jerked his head toward the end of the hall. "Let's go to my office."

Ryan kept up with his long strides as his feet went on autopilot. They had to move fast. "The shell company set up?"

"Years ago, and before you ask, I just checked in with the legal team twenty minutes ago to make sure it's ready to go."

"Good. Let's move on it." He nodded his head at a couple stepping out of the elevator. Once inside, he turned to Ryan. "I want the purchase of the estate done by day's end."

"The family's putting up a fight over the grounds. They're willing to convey all the paintings, antiques, collectibles, but they want to keep three acres. Apparently, there is a family gravesite—"

"Nonnegotiable. I'll pay whatever they want, but I will have the entire estate."

"They say money isn't the object."

He blew through his nostrils. "With the Wynters, money is always the object. The last surviving heir can't afford another bankruptcy, and he doesn't know how to live without money—a lot of it."

They rose the short distance in silence, and when the elevator doors opened, he barreled forward and cracked open the door to his office. Clarisse straightened from bending over a pile of papers on his desk. She nodded but didn't speak and scooted out through the adjoining door to her office.

"How much are you willing to spend?" Ryan settled into one of the chairs arranged in front of his desk.

"Start at $25 million. Go up to $100 million if you have to. I don't care. Before midnight tonight, Ryan, signed papers —" he aimed his finger down to the blotter on his desk. "— right here."

Ryan scratched his chin. "Alexander, I have to ask. What are you doing?"

The man had done well in helping him make today happen—one of the greatest days of his life in the last few decades. He deserved to know the truth.

Alexander sank into his chair and leaned back. "Keeping a promise."

He always kept his promises, and this one was long overdue—forty fucking years overdue.

2

Alexander's legs complained from standing on the asphalt, but the crumbling house behind the iron gate demanded a five-minute study. The once-grand drive was cracked and littered with dead leaves. "You haven't aged well, old girl." As if in answer to his mild insult, a loose shutter banged in the chilly air of the Connecticut fall.

He stepped back and gazed at the two large W's embedded in each of the gate's swing frames. To think he'd once been shut out by this rusted gate. The woman who lived behind it had stood on the other side, not ten feet away, and obliterated his life. He regripped the handle of the sledge-hammer hanging heavy along his side. Time to even the score.

"Set it up, Tony."

The metallic screech of the ladder snapping into place startled a few birds from a nearby oak. Alexander climbed to the top, his coat flapping in the incessant gusts. Let the wind try to push him off. He was doing this. Two precise hits on the W and the metal oval hung sideways. One stubborn screw refused to let go, just like the witch who'd lived behind it for the last seventy years. One more dead center hit and the inlaid plate shot to the ground. The other W met the asphalt without a fight. Disappointing, really. The sledge-hammer fit his palm so beautifully. After all the devastation she'd wrought, her family's emblem should have put up a better fight.

As he descended, he shrugged off Tony's outstretched hand. Today was a day for doing things himself, and his muscles vibrated from the challenge of dismantling this cruel place, with his own hands if needed, brick by brick.

After freeing the inelegant padlock and unwinding the chains, the gate swung open with a groan. The flimsy plate made a satisfying scrape under his shoe as he strode through the two stone pillars and onto the former Wynter estate.

Tony cleared his throat. "Sir?"

"Follow me in the car. I'm walking in." Promises made, promises kept was his motto. He'd told Alice Wynter the day he took possession of her property he'd walk right up to the front door, sledgehammer in hand. Her replying smirk and her words—"Over my dead body"—echoed in some far-off corner of his mind. He hadn't wished her real harm, not then and not now, but he had no qualms about treading the ground that now covered her corpse.

He took his time advancing on the house as his mother hen assistant crept behind him in the Mercedes, the engine purring like a sated lion. He tuned into every bird chirp in the trees lining the drive, every leaf crunch under his shoe, every crack he stepped on as he fulfilled the first of three promises he'd made the last time he was here.

The first, that one day as the new owner of Wynter Estate, he'd stride in by the power of his own legs.

The second, he'd stand before Charles once more and say all that needed to be said.

The third? Well, that last one was hard as hell to even think about. He'd deal with his thoughts about Rebecca, later.

He took the front steps two at a time and paused at the white double doors with their ostentatious lion knockers that had once barred his entrance. He lifted the sledgehammer, and a hand fell on his bicep. Tony had ghosted up behind him and now stood with a set of keys dangling from his index finger.

"That's a first," Alexander said. In eighteen years, Tony had never intervened in his actions.

"Yes, sir."

Alexander exchanged the hammer for the keys with a slight scowl the man didn't deserve, but today he was incapable of pretension.

The door creaked open. A swath of light cut into the large entry hall, and a breeze blew dry leaves in over his feet to skitter across the marble. Two strides and his feet landed on the round inlay in the center of the circular portico. His skin prickled at the lack of life. He drew in a long breath, held it for three seconds, and pushed out the air in his lungs. So much was off. Stillness surrounded him, not the ticking of the grandfather clock and ice clinking against crystal tumblers. The smell of paint thinner and mold filled the air, not the expected lemon furniture polish. So much was right, too, like no Alice Wynter with her pinched, disapproving face.

He stepped up to the bottom stair of the split staircase, the red carpet fraying on the edges. A box with paint cans and an abandoned brush, stiffened with dried yellow paint peeking from out the top, stood on the first step. Someone had the presence of mind to touch up the place before it was sold. How quaint given he was going to gut the house.

At the top of the landing, the family portrait still clung to the wall. He glared at the likenesses of Alice Wynter, her husband, and one son. "Unwanted and abandoned." The last time he'd stood in this spot, four people smiled out of that painting. She must have had a new one commissioned, leaving out the son Alexander had the audacity to love and the reason he'd been banished from this place.

"Typical," he muttered under his breath. The Wynter family once had everything material, but nothing truly important. What he wouldn't give right now to have brought a blow torch along with his sledgehammer. Oil paint caught fire quickly.

He parked that old anger which arose whenever his mind dwelled on the hateful family matriarch and turned away, otherwise, he'd never get through this day. He turned to his assistant. "Tony, go see if there's any wood outside? I feel like having a fire."

Where to start? He had choices. Assess each room, one at a time? Go straight to Charles' room? Or had the old woman dismantled that small bedroom as she'd promised? To his left, a thin strip of sunlight cut through a crack in a set of double doors.

The pocket doors slid open easily, and sunlight hit him square in the chest. Abandoned furniture, some cloaked in sheets and tarps, and others left exposed to collect dust, piled like Lincoln logs against the far wall. He strode to the middle window framed in powder blue velvet curtains. Through wavy cylinder glass, Alexander's gaze swept over the priceless view that would make a realtor orgasm on sight. Tall oak and maple trees, now a tangle of bare branches, hugged the edges of a thick grass carpet that rolled away from the house for several, undulating acres, the Connecticut River a sliver of sparkling reflections in the distance. That wasn't what interested him. Rather, his full attention landed on a brick walkway lined by boxwoods that led straight to a walled square, the family gravesites. *That's where he lies. In there.*

He couldn't get any oxygen into his lungs.

He swayed a little on his feet, and his hand landed on the nearest piece of furniture, a small Sheraton writing desk. It was a tiny, delicate thing designed for a woman. *Jesus.* So this is where the head bitch had sat writing her letters to other society members about him and his deplorable ideas, how he had corrupted her son, Charles, and led astray "that young girl Rebecca."

One such letter forwarded to him years ago by his friend, the Duchess Marchand, floated up in his brain like a ghost. *Alexander Rockingham is the devil incarnate, and I will make sure he never sees either of them again.* His fingers curled into a fist, and he smashed his knuckles down on the desk. His forehead pricked with sweat. He'd grown used to that bone-deep ache in his chest, ever present like an old war wound, but seeing where she planted herself, overlooking her family's Memorial where her son lay six feet under? An assassin's knife spearing his heart couldn't have called up more pain.

"You didn't deserve him," he gritted out. He leaned down and grasped one table leg, dragged it through the house, and let it bang down the stone steps of the front entrance. He tossed it in the middle of the drive to deal with later. Nothing was as important as getting inside those Memorial walls.

His legs got him to the stone archway of the Memorial, and he stood there for long moments, his stomach churning with nerves and disgust. Inside, tufts of yellowed grass clustered around black rail fence that cordoned off several gravesites. A stone bench for someone to sit and reflect on lost loved ones lay lopsided, having lost one support leg. Dead tree branches littered the base of a large maple tree in the corner. Having everything and valuing nothing.

He moved with slow strides, his gaze bouncing from headstone to headstone. Some names were etched clearly in polished granite, some so worn by age they were nothing but grooves giving them the appearance of children's art projects, tiny hands pressed into clay molds for posterity.

He paused at a dirt mound, not yet tamped down by rain or taken over by nature. Alice Wynter's grave marker was an angel with a trumpet raised to the sky. The wretched woman was probably barking orders to the heavens as he stood there. *Keep him out. He's the devil. Corrupted. Evil.* God, his gut roiled—not for the remembered words but for all the retorts he'd swallowed over the years.

He turned, and found the only thing that mattered. A black granite headstone rose from the ground in the center of the graveyard. He choked down the lump that rose in his throat as he took in each letter of the name etched there.

CHARLES DURHAM

JULY 12, 1959 - JUNE 8, 1981

Fuck the Wynters. They hadn't the respect to include their own son's last name on his headstone. The black color of the granite raised more anger. Nothing that hateful family did was without meaning, and the black sheep reference might have him knock that trumpet off the shrew's marker with his sledgehammer.

Instead, Alexander crept closer to where Charles lay. With a long inhale, he placed his hand on the modest stone, warmed by the fading sunlight streaming through the trees. At least there was that.

"Charles, I'm here." His rough whisper hurt in his throat. "You're where you asked to be ... in the sun."

Because he said he looked better with a tan. Wasn't that what he'd said, lying in that hospital room? Alexander's throat closed, and he had to force air into his chest.

For four decades, he'd caged the agony of losing Charles,

never letting it fully out because he knew this day would come. Today, armed guards couldn't throw his ass into the street like they had many times, including the day of Charles' funeral, because he just couldn't stop trying to get inside. He would stand here like he'd promised that bitch staring at him from the other side of the locked front gate. Tomorrow that thing was scrap metal. Today? He scrubbed his chin, not quite sure what to do first. Ask Charles for forgiveness for taking so long to get here? Ask if he was all right?

"Rebecca, you should be standing here with me." The words were lost in the wind like she had been the same day Charles had died. The three of them—once so close air couldn't get between them—were now as far apart as three people could get. One was dead. The other was just ... gone. The raw absence of them both cut his heart as if they'd been ripped apart only yesterday.

His hand grew raw from worrying his five o'clock shadow. He hadn't had two nickels to rub together back then. Now? At sixty years old, he had everything. He could have anything. He could fix anything—except them. He couldn't bring back Charles or save Rebecca from running away from him.

"If there is a God ... " Was there? It was one question he'd never been able to answer. He was done hedging his bets, though. He, a man who didn't get on his knees for anyone, dropped to the ground and began to pray.

Truth told, he couldn't have anything. He had lost everything that mattered long ago.

3

Eric pulled up to the object in the middle of the limestone drive. That wasn't ... It couldn't be ... Oh, yes, it was. A Sheraton writing desk lay on its back, legs pointed heavenward like a submissive dog.

He put on his sunglasses, lifted himself out of the driver's seat, and stifled a mild groan. Annoying jet lag. His brain seemed to be floating in molasses—and on fire. He stood over the antique and scratched his stubble, then turned to squint up at the Wynter country estate home. He still didn't understand why he was here or what Alexander was doing with this crumbling place. And the price?

"Two hundred million." Eric sighed. "I don't understand, Alexander." The man didn't do things rashly. Something was afoot, not that Eric was displeased to be here. Yesterday morning he'd been at the bottom of the man's exclusive guest list. By that afternoon, he'd been summoned to the States by Ryan Knightbridge, Alexander's nephew, for his "estate settlement genius"—exact words. A tad exaggerated, but he'd take it.

A man with the broadest shoulders he'd seen outside a

comic book launched across the pebble drive toward him. His black, formal, coat flapped in the wind.

"Mr. Morrison?" The man extended his hand. "Tony. Alexander's assistant. We expected you—" Tony turned his handshake, glanced at his Rolex, and then glared at Eric "—tomorrow."

"Eric." He flexed and broke Tony's grip. "Caught the first flight from London." He leaned to peer at the house over Tony's shoulder. "Alexander inside?"

Tony folded his arms over his chest. "Mr. Rockingham doesn't do surprises."

Did the guy think to scare him off to a hotel for twenty-four hours? Not when he finally had an opportunity to serve Alexander. "Yeah, well, I was also told he was in a hurry. So, this desk—"

"Mr. Rockingham is walking the property. You can wait inside."

Okay, Eric wasn't getting anything out of this guy. He scanned the front of the house and noted the walkway to the side yard and presumably a pool and gardens beyond. *Perfect.* "I could use a walk. I'll take a look around." He darted around the human tank.

"Inadvisable."

Eric twisted to glance back over his shoulder at Tony. "Excuse me?"

"Just give him some space." Tony reached into his jacket, drew out a pack of cigarettes, and held it out to him as if in a peace offering.

"I don't smoke."

Tony patted his chest. "Damn. Come with me. I'll show you inside."

Okay, they were playing the who's-got-the-biggest-cajones game. *Whatever.* He followed Tony toward the house, because why not? The man needed a light, and Alexander needed space. Eric needed to keep his ass here and closer to Alexander than he'd ever imagined possible. He wasn't going back to watching Alexander from the sidelines as he had for the last seven fricking years—one of his endless guests at the man's home-turned-BDSM-playground—dreaming, fantasizing, lusting after Alexander like a teenager on steroid-induced hormones.

He stepped inside the entryway and froze. Okay, now the $200 million price tag made sense. Artwork crammed every inch of the walls. He counted a Kirchner, a Botticelli, a DaVinci line drawing, and at least five—no six—Jean Metzinger oils. He let out a whistle. Was the final heir, Marston Wynter, stupid? Sure, the man had been banned from every auction house and reputable seller activity due to that little illegal ivory-selling stint a few years ago, but he could have gotten someone to offload this hoard.

"Guess the bad reputation stuck." He turned toward Tony but found himself alone.

Well, no time like the present to start earning his genius reputation. His footsteps echoed a little in the portico as he strode by an art auctioneer's dream. He had never understood people's obsessions with owning things and collecting property like Monopoly board wins. The world offered so much to explore. Of course, he'd be out of a job if everyone lived as he did—plane to hotel, to plane, to yet another hotel.

He strode to a Gustav Klimt painting, a beautiful woman awash in blues and purples. His cock woke up at the sight of the image thanks to the memory of meeting Alexander for the first time at a Paris art auction. Alexander had failed to win a Klimt that day but succeeded in becoming Eric's singular obsession. Jesus, let his dick behave today. Nothing like punching a hole in your pants while talking about auctioning antiques ...

A gust of wind blew over him as the front door slammed

open. He startled at the bang and turned as Tony strode by him to a box on the stairs.

"Alexander back?" Eric asked.

The man glanced up at him, a small square can in his hand, and walked by him and out the front door without a word.

Eric moved to the open doorway just as Tony handed Alexander the can. The man popped open the plastic top, emptied its contents over the Sheraton desk, and tossed the can to the side. He pulled a handkerchief from his pocket, ignited it with a lighter, and dropped the small linen square onto the desk to create an instant bonfire. In the middle of the driveway. In front of the Wynter estate. Using an antique Eric could have sold for, what, half a million?

Eric stepped outside and sidled up to Alexander.

"Eric." Alexander didn't take his eyes off the blazing piece of furniture.

He swallowed. "Alexander. Last year at auction a Sheraton desk just like that went for $475,000."

The man's blue eyes turned his way. "It belonged to Alice Wynter. I have as much use for it as I had for her." He held out his hand, which Eric took. "Whenever you're ready, I'll meet you inside." He dropped his handshake. "Tony, take a walk around the perimeter. Check things out."

Tony nodded once, and Alexander's broad back disappeared into the house. For long minutes, he stared at the yellow flame dancing up the desk legs and breathed in the acrid smoke as the surfaces curdled and blanched in the flame's heat. Was Alexander losing it? He drew out his phone and got Ryan Knightbridge's voicemail.

"Ryan, want to give me a call? I'm at the Wynter estate standing in front of a bonfire fueled by a half a mil antique. This isn't an ordinary estate sale, is it?"

4

Alexander flipped keys over the ring he'd been handed thirty minutes ago. One of these opened this door. If not, one kick would get him inside. He tried the one key that looked as new as yesterday, and it worked. The wood frame gave off a loud crack as he turned the knob and pushed open the door to Charles' bedroom. He stepped into the musty air and met a time capsule. The same walnut furniture and the same red and blue checked fabric covering that God-awful wingback chair in the corner greeted him.

"You didn't have the stomach for it, did you, Alice?" he asked the lifeless space. The woman had promised to take a blowtorch to the room or at least the queen-sized bed where he, Charles, and Rebecca had been found, tangled in that Queen Anne bedspread by Charles' brother, Marston. As usual, the hag's bitter words had no real teeth. To this day, he could not understand why Marston had run his mouth to his parents like a four-year-old tattling on the other kids.

In a rare masochistic moment, he forced himself to focus on the most familiar of the room's details, starting with the bed, and then up to the sailboat print, now faded under dusty glass. He strode over to get a closer look. The print resurrected the cry of seagulls and the cut of a sharp, salt-tinged wind.

"Charles, you and that ridiculous little schooner." How Charles had avoided frostbite when he'd taken it out in Boston Harbor one January, he'd never know.

He pulled the photograph he'd been saving for this occasion from the lapel pocket of his suit coat. It was square, yellowed, and curling on the edges, and his most prized possession next to the letter Charles had written when he'd sent the picture. It was the last communication he'd had with him. He stared down at the picture of two young men—so young, so foolish, so unprepared for what was going to happen to them—pressed on either side of a young woman, her rose gold hair sparkling in the sunlight. Rebecca. Jesus, he'd been so naïve.

He set the picture against the small hobnail lamp by the bed and shut his eyes. He needed one minute to shake off the sadness that arose whenever he pulled out that photograph. What had he expected today would bring? Rainbows and angel song? This day was bound to raise regrets.

A man's throat cleared. "Forgive the intrusion … "

His eyes snapped open to find Eric standing on the threshold, hands stuffed into his jean pockets. Alexander should fill him in. The man had shown considerable grace given what he'd witnessed so far. "Come in."

"Forgive me for being early. I know you expected me tomorrow." He stepped in closer. "This Marston's room? I understand the items that Alice specifically willed to her son have been—"

"Sons. There were two. Marston and Charles. This was Charles' room."

"Oh, I didn't know. I've been here once. Ten years ago

when Raymond Wynter thought of selling. The paintings downstairs, though? Jesus. Leaving them like that ... "

Alexander chuffed. "No one wants to touch Marston since he sold ivory across state lines."

"I'm impressed you knew that."

"The art world is a small place, and selling the entire estate and its contents in one transaction made things easy for him. He likes easy."

Eric's eyes brightened as he stared at the print above the bed. "Is that a–"

His hand rose, stopping the man's advance toward it. Rude and aggressive, but no one was laying a finger on the contents of this room. "You won't touch a thing in here."

Eric raised his hands in a surrender gesture and stepped backward.

Alexander nodded once. "Forgive the emotion."

"No apologies necessary." The man's eyes softened as if understanding, though how could he know the rage running up and down his spine at any hint of dismantling this room?

A man's heavy footfalls pounded up the stairs. So, the prodigal son had finally arrived. He was surprised it had taken Marston this long, once he discovered the identity of the buyer.

Marston Wynter filled the doorway. "Knightbridge Associates was you." Spit flew from the man's lips. The eldest Wynter son always had been a blowhard. The extra fifty pounds on his frame was unexpected, but little else had changed. *Shocker.*

"Marston." He glanced at his watch. "Less than twenty-four hours. I'm impressed."

"Fuck, the ink's not even dry."

Eric strode forward and extended his hand. "Eric Morrison."

"Who the hell are you?"

"He's with me." Alexander noted the man's manners hadn't changed, either. "And, you're trespassing."

Marston sneered. "Felt good to say that to me, didn't it? I had expected something more original from you, Alexander." He breached the room, crossing the threshold. "At least that's what my brother called you. Original."

"I thought you didn't have a brother."

"Oh, I had one all right, until you took him away, corrupted him and Rebecca, you sick bastard."

"Hard to take someone away when you're banished from their deathbed." Alexander bore down on the man. "Leave."

"So you can continue your redecorating?" Marston angled his head toward the front of the house where the bitch's precious Sheraton had been reduced to ash. "A bit dramatic, even for you."

His fingers curled into fists. "Don't pretend you know a thing about me."

The man let out a hiss worthy of a viper. "Visiting mother's grave. I'm allowed to do that, you know. State law."

"She lies outside this house. If you're smart, you'll back out of this room." Fabric strained across Alexander's chest and arms as every muscle tensed to finally land a punch on that smug face. If they'd been alone, he might have done it. "Eric and I have business to attend to."

Marston glanced at Eric and then back to him. "I'll bet you do." He spun on his heel, but before stepping through the door, he paused. "Try not to mess up the sheets too badly, will you? You know how Mother despises freaks, and your presence might raise her from the grave."

"Let her." Let the she-devil even try.

Marston huffed an amused breath but sauntered back to the hallway.

Alexander filled his lungs with stale air and stretched his

neck from side to side. *Fuck*. His hands cramped as if itching for a fight, and his heart clawed at his ribs as if wanting out to join them.

"Thought you were going to punch him." Eric half laughed but then stilled.

"It's this house. Forgive my outbursts, but I'm incapable of giving a shit right now." He stretched his fingers and turned to Eric, a man who didn't deserve to be in the wake of his past. "I've waited almost forty years to be standing in this room."

"Then you should take your time."

So, Eric did understand. "Inventory everything. We're going to auction the antiques, paintings, whatever is of value. Donate the proceeds. Every cent goes to CAG-LBTY. Do you know what that is?"

The man straightened. "The Connecticut Alliance of Gay, Lesbian, Bisexual and Transgender Youth. They could use the money."

"Let that bitch's precious Renoirs, Persian rugs and ridiculous Rochard French doll collection, clothe and feed the very people she railed against. And, Eric. . ." He moved closer to him. "It probably goes without saying but I'm going to say it anyway. Any personal items we find, you bring to me. Not Tony. Not Ryan. Are we clear on that?"

Eric nodded. "Whatever you need. Why don't I go check into my hotel, get over this jet lag, and we can start fresh tomorrow?" His gaze stalled on the yellowed photograph propped against the small lamp. "Give you time to go over the house yourself."

The man also was observant. He would be, given his job. "Good. Dinner tonight. Eight o'clock, suit? We'll talk then." He turned away. He had no more words left in him. At least none that wanted out.

Eric left him, and he sat on the edge of the bed, blessedly alone except for the memories that had their hooks in him like they always would.

5

_____

"Come on," Eric growled at his phone. Three eternal minutes later, the blue dot signaling where he was on the map finally populated with winding streets and historic points of interest.

"Starting route." Siri's male, Australian, voice cut through the incessant pinging of rain on the car roof.

"About time you showed up, hoss."

"Turn left onto Johnson Street. Then stay right."

Eric spun the steering wheel into the driving rain toward the Grafton Inn, now that he knew where it was. Jesus, don't let the place be a dump, though he doubted Alexander frequented anything less than a Chateau Relais property. Plus, yesterday, his *other* assistant, Clarisse, said Alexander had suggested the place, something about a renovated Connecticut Inn from the 1700s blah, blah, blah. How bad could it be?

Eric urged the car forward. Sheets of rain blew sideways across the road and water blanketed the asphalt. This was going to take a while.

His phone vibrated, cutting off the route guidance. Now

what? One glance, however, had him pull over and scramble for his phone's on button.

"Ryan. Thanks for calling me back." He pushed the car into "park."

"Eric. You made it a little early, I see."

Jesus, what was with everyone pointing out the fact he'd jumped on the first plane to get to Alexander? Didn't everyone do that when the man called? "I did."

"I spoke with Tony earlier."

Of course Ryan had. Or, perhaps spy Tony had called *him*.

"So did I. Also witnessed a half a million dollar antique go up in smoke and met Marston Wynter." Or re-met him. The man clearly didn't recall their brief encounter from a few years ago. "I learned the Wynters had a second son. It's been an interesting and informative day so far."

The male voice on the other end of the phone chuffed at Eric's sarcasm.

"Sorry. Jet lagged." Eric sighed heavily. "Just trying to avoid any landmines. Anything I need to know?"

"No."

Okay, then. Perhaps he'd push it a little. Sure, Alexander had said to only come to him, and given how he'd seen the man handle people who ignored his concise orders during a play scene, he probably shouldn't tempt fate. Or, rather, he'd love to under better circumstances, like once he convinced the man to secure him to a St. Andrew's Cross with one or two niggling limits in place because he'd let that man do pretty much anything to him. In the meantime, he needed some answers.

"Well, Alexander seems ... " How did Eric explain this next part? *I've waited almost forty years to be standing in this room.* His chest ached a little when he remembered Alexander's unshielded, vulnerable words.

"What? How is he? Is everything okay?"

Good. It was about time someone was worried about the man. "Everything's going to be fine." Because he'd make it so. "It would help to know what I'm dealing with before I suggest he sell sentimental items. I mean, did you ever meet Charles Wynter?" He doubted it given the likely age difference, but why not go there? "Alexander seems—"

"No." Another clipped answer from Ryan. "Just follow Alexander's lead."

"Okay, then. Guess I'll carry on."

"Thanks, Eric." The line went dead.

Oh, yes, there was history here. *Damn.* Ghosts were the hardest competition to deal with. From his quick glance at the photograph in that bedroom shrine, this Charles guy had been a looker. The woman with red-gold hair sandwiched between them raised another mystery he'd solve another day. For now, his mind filled with images of a younger Alexander, undeniably happy, his arms intertwined with this mysterious second Wynter son. An odd twinge went off in his chest at the thought the man had loved and lost. It was as if a little bit of the magic in the world dissolved with the realization Alexander was human after all and not the indefatigable man he'd built up in his mind.

He scrubbed his chin. He should go back to the Wynter house. Tony drove off right after him, no doubt dismissed by Alexander. That meant Alexander was alone. A gust of wind swayed the car a little. The weather was *not* cooperating. He pulled back onto the street, but didn't turn around. He'd go to the Grafton Inn, get cleaned up, handle his throbbing cock, and take a nap. At forty-eight years old, he didn't handle jet lag as well as he had when younger. He'd meet Alexander for dinner, hopefully alone, and let him know he was up for anything that helped—*anything*—including himself.

"Get in the left lane," the navigation app called out.

"So bossy, hoss." Just the way he liked it, especially if orders came from a certain silver-haired, six-foot-four, grieving man who really needed a distraction. Sex was a spectacular diversion from loneliness. His whole life stood as evidence.

6

The red taillights of his Mercedes finally disappeared around a bend in the driveway. It had taken some persuasion to induce Tony to go the Grafton Inn without him, but Alexander needed to be alone with his newly acquired real estate. He blinked rainwater from his eyes and ascended the stone steps slowly despite the precipitation beating down on him like tiny fists from heaven.

In the blue, front parlor, he wrestled an armchair to the window, letting it down with a hard thunk right where Alice Wynter's desk once sat. Water beads clinging to his coat rolled off to wet the chintz. As he lowered himself to the cushion, a tobacco scent rose up. So this had been Raymond's chair. How had that man stayed married to that harpy all those years?

He scrubbed his hands over his hair, and a loud roll of thunder answered his growl. Let all of hell storm. He'd fulfilled every promise he'd held close for four decades, and he was going to dwell in that victory for as long as he damn well felt like it.

A long whistle sounded from the portico as the sudden

nor'easter winds rushed through leaks around the front door, and the chandelier's light died. Darkness enveloped him. Who cared if the electricity went out? He didn't need light. Through the window, the archway that led to the family gravesite remained visible in the rising storm.

He settled his forearms on the tufted armrests and, for a change, allowed his mind to wander wherever the hell it wanted. Memories he'd driven into the ground rose up like the dead.

Knife-cold wind searing his face as he rounded the corner in Harvard Square.

Two angry figures kicking a boy lying in a fetal position in the snow.

The ache in his knuckles as his fist landed on the nearest guy.

The smell of beer and cigarettes rising.

And, later, warm flesh against his under cheap sheets in a dorm room.

The first time he'd stepped onto that marble portico, thirty feet from where he now sat.

The young girl with rose gold hair flying down the stairway to launch herself on to Charles, their eyes lit up with so much joy to see one another.

The three of them trading kisses, mouths on each other, everywhere ...

Like a runaway train, his mind barreled forward to Charles tumbling to the dirty floor of that horrible Chinese restaurant on San Francisco's Market Street. Rebecca's eyes lifting to him as she crouched next to Charles, and the silent message swimming in all that pale gray. *Nothing was ever going to be the same again.*

"Enough." His lids snapped open. He'd drifted into dangerous territory.

A crack of lightning momentarily lit up the Memorial's entranceway. Shadows darted across the stone wall. He leaned forward as another flash across the murky sky illuminated something. No, *someone*. Who the hell would be sneaking around during a storm? Another crack of lightning lit up the figure long enough to see it disappear through the stone arch.

Of course. "Marston Wynter, it's time you and I end this game." Alexander stood and headed outside.

The wind whipped his coat around his legs as he took his time on the slick bricks leading to the Memorial. The solar lights did little to light the way. They looked as tired as he felt. He paused in the archway. A lone figure hunched over Charles' grave marker, an inadequate trench coat fluttering around a thin frame. It was a woman. She turned. A flash of lightning shot across the sky illuminating her face. Pale gray eyes pierced the gloaming, and rose gold hair spilled from underneath a beret dripping with rainwater.

Water ran down his neck and seeped under his coat collar, and he pushed hot, heavy breaths in and out of his throat. "No." His word was no more than a whisper lost in the wind and rain. Adrenaline kicked through his system. Muscles tightened in his chest. It couldn't be … The woman shifted on her feet, and he froze. If he moved, she might disappear, proving she was a trick of the shadows formed from branches and headstones. Perhaps she was a former servant coming to pay respects. His brain offered many possible answers to the identity of this woman. He hadn't seen her for nearly forty years, but his gut knew the truth.

Her chest expanded as if taking in a long breath and then she gave him a familiar, hesitant smile. "Hello."

His brain caught up. "Rebecca."

7

Rebecca's hand flew to her throat, fingers landing on her thrumming pulse as in four strides, Alexander closed the distance between them. Leaves skidded under her feet, and the ground tilted sideways. His hand gripped her bicep and yanked her upright.

"Jesus, Rebecca." His blue eyes seared through the darkness.

She found her feet and pulled her arm free. "H-hello, Alexander." *Stammering, great.*

He ran his hand down his face. "How are you here?"

"I heard the place sold. I wanted to see Charles one last time." Her voice, breathy and pitchy, belonged to a little girl, not a grown woman. Alexander's presence always had knocked her a little off balance. Seemed time hadn't changed his impact on her.

A crack of lightning made her jump.

"The storm's getting worse. Let's go inside." He moved to touch her again.

Inside? No, no, no, she couldn't go inside that house. She

stepped backward, and his hands circled her bicep once more.

"It's mine now," he said. "As of yesterday."

"That means … "

His attention drifted over her shoulder toward Charles' headstone. "Yes. This is the first time I've seen him."

"Alexander, I—"

"Inside."

No one had spoken to her in such a commanding tone in years, but her insides reacted as if no time had passed between them, as if she was still that young woman who'd knelt at this man's feet in a nanosecond if he'd desired it. He tugged her forward, and she let him.

"We'll talk," he said.

That was the problem, though, wasn't it? She and Alexander never *just talked.*

Inside, Alexander shrugged off his coat and hung it over one of the staircase railings. "Electricity's out. I'll start a fire." He strode into the formal living room, leaving her standing in a pool of rainwater in the entrance hall with its over-the-top marble floor and columns. Did he expect she'd follow him? Should she? Her heartbeat danced like a timpani drummer had taken command, and it made it hard to think. Her legs itched to run as if the memories this house exhumed would kill her. Well, they could. If Marston caught her here … Her hands found their way to her throat again as if that would help her breathe better. Of all the places in the world for a reunion with Alexander— something she'd worked very hard to avoid—it had to be here?

A glow grew in the large archway separating the entry- meant-to-intimidate from the formal living room. She jumped when a loud, crackly, pop echoed off the marble.

"Rebecca? Are you coming in?"

At the sound of his deep, gravelly voice, she released a

breath and hesitantly walked into the room where she'd lost everything. Alexander crouched near the fire, the flames lighting up the angles of his face.

"This place hasn't changed much." She moved closer to the beckoning warmth.

"It will." He stood and placed a poker in the andiron set. He gestured to the familiar long couch, the chintz now faded and worn, a tarp thrown casually to the side. "Sit."

Her legs moved at his direction. Okay, one thing hadn't changed. Sit. Stay. Bend over. Commands she'd heard a hundred times a million years ago had the same effect today. Her body reacted without question to Alexander.

She took the offered seat and rubbed her chilled, chapped, hands together. Why hadn't she dressed better? Why hadn't she run when she saw him? Why had she come at all?

He lowered himself to an armchair a few feet away, his deep blue eyes trained on her. Silver flecked his temples, and lines etched his forehead, but he still exuded the same intimidating masculinity she'd lost herself in so many years ago.

"You look good." His gaze traveled her body. "Well."

"Not as good as you."

It was true. Men and their supernatural aging abilities. It really wasn't fair. But then when had she ever thought life was fair? Genetics gifted this man with a striking face, with height, a powerful physique, and with courage—a character trait she lacked. He looked like wealth. Always had, even when none of them could afford a cup of coffee.

His blue eyes, more guarded than she recalled, studied her with unwavering intensity. "I didn't see you drive up."

"I left my car outside the gate. Walked inside."

"I did the same thing."

"Just like you said you would." He'd said he'd be back and stride in with a sledgehammer. Weren't those his words?

"I kept all the promises I made that day, even the ones I didn't want to keep."

Prickly heat filled her face, and her fingers would not stop shaking.

His finger went to his lips. "Where have you been?"

Okay, he was cutting straight to the chase. She forced a small inhale. "Everywhere."

His nostrils flared. "Not everywhere." His stare had once been like standing in sunlight. Now a chill ran through her body from head to foot.

A stupid thought flitted into her paralyzed mind. This is how deer felt before the truck plowed over them. "You live here now?" she blurted. "Not in D.C. anymore?"

His brows arched up. How could he be surprised she'd checked up on him? She shrugged. "I wondered where you were. I looked you up on Google. You were at a charity auction or something. I almost reached out to you, but so much time had passed, and I wasn't sure. I mean, given how things … ended."

"Oh? I tried reaching you, as well. Unfortunately, when we parted there was no internet, and, well, by the time there was, I had stopped looking. I figured you meant what you said." His jaw tightened ever so slightly.

Oh, if you knew. "You have to believe me, back then, it was … hard for me, too."

"Define hard."

Fear sliced through her chest, and she was so, so tired of it. She swallowed. "Walk through fire hard." There, the hard, cold truth. "We loved each other." She looked down at her twisting fingers, her voice dropping. "More than love if there is such a state." She lifted her eyes to stare into those blue irises that bore down on her like a laser. "I would have died for you."

"Then we're even." He picked a piece of lint off his trousers.

This could be her moment. She could say she was sorry. She could drop to her knees and beg forgiveness. She could say and do so many things if only... All the words she wanted to say rose up into a sharp point, but where would she start? Could he ever understand what she'd done for him? *No, why would he?*

"I'm sorry." She swiped at her cheeks. Jesus, she had started to leak tears. She stood and held out her hand. "I should go. It really was good to see you, Alexander."

"Going somewhere?" He glanced at the window. "The storm isn't abating."

"Thank you, but I'll be fine." She jutted out her hand again. *Please take it. Please show me you don't hate me.*

He stood and finally took her offering. He turned her hand and ran his thumb over the pad of her palm. Then, took possession of her other hand. "No ring."

She shuddered at his caresses. "Divorced."

His other hand lifted a lock of her hair and twisted it around his finger. "Still like a sunset made of rose gold."

"My hairdresser loves me. Vain, I know."

"No, beautiful." His fingers gathered more of her hair.

His possessive move had once comforted her. Now it sent a warning. Run. Leave. Do not get sucked in, because then she really would have to tell him things. She knew this man —or had—and he'd want more, always more. "Alexander—"

"Hush. No more handshakes. We're past that." He circled her waist with his free hand and pulled her closer.

He was right. She hugged her mailman for God's sake, though Mr. Evans didn't entwine his fingers in her hair or stare down at her like he'd devour her soul. But then, that's the way she and Alexander had constructed their relation-ship, hadn't they? He commanded, and she obeyed, with

Charles in between them doing whatever he wanted. God, what she would do to go back, start over. She'd do so many things differently.

Her arms wrapped around his waist, and her face found his pec, as strong and solid as she recalled. His familiar scent of warm, freshly-laundered, cotton got into her nose, and her shoulders slumped.

"Alexander, someday I hope you'll forgive me." They were such inadequate words to say, lost in his shirt.

"Oh, I will." His nose nestled in her hair, and his pull on her scalp intensified. Air rushed from her lungs when he yanked her head backward. "When you tell me the truth. How is it you are here? And, why? Out with it, and no lies."

Nerves ignited up and down her spine. He was going to make her tell him the real reason she'd broken things off with him. Why had she thought she could sneak in and out without being caught? Perhaps one small part of her had known this would happen, which meant only one thing. Their sudden reunion was a sign for her to finally make peace with the man who was the single most important influence in her life. It was time to come clean—if those blue eyes didn't sear her in half first.

8

_____

Alexander released her hair and stepped back. Crossing his arms over his chest, he glared down at Rebecca. "Start talking."

She swallowed, her bottom lip trembling. Let her cry. He could handle tears. He couldn't handle any more pretenses, and coincidences were for foolish men. Rebecca was here for a reason, and it wasn't to visit Charles' grave because the Wynter estate sold.

She sank to the couch. "Alexander, I ... " She stopped short and then sat up fully. "I've known where you were for the last ten years."

His forehead tightened. She'd been thinking of him? Looking for him? "Explain."

"You're not a hard man to find. I mean, Google. Then when I heard the place sold, I had a feeling you had bought it." Her lashes flicked up. "I'd hoped you'd bought it."

Suspicion, shock, hope—all crashed in on him. "You came to see me?"

"No. Yes. Maybe. I knew you probably didn't want to see _me_. That's why I snuck into the Memorial. I wanted to stand there one more time. I haven't been able to get inside for many years."

"Bullshit. I knew how much time you spent here after the funeral. I tried to get inside myself a few times. Climbing the fucking wall like an escaped convict." Until he grew a pair and moved on. "That bitch or Marston would have let you—"

"No. No one knows. He can't know. He can't." She jerked to her feet, her voice shrill.

What the hell? Why would it matter? He strode forward. "Did he do something to you? Marston?" The pussy wouldn't dare, but if he had tried something …

"What didn't he do?" she spat. "He threatened me regularly. He continued to threaten you." There was that Irish temper he'd loved.

"Empty and nothing new. Bogus charges—"

"Not bogus. Real." Her fists ground into her belly as if she'd been stabbed and staunched a wound. "I was seventeen. You know the law."

"I know exactly how old you were. I was there." He had never seen her as a young teen, but rather a full-grown woman like the one standing before him now. He'd treated her as such, and she'd blossomed. *Such a mistake.*

"Then you remember why we had to run away. How they cut us off … "

Oh, how he knew. He turned away, scrubbed his chin. "How else could that bigoted, homophobic family deal with their sexually aberrant son but carve him out of the family like a rotten piece of meat?" After Marston caught the three of them *in flagrante delicto*, they'd ditched school and ran away to San Francisco like a bunch of 1960s hippies. It wasn't their most intelligent decision, but they'd been free. As for the narrow-minded Wynters? They cut Charles off altogether. That old feeling of wanting to punch his fist through a wall nearly knocked him off his feet, but his intellect righted him. "It was expected. We proved we didn't care, and the society-hungry Wynters would have never gone through with their other threats." He faced her once more.

She shook her head. "You forget Raymond was friends with the DA and—"

"Nothing but a lot of bluster. Any statutory rape charges would have implicated their son, too." He yanked his tie loose. His skin prickled from the heat rising in the room.

"You know the Wynters. They would have said he wasn't there, and he wasn't strong like you. He was ... "

"Sick." Jesus, he was so damned tired of reminiscing about how reckless he'd been back then. He'd been a young man in love with two people, harboring some romantic notion they'd be able to form a life together. Yet would he have done anything differently? Hell, no.

"You remember the day you had to make the call to his family?" Her voice was barely a whisper but broke through his rage like a missile. "The day Charles collapsed in that horrible Chinese restaurant?"

"Branded into my brain." How did you forget your best friend and lover collapsing and then have his cruel family jet in only to throw you out into the hospital hallway like trash? "Along with the day you ditched me as I stood locked outside that front gate." His throat tightened to the point he could barely swallow.

"The day he died." She lifted her lids and leveled her watery, gray eyes at him. "That was the day I got their final offer. Right here in this room. That bitch said I could save myself and you. If I cut you out of my life, disappeared, they wouldn't pursue statutory rape charges. They promised to remain hands off. The price for your freedom was my penance."

Hands off? Bile rose in his throat, just as it had the time he tried to get inside to see Charles, and Alice instructed security to shoot him. Later, the day of the funeral, he had gained entrance, throwing himself over a stone wall in the back. If the cops hadn't arrived and hauled him away for trespassing, most assuredly, that bitch would have pulled the trigger herself. She believed she was above things such as the law. His anger flared to new life. "And you took that deal."

"Yes." She rose. "I loved you, Alexander. Enough to let you go. Now it's time I go."

When she tried to step around him, he blocked her path— a move uncharacteristic for him—but they were not done. None of this made sense, not back then and not now. She'd spoken her peace. He had some words for her. "I loved you. I loved Charles, and I was punished for that. You didn't trust our love enough to stay with me? Fine. Consent is vital in my world, but I will not be lied to. Never again. What aren't you telling me?"

She moved to speak but then snapped her lips together. Instead, she rushed toward him, pressed herself against him once more in an awkward hug. "If there was any other way, I'd have done it. I would have done anything for you."

He grasped the back of her head with such force she gasped. Her delicate neck bent and a waft of familiar lavender cut into his senses. A silver chain disappearing into her cleavage glinted in the firelight. His breath stilled as his finger slipped under the thin strand and pulled. A moonstone teardrop slipped out from its hiding spot.

My God. His heart thumped under his ribs. "You still have it." Her eyes rimmed with new tears.

"You said nothing bad could happen to me if I wore it."

He stared at the pendant, the firelight dancing inside the stone. It was a cheap necklace, a talisman bought at a greyhound bus stop and given to a frightened, orphan girl who had the guts to run away with two men, committed to protecting their idealistic faith in a different kind of love.

He fixed his gaze on her eyes. "Was I right?"

She nodded slowly, as much as his firm grasp on her hair allowed. "You're always right."

He let the necklace fall back to her skin, and his anger drifted. She'd loved him once, of that he was certain. Perhaps a piece of her never let go. There was one way to find out, for desire never lied. He inhaled her lavender scent, and his lips took possession of her mouth.

9

Eric stilled in the archway. Alexander, tie skewed and shirt open, held the back of a woman's head in a greedy hold, his long fingers threaded through wild red hair. Who was the woman? Her skin was so pale against Alexander's. He kissed her as if punishing her with his mouth, oblivious to the fact Eric had breached their personal space.

He should turn away. Hell, he shouldn't be here. He had taken his life in his hands crossing that creek and sloshing up and over the bridge to bring Alexander dinner—the meal he'd forgotten to join Eric for. He'd chalked it up to the man still grieving. *Clearly not.*

Alexander's fingers curled tighter into all those red strands as he deepened his kiss. Eric's mouth watered, and the front of his pants shrank five sizes. One second of observing Alexander's dominance and all Eric's earlier efforts to drain his cock of need were for nothing as his erection strained against his zipper.

He swallowed, and shifted his weight. His soggy shoes squeaked against the marble, sending off an echo that could wake the dead. Alexander's face broke contact with the woman and turned to him.

Eric glanced away. His options were limited. Step back out in the storm. Go to another room and wait out …

"Eric."

Damn. Caught being a voyeur. He turned to face the man and prayed like hell he wasn't blushing. The woman had shrunk behind him.

He lifted the bag. "I brought you dinner." Lame, but true.

"Ah." Alexander scrubbed his salt and pepper five o'clock shadow. "Time got away from me."

Eric stepped closer and held out the bag. "I'll leave it and head back out."

"No, come in." Alexander crooked his finger. "You're soaked. This is Rebecca Beaumont."

She stepped out from behind him, her cheeks aflame. His heart hitched a little at the vulnerability in her red-rimmed eyes. She'd been crying.

"Eric Morrison." He offered a handshake. "I'd forgotten how vicious New England storms could be."

Her hand disappeared into his palm. "Alexander and I are old friends."

I can tell.

"Eric is helping me settle the estate." Alexander gave him a half a smile on that word, and Eric's belly gave a lurch worthy of a teenager with a bad case of puppy love.

"I don't mean to intrude … " *Or stare.* In this light, Rebecca's high cheekbones and pale gray eyes cast an otherworldly vibe. His first thought was that she'd stepped off a film set from Lord of the Rings, like—what was the name of that elf colony? *River-something.* He was snapped back to reality from the crinkle of the food bag as Alexander took it from him.

"Not at all." Alexander peered into the bag. "Eggplant Parmesan from the Grafton. My favorite."

"Still?" Her tentative smile lit up her face. "Is it as good as Bertrands?"

"Better." Alexander winked, and Eric's eyebrows shot to his hairline. The Alexander Rockingham he knew didn't do anything as frivolous as wink.

Eric cleared his throat. "If you're planning on going out, you should know the bridge is almost washed out." What else would he contribute to this tête-à-tête he'd witnessed—or rather, had barged in on.

Alexander frowned. "Tell me you didn't take any chances."

"No big deal." He shrugged. "I survived Hurricane Katrina. A little Nor'easter won't be a problem."

"Well, that's it. You're staying. In fact, we all are."

"What?" Rebecca's eyes flared with fire and her cheeks colored. Yep, she had that enchantress, elf queen, vibe going on.

Alexander turned to her. "Do you have someone you need to call?"

"N-no. But—"

"Then it's settled. Nine bedrooms, and I'm sure there are linens somewhere. I'll have Tony bring luggage in the morning before he heads back, and Eric, we can start fresh. Let's eat."

"I didn't bring much." She half-laughed. "I jumped in the car, and here I am."

"We can handle that." He circled her shoulders, and the overhead chandelier in the entry hall burst into life, throwing harsh and unflattering light over them and the space. He glanced down at Rebecca. "A sign?"

"A sign," she whispered. Alexander looked down at her mouth as if he wanted to devour her again.

Oh, yeah, that watery, vulnerable smile of hers had a million dollar movie contract written all over it. Eric had definitely, most unequivocally, interrupted a reunion. Rebecca's eyes held a wild need, a look he recognized, as it imitated what he saw every damn time he looked in the mirror and thought of Alexander.

"Very good. Let's eat in the kitchen." Alexander steered her toward the hallway.

The man's invitation could have been merely a polite offer meant for Eric to turn down, but like hell he'd leave. He didn't get this far to once more be relegated to the bottom of Alexander's invitation list and have this old friend, this elf queen, snatch him right from under his nose.

He fell in step behind the two of them. He'd thought he'd attempt to seduce Alexander tonight. Well, he could knee that fantasy right in the groin and move to plan B. "Raymond was a notorious wine collector. Let me see if there's anything left in the cellar."

"Excellent idea." Alexander's eyes flashed. "Rebecca ... " He placed his hand on the small of her back, guiding her toward the kitchen.

If there is a god, there would be something alcoholic in this house. Drinks would loosen some tongues, and he was going to find out everything about the woman Alexander's eyes and hands couldn't leave. Alexander growing spellbound by this elf queen, this movie star witch?Not on his estate watch.

10

———

"Downward dog." Rebecca tore off another piece of garlic bread and nibbled it.

Eric waved his hand in the air. "Everyone says that. I'd choose wild thing. I mean if it was the last yoga pose I could ever do, why not go all the way?"

"You're a hedonist." She clinked her wine glass against his. "I like it."

Alexander studied her smile, now aimed at Eric. The flirt kept touching his arm. When they'd been involved, he'd allowed no man other than Charles within five feet of her.

She cocked her head at him. "What?"

"Mmm, nothing." And everything.

God, she was still so beautiful. Gray eyes that looked more blue under the artificial light and with tiny laugh lines that only made her look wiser and more womanly than the young girl he'd known. Her full, peach lips teased the edge of her wine glass as she peered at him. Her pussy lips were a similar peach—or they had been when he'd had the privilege of worshiping that part of her years ago. Did she still have that smattering of freckles across her back that resembled the star constellation, Delphinus?

"And, you, Alexander?" Eric refilled his wine glass with a wonderful Cabernet the man had liberated from Raymond's stash in the basement.

He gratefully accepted the wine. "Last yoga pose forever? Tree."

"Of course. Then you'd have a great view of everyone in their various, uh, positions." He winked. It appeared Rebecca wasn't the only flirt in the room.

Alexander laughed. Eric had been quite entertaining—and helpful, despite his slight possessiveness arising from Rebecca's obvious and instant affinity with Eric. She'd always been good with men.

Alexander threw down his napkin. "Change in topic. If you could only visit one place for the rest of your life, where?"

"Oh, easy." Eric leaned back in his chair. "I'd go back to South Africa." He slanted his eyes toward Rebecca. "Go ahead. Top us all, Miss Travel Writer."

Eric's little get to know you game had been good at teasing out bits of Rebecca's life. Tonight that void in his mind, the blank spaces about what she'd been doing, had been filled with images of street festivals in India, hiking in Nepal, all the things she'd described with big hand flourishes and laughter. Thank God she'd had a good life. Her chosen profession under the pseudonym of Anne Broadstreet also explained why his few attempts to find her were thwarted, though, truth told, he hadn't tried very hard. He should have tried harder.

She sighed. "I know what you're thinking. It was all resorts and first-class travel. Well, think again. I'd go to South Africa, too, because I was stuck in Johannesburg the whole time."

"Museums?" Alexander ran his finger over the step of his wine glass, let his gaze liberally travel her face, her hair, drinking in all the light she still emanated.

"Nightlife."

Eric's hand flew to his chest in mock horror. "I feel for you. The horror of having to go out and have fun."

"Ha. Says you. I was in my forties then and being jostled around on a lighted dance floor right out of 1976 was no fun." Her eyes clouded in thought. "But, I remember it was a magical place, even though I was there for just three days."

Eric rocked his chair onto its back legs and stretched out. "There's something in the air in South Africa. The wildness of it. The woods. The mountains. The desert. Then there's the generosity of the people, how what's theirs is yours. Ubuntu."

Rebecca's forehead crinkled. "What's Ubuntu? I'm unfamiliar with it."

"It means humanity," Alexander said. "Humanity toward others. A universal bond of sharing that connects all of us."

Eric's gaze shot to him. "I am because we are."

"That's beautiful." Rebecca's smile was, too.

Alexander twirled a lock of her hair around his finger, and her lips parted. "You're beautiful."

Eric's chair slammed back down on its legs. "Ubuntu makes me think of your home, Alexander. How you connect people."

A sliver of irritation arose. He dropped her hair and stared hard at Eric, who knew better than to raise even a hint of his home's true nature. Alexander would deal with the why and details of how his house doubled as a BDSM club with Rebecca later. During dinner, he'd had an urge to take her there, show her who he'd become since they'd parted ways.

She settled her chin on her hand. "You like to entertain, Alexander?"

"Yes." Though entertaining was in the eye of the beholder at Accendos. "As for where I'd go? The Grand Canyon."

Eric glanced at him as he poured more wine for Rebecca, which she did not need. "Grand Canyon? Seriously?"

Alexander took the wine bottle from him and corked it. "It's the one wild place I haven't managed to visit."

"Speaking of wild." Rebecca took another sip of wine. "It may be one of the few unique places left in the United States soon. It's amazing to me how homogeneous the world is growing."

Eric raised his glass. "To fighting homogeneity."

Alexander met his toast, as that was something he could most definitely get behind.

Rebecca cocked her head at him as she also raised her glass. "Uniform is not something I could ever see you being."

"Nor I," Eric interjected. The man wore a half smile Alexander could not decipher.

"Well, gentlemen." Rebecca put down her glass. "I appreciate the good food and conversation, but I really must go to sleep. I'm not the night owl I used to be."

Alexander rose and eased out her chair.

"Still a gentleman, I see." She touched his arm. "I'll take my old room, that is if it's still a bedroom?"

"It is, and I'll be next door in the guest. If you need anything ... " Alexander dipped his head. Her face twisted as if she wanted to ask him something. He wished she would. He wanted to answer all her questions, but timing was everything.

"Goodnight. Eric, it was wonderful to meet you." She held out her hand and the show-off raised it to his lips.

"The pleasure was all mine." He held her hand a few seconds longer than Alexander liked.

"Eric, take whatever room suits. Get some rest. Work tomorrow." The kitchen chair screeched across the floor as he pushed it back to the table.

"Thank you, Alexander." The man had the wits not to smirk at him. He liked the guy, and he had no doubt of his professional abilities, but Rebecca brought out an uncharacteristic streak of jealousy Alexander had thought gone forever. Apparently not. Perhaps everyone was just overtired.

"Goodnight, Eric." He followed Rebecca into the hallway. Tomorrow, he would take her for a walk, tell her all about himself—if he could wait that long.

11

Alexander threw off the sheet and swung his legs over the edge of the bed. Sleep wasn't happening. He stared at the scratched hardwood underneath his feet. He couldn't blame his failure to sleep on the house creaking in the fading storm winds. Rebecca lay next door, and he still had so much to say to her. He also wanted nothing more than to wrap his body around her, skin to skin. Despite everything that had gone down, he still wanted her with a vengeance.

He stood and pulled on his trousers. He needed to work. Tomorrow's to-do list became tonight's action plan. At the top of his mental list was figuring out how to keep Rebecca close, at least not disappearing again, followed by designing a battle plan for Marston's next counterattack. The man was entirely predictable. Eric could handle dispersing the contents of the house.

He swung the door silently open to the hallway. At the end, a glow seeped from under Charles' bedroom door. *Tell me Eric didn't choose that room.* His strides ate up the worn carpeting, and he didn't bother to knock, instead throwing open the door with a loud bang.

Rebecca shot up from where she sat, fully dressed, on the bed. She held the photograph that he'd left in her hand. "Oh, God, Alexander. You scared me."

"Can't sleep?" *Planning on running?* That had been another thought he'd had as he'd tossed and turned over the last hour. He had the means to track down the most determined recluse but had hoped he wouldn't have to where she was concerned.

"Not really." She glanced down at the image of the three of them. "You kept it."

"I did." He stepped into the room and shut the door behind him.

Her eyes ran over his bare chest and then quickly turned to set the picture against the hobnail lamp. She ran her hand over the nubby Queen Anne bedspread. "It's the same one."

"Everything's the same." He joined her on the bed and took her hand. "Well, perhaps not everything. I apologize for my earlier emotion. Before Eric arrived."

"Emotion." She laughed a little. "You always were so polite. You had every right to be upset. We both do, actually." Her eyes clouded in thought.

"One thing is the same, though." He tucked a piece of hair behind her ear.

"My hair?"

"Your lips."

She didn't break eye contact. "You know, when you used to look at me like that, I believed you could see all my secrets."

"Have many secrets?"

"A woman's allowed some, isn't she?" She twisted her fingers together.

He drew closer, laid his palm over her hands. "Tell me one."

She smiled. "I looked you up a lot on Google. Not just once."

A laugh jumped out of his throat. "I'm an easy man to find. You, however—" he raised her chin with his index finger. "—did a good job of disappearing. Now I know where you disappeared to, Miss Globe Trotter." He couldn't seem to stop touching her skin still freckled and smooth.

"I couldn't seem to settle down in one place for too long."

"Bad memories will do that to you."

"The memories weren't all bad. There was this." She ran her hand over the bedspread again. "It was good, wasn't it? Like magic?"

"It was better than good, but we were naïve, and I don't believe in magic anymore."

"What do you believe in?"

"Creating and then controlling your destiny."

One side of her mouth pulled up. "An impossible luxury in my world. Nothing is in my control and my choices are limited."

"My world is different."

She squared herself to face him, one leg propped up between them. "I'd like to know more about you. Eric and I did most of the talking tonight. What's your life like in Washington? You have someone special? I should have asked before."

"No, I don't. You?"

"No. Hard to have a relationship when you're always catching a plane."

So neither of them had been able to replace the other. Sadness climbed his throat, and he was getting damn sick of it.

Rebecca leaned back on her hands. "Eric is kind. Respectful, especially given what he walked in on. How did you two meet? At a charity gala?"

He laughed. "I do considerably more than go to events, but, Eric and I did meet at an art auction. Later, he became part of my circle. He's very good at what he does."

"You two have never? I mean, I see the way he looks at you."

"And what way is that?" He reached over and grasped her wrists, pulling them to his lap.

"Like he wants to be where I'm sitting right now. That hasn't changed, either. Everyone wants to be as close to you as possible."

He intertwined his fingers in hers. "Do you like being this close to me again?"

"Yes."

The way her delicate lips parted only strengthened his need for her. "Do you remember? Kneeling at my feet. Giving yourself to me?"

She nodded slowly.

"It was an honor, Rebecca." His mind's eye recalled her so clearly, sneaking innocent glances up at him from under lashes darker than you'd expect from a natural redhead.

She raised her hand to his chest, and her fingertip circled the small crescent scar on his right shoulder, but she wouldn't meet his eyes. "I should have done more." Her chin fell and her hand slid back into his lap.

"I know what you're thinking," he said. "The day of the funeral, when you heard the gunshot, you should have come to see if it was me security shot. It was. The cops put me in the ambulance, in handcuffs, but you didn't know." He lifted her chin. "Don't blame yourself. You were scared."

"I did know, and Alice Wynter made sure I was too scared to do anything but cower inside." She raised her gaze. "I'm not afraid anymore, though."

"Good." His hand came down on her thigh. "I'm not the fledgling Dominant I was when I met you."

"I would never have called you a fledgling."

He chuckled. "Compared to now? Consider the man you first met an amateur."

"And now?"

"Now it's my life. You need to know that." He ran his fingers through her hair, and her lashes instantly fell. "If you need a penance, I could sit you in a corner on a vibrator and edge you for hours. Make you beg to come."

Her teeth grasped her bottom lip, and she swallowed. "I probably deserve that."

"Deserve or desire?"

Her eyes rose to his. "Both."

"Still interested?"

"Yes, though it's been years." She flushed a beautiful, coral peach.

"Then spread your knees."

She blinked hard. "I'm not … I don't jump in … We can't … I mean, Eric … " Her gaze darted to the door. "He would hear."

"He knows all about the kind of life we once lived, though not our specific story." He cradled her chin in his palm.

She swallowed hard again. "I'm not that young girl anymore."

"Thank God. You turned out as I thought. Elegant. Provocative."

"And you did, as well." She flicked her tongue across her bottom lip. "You're … still dashing. Such an old-fashioned word, but it suits you." A warm flush rose in her cheeks.

He lifted her chin once more. "Even after all this time, tell me you don't want me. Say it, if it's true."

"I could never not want you, Alexander."

"Then tell me you do."

"I do."

He arched an eyebrow. He needed more.

She gave him more.

She swung her legs over him so she straddled him. She mashed her mouth into his, and hell, he would take that as a resounding yes. He'd let her have this little topping victory for a few seconds because memories that he'd previously been stellar at tamping down broke through the damn. Flashbacks rose up hard and clear about how it felt to settle his weight on her in sheets damp from their sweat, Charles' limbs entwined in both of them.

He took over the kiss, pushing her tongue where he wanted it, punishing her lips and letting his hands go where they'd wanted to for the last thirty-eight years. He explored every inch of her shoulders, palmed down her back to grasp her ass, and hoisted her closer. Her soft moan at the contact was all his cock needed to lengthen fully and press into her crotch.

He twisted her hair around his fingers and yanked her head back to break the kiss. "Next time you want to kiss me, you'll ask me for permission, won't you, mo rúnsearc?"

Her lips parted on a sigh at hearing his endearment for her. *My secret love.* Her eyes misted. "Yes, sir."

She had been one of his greatest secrets, a female on the cusp of womanhood who he'd taken before he understood the more profound responsibilities associated with dominance and submission. He'd surely go to hell for his recklessness with her. He supposed he'd deserved her complete abandonment. He'd overwhelmed her senses. Now, he was older and wiser.

"Say it. I need the words."

"I want you."

12

_____

His hand curled around the back of her neck. His large palm engulfed her head, held her captive. *Captive, yes, please.* She shuddered as he traced the shell of her ear with his thumb.

"If you could see what I do. The light in your eyes."

She was then on her back. His body pushed her into the mattress, and her breath grew shallow under his weight. God, she'd missed that overpowering mass of a man covering her. All along her spine, her legs, nerves that had lain dormant lit up, and her hands could not stop roaming over all his hard male muscle.

His hand kept her neck captive, the other lazily trailed down her side to her thigh. He hitched her leg up around him. Her spine arched to meet him, her crotch seeking to rub against him, anywhere and everywhere.

"Feel that?" He ground his steely erection into the apex of her thighs. "That's what you do to me. That's what you've done to me every moment for the last forty years when your memory came up."

His words broke every latch around her heart. How foolish she'd been. He'd missed her. All this time she hadn't been alone in those feelings. A hot tear escaped and ran down her temple. "I missed you. Every day."

His blue eyes narrowed. "You want me, Rebecca? Want to serve me again?"

He wanted the words. She'd give them to him. "I never stopped." She mustered as much courage as she could. "I love you, Alexander. Still." From the second those blue eyes caught her outside in the pouring rain, any other choice that didn't end with him, vanished. In his presence, it always did.

Perhaps that's why she never gave into another man after him, never allowed herself to truly love another. She'd never stopped loving this man pressing her body into a mattress in the house where it had all begun.

He lifted himself from her, earning a small whimper from her in protest. For the briefest second, panic set in. He wasn't leaving, was he?

"Facedown. Ass up."

She twisted to lie on her stomach, and he yanked her panties down so they stretched across her thighs.

"Alexander." His name came out as light as a breath.

He landed a sharp crack to her ass. As all the air in her lungs rushed out, and the sting traveled through her whole body, her clit roared to life. She fisted the sheets. "Sir."

The honorific was the one bit of formality they'd adopted between them so long ago, back when protocol was scanty at best. She was now in even newer territory, but damnit, she would not stop whatever was happening. Alexander had been a god in her world. Then he was gone. Now, she was face first in a bed where ...

"Rebecca. Stay with me."

Had she been that obvious? He unfisted her hands from the sheet. His voice was in her ear, murmuring soft nothings as the sheet grew wet under her cheek. She'd begun to weep.

"You aren't ready for this." His voice was gentle, kind, and she didn't deserve it. She didn't want that. She wanted rough. She wanted the beast that lived under his polished exterior.

"No, no. Please, sir."

"What is it you want, Rebecca?" His voice was stern, his breath hot against her neck. "Tell me the thing you don't dare speak aloud. Give me the words."

He was going to make her admit her need.

"I don't know how … " *Liar. Coward.* "Nothing's changed since … "

"Since I last took you from behind in this room? On the floor next to this bed while you took Charles' cock in your mouth?"

Her muscles quivered with ripples of desire twisting her spine. "Yes."

He yanked her hips up in the air, and when his mouth met her pussy, her jaw dropped open in a long moan. She took in a mouthful of sheet to keep from groaning too loudly. A red wash grew behind her eyes, a blind lust that had been banked behind acres of mental concrete and fear. He licked her deeply and thoroughly, his mouth sending one message—this body was his. It always had been.

A hot wave built between her legs, more intense than she'd ever been able to produce for herself. Wet sucking sounds filled the room, and she cried out as she began to crest. The devil knew it, too. He broke contact with her, returned her knees to the bed. She growled into the sheets in frustration.

He forced her knees wider apart, and a shameless trickle of her juices slicked each of her thighs. "Keep those wide, Rebecca. Show me what you have for me."

Her breath was hot in her throat, and she had to keep swallowing to keep her mouth and throat occupied. She didn't think this was possible again, to feel so much lust, a bone deep, aching need to be penetrated in her pussy, her mouth, anywhere he wanted. His touch unearthed needs she'd buried long ago.

Dominance, flogging, bondage weren't just part of her youth. They were front and center in her dreams, tucked away like treasured memories of when she could afford such luxuries as trusting someone so much you'd hand over your body to be used, pleasured, and worshipped. She hadn't indulged in such things in decades, but god, the way Alexander handled her in the last three minutes? Please let this not be a dream.

The soft rush of fabric hitting the floor only made her desire grow. The bed jostled, and wiry hair hit the back of her thighs. She gathered fistfuls of the sheets again as the broad head of his cockhead barely breached her.

His large palms came down on her hips. "This is mine."

"Yours." She fought the urge to ram herself backward, to wait for him.

He pushed inside her inch by excruciating inch. He was so wide it hurt, as if he grated against a sunburn. She must have winced as he stilled with his fingers running up and down her spine. His mouth was on her neck, suckling and scratching her with his evening beard when she wanted him to just fuck her. She needed to be rubbed raw, filled, over-whelmed. She pushed backward.

"Stop." His bark made her freeze. "Do that again and— "

"I'm sorry, Sir. I won't. I'm sorry, Sir." Her rush of words was nothing but whispers.

He rammed into her to the root, and she cried out at the stab of pain. Yet the mental picture of him behind her, buried so deep inside, was enough to make her pussy weep uncon-trollably. Her need for him in this moment was terrifying, overwhelming, but she craved it like a junkie. Despite his earlier bark, she pushed back against him, wanting more of his thickness to rub, scrape, force open her walls.

His voice rose over the pounding in her ears. "Do you deserve this? Me?"

How did he understand her so well? She clung to one tiny piece of disbelief that she deserved to be here. "I want to."

A sharp crack from his palm made her flesh jiggle a little, and a sting spread across her backside. "Then, stay where I tell you."

She nodded.

His chest engulfed her body, his arms thick as he braced himself alongside her. He started a rhythm, a retreat and withdrawal, his palm coming down on her ass. The sting kept her present, away from dangerous thoughts like how they were in the Wynter house, fucking like animals, as they had been the night Marston found them. His fingers dug into her ass as he held her fast, holding her in place for his use. *His use.* A small moan escaped her throat.

After long minutes, he pulled out and twisted her so she lay on her back. His strength, his ability to move her around, only made her body ache for him more. He hooked her legs in the crook of his elbows, bending her in half in an impossible angle so one palm could hold her wrists above her head, the other palm resting around her throat. He'd positioned her for one thing and one thing only—taking his cock.

His blue eyes found hers, and she was trapped, captivated by his eyes, his strength, his utter command of what was happening. His mouth was on hers in a sloppy, impolite kiss. Her body grew limp as her legs flopped like a rag doll from his punishing thrusts. She couldn't hold back anymore, and her nerves exploded between her legs. He released seconds after her climax, his teeth latching onto her shoulder. He had taken her so brutally her mind emptied until only one thought remained. *Alexander. Here with me.* She didn't deserve him. She didn't deserve this second chance. She was taking it anyway.

13

_____

Eric jabbed at the massive piece of wood with the poker, more for something to do than to reposition the log. A shower of sparks flew up the chimney. He should go to sleep. Fucking jet lag. Either that, or the fact he was a few hundred feet away from Alexander who slept upstairs without him, thanks to a certain redhead.

Still, he learned a lot about the man today. Had he known Alexander's story before, he'd have parked his ass more in Washington D.C. and not been the waiting wallflower. He'd always suspected he and Alexander would get along fine— bouncing back and forth between men and women. Now with semi-confirmation on that front, like Alexander might be bisexual as well? Yeah, his hugging-the-sidelines approach to the man was officially getting pitched.

He quit annoying the dying fire and put the poker back where it belonged. He reached for his jacket and pulled out the moleskin journal he'd picked up at the airport this morning. No time like the present to get started on the art inventory.

He turned on every light he could find to illuminate the

front room and glanced around. A curio cabinet held an impressive collection of jade eggs. Why would anyone leave these behind? Marston must be kicking himself for his past indiscretions. As he added up the trinkets and art in the front room, his mind spun, mentally assigning items to Sotheby's, Christie's, and Phillips. His standing at all the major auction houses was about to go up.

After filling four pages of his journal, he strode into the entryway. He took the grand staircase two steps at a time and halted at the top landing. He studied the large family portrait, another odd thing to leave behind. He couldn't help but assess the lines and paint to see if the other son—the one not depicted—had been painted over or left out altogether. In his work, he'd seen it all—outlines of pictures that once hung on walls leaving a conspicuous mark on faded wallpaper, photographs strategically cut to remove unwanted remembrances, and, once, cigarette burns obliterating a face in a painting.

He stepped closer as the light from downstairs cast eerie shadows over the likenesses. Alice Wynter had a cruel smile, even in a painting. The last time he was here, he considered her unremarkable. Marston, however, he remembered *very* well. The man's shrewd eyes assessed his every move, and Marston asked if he'd like a drink. He'd thought nothing of it at the time— merely a friendly offer. Today? The man had forgotten they'd ever met.

He turned to his left and into a hallway leading to the master bedroom, pulling out the small flashlight he had hung on his keychain, and sending the beam of light down the red oriental runner. From the threadbare nature of the center of the carpet, someone had trod this hallway often.

As he traversed the hall, his small light illuminated the illogically-placed paintings hung on either side. A Lawrence Harris landscape hung next to a pastoral Alfred Fenton, a pair of Schut scenes near an unknown abstract painting. Now the guards peppering the place when he visited ten years ago made sense. He chuckled inwardly. The rich—always expecting a home invasion where marauders would loot them of all valuables. All except Alexander, who invited in every stray cat that slunk by.

Eric stopped in front of an odd scene. "A Caravaggio. What do you know?"

He ran his fingers over the frame. Was it wood or plaster? The painting didn't hang as flush as it should. He lifted the frame ever so slightly. Papers had been taped to the back, probably proving authenticity. *Still, odd.* He flicked on the hall light. The painting was over four feet wide, but he was able to grasp the sides and detach it from the wall. Ignorant private owners had no idea how to properly hang artwork of this importance.

He balanced the frame as he examined an envelope taped to the back. An outline of a bird had been sketched on the front. He should leave it. No, he'd bring it to Alexander. Perhaps the man was having trouble sleeping, as well? He detached the envelope and headed to the other wing. Light seeped out from under the door of Charles Wynter's old room, so he headed there.

A low rumble followed by a woman's keen froze him momentarily. He crept toward the door but stopped short at Alexander's muffled voice. The words still drifted into the hall. "Come for me." A female moan answered.

He'd been too late … again.

Time for plan C. If only he knew what that was.

14

Eric's eyes snapped open. There is a god. Someone in this house was brewing coffee. After a quick shower, donning clean clothes, and enjoying five minutes with his toothbrush —thanks to someone dropping off his bag at the crack of dawn outside his room—he followed the thick scent of roasting java to the kitchen.

Rebecca leaned against a granite countertop, her head cocked and one hand on an old-fashioned transistor radio.

"Morning." She smiled over her shoulder and straightened.

He nodded toward at the large coffee pot. "If that's full strength French roast, you are officially my favorite person."

"Want some?"

"Is there any other answer than yes?"

"Never." Alexander strode in, cradling an armful of wood. He dropped his load of firewood by a small stone fireplace already crackling with a small fire. Rebecca poured Eric a full cup and then turned to lean against the counter, her eyes traveling Alexander's form. The man dusted off his hands, and his mouth inched up into a sated smile beamed toward her. Her seducing eyes dropped in an obvious obeisance. Eric took a long swallow of coffee, burning his tongue, before he did something stupid like let his hand drift to his cock as it had throughout the night powered by what he'd heard coming from Charles Wynter's room. It didn't help that Alexander had switched his suit for jeans, a sweater, and boots, which officially slid into his most-favorite-Alexander-look.

Alexander finally ripped his gaze from Rebecca to rest those blue eyes on him. "Did you get your things?"

"Yes, thanks." How Tony, or whoever left it, knew which room he'd taken, he'd never know. He was grateful, none-theless. The rain pinged against the windows like tiny pebbles trying to break the glass. He should have brought his hiking boots. Any foray outside would ruin his new Edward Green shoes—if yesterday's excursion hadn't done the job already.

Rebecca gasped, pushed off the counter and raised a finger. She pointed at the radio. "Beatles." She twisted to face Alexander. "You know what that means."

He grasped her hand and yanked her toward him. She twirled under his arm.

"I'd like to be … under the sea." Her pretty voice cut through the somber morning like a spring breeze. Or, perhaps, the magical caffeine had begun to work.

He leaned against the counter, his mind wrestling with the fact Alexander Rockingham was dancing in a kitchen. For a brief second, the man locked eyes with him, and Eric absorbed some of the happiness radiating from him. He felt like an intruder. He'd take his coffee outside. Rebecca's hand grasped his forearm before he got two steps toward the doorway.

"Eric. You have to dance." She pulled on this arm. "Nobody sits while the Beatles are on!"

She pulled him so his arm bumped against Alexander's. The man didn't budge, which only sent a shot of lust through his system. They locked eyes for a second time.

"Charles Wynter rule." Alexander's eyes sparked.

Had he ever seen Alexander this casual, this carefree?

Rebecca gripped his hand. He'd rather parade down Broadway in a Speedo than dance, but, when in Rome ... "Okay, but I'm terrible," he said. "Two left feet."

"No one is terrible when the Beatles are on." She raised his arm and ducked under in a graceful circle. Okay, the woman could move. She pulled and pushed, leading them. She also had a lovely smile—genuine.

He bowed formally after the song blessedly ended and retrieved his coffee cup. "Well. Thank you. I'm awake now."

She panted from exertion or perhaps it was happiness. Her face glowed, but then from what he'd heard last night, she had reason to.

"That was the third Beatles song I've heard this morning," she said. "It's like this house is trying to remind us."

Alexander smiled at her and cocked his head toward Eric. "Rebecca believes in signs."

"They're everywhere if you look. Remember how Charles thought birds were messengers?"

Eric's brain clicked into gear. "Speaking of which, I hope you didn't mind, but I took a look around last night. I found a rare Caravaggio. I believe it's called Cardsharps."

"That painting's been missing for years. It's probably a copy." Alexander reached for the coffee pot.

"I don't know. There was an envelope taped to the back of the painting. I didn't open it." He withdrew it from the pocket of his fleece. "There's a bird drawn on the outside. Kind of crude ... "

Alexander snatched it from his grasp. Eric startled at the man's jarring move. When Rebecca clicked off the radio and sidled up to Alexander, a prickle moved up his spine. Something was very wrong.

"It's … " She looked up at Alexander.

If Eric didn't know better, he'd say the man stopped breathing altogether. "You know what it is?" he asked.

Rebecca looked at him. "This bird is a raven. It's meaningful to us."

If he felt like an intruder before, he was a full-on voyeur now. "I can leave you two alone." He didn't budge, though. He could play the offer-to-go-but-don't-go game, too.

"No, stay." Alexander lowered himself to the farmhouse bench. "You're about to handle one of the most personal things I've done in my lifetime. You deserve to know at least a little more as to why I needed this house. Sit." He gestured to the chair across from him.

Needed. He'd often heard how someone just "had to have" something. However, he recognized honest words when spoken. He sat, grateful not to have been dismissed.

Alexander handed the envelope to Rebecca. "Read it."

She gently ran a fingernail under the yellowed scotch tape and drew out a piece of folded paper. A sad smile spread across her face as she scanned the words across the lined notebook paper.

"Out loud," he said.

She took in a long breath. "Charles Durham Wynter. Note Number 473 or thereabouts." Her voice hitched a little, and she pressed her lips together for a brief second as if swallowing some emotion. "The raven is the most misunderstood bird in the Wynter kingdom. I know how it feels to be accused of being the harbinger of death. Well, someone's got to do it." A half-laugh crossed her lips. "And if you found this note, what are you doing sneaking around and taking paintings down?" She sniffed and looked up at Alexander. His blue eyes were glassy, all traces of joy erased.

Alexander's spine straightened and his eyes cleared. "That reminds me. I brought his last letter to me. It's in my jacket in the front room. Rebecca, will you go get it for me?"

She nodded and disappeared, leaving him alone with Alexander. Because he didn't know what else to do, he reached for Alexander's cup, cold to the touch. "More coffee?"

"Please."

After handing him a refreshed cup, Eric sat back down. Should he speak? He wasn't sure of the boundaries between personal and professional yet. He dug into people's lives for a living, but some lines shouldn't be crossed, like asking the barrage of questions pinging in his brain as fast as the rain outside. What was Charles like? What's up with Rebecca? Is she staying? Why hadn't he heard of her before now? As if Alexander had ever said much about himself.

Alexander sighed heavily. "Thank you, Eric. You did as I asked. Brought that envelope to me." He nodded his head toward it but didn't touch the note on the table. The man's fingers strained around the cup.

Eric fisted his hands in his lap. Alexander didn't get undone by notes from the past. The man was ... Hell, he didn't know. Over the years, he'd built him up in his mind so much he was sure the unflappable Alexander Rockingham was above past regrets and past hurts.

Alexander stared at the kitchen fireplace, lost in thought. "I met Charles at Harvard. We became ... involved. Lovers. He invited me here during our last Christmas break. That's when I met Rebecca. She was the daughter of one of the Wynters' oldest friends. When they died the Wynters had taken her in."

Eric swallowed, the sound too loud in his head. He didn't want to miss a word of this confession, if that's what this was.

"I was captivated by her. By both of them, actually." He turned his head toward Eric.

"She's quite attractive." *Can you be any more unoriginal?*

"You think she's beautiful now? Hell, I spent the first two days resisting the urge to jump those lecherous old men Raymond was so fond of hanging with if they so much as looked her way. Which they did—often." He took a deep breath. "We became lovers that week. All three of us. And we were caught." He glanced up to the ceiling. "Upstairs. Marston found us. Twenty-four-years-old and he still ran to his parents to tattle-tale like some kindergartener scoring points with the teacher. Alice and Raymond did what parochial socialites of that era did. Cut off Charles' funding. Instead of going back to school separately, we went to San Francisco together. Lived there for five months, squatting in friends' apartments, taking on odd jobs, until … Charles … Well, we didn't know he was sick when we fled Connecticut." His last words were so laced with pain Eric's lungs seized.

"AIDS?" He didn't know where he got the balls to ask, but what did he have to lose? How about everything—like having Alexander clam up?

"Yes, though back then no one knew what it was."

He was a kid when the news about the fatal disease no one knew anything about broke. All he could recall was the pure terror in people's voices, the acronym spoken in whispers. No one knowing shit. "I remember."

Alexander eyes clouded as if studying some faraway memory. "It wasn't long after that I stood outside the Wynter's front gate and watched a hearse disappear up the driveway to this house. Guards stood on the other side—men that had been given the orders to shoot if I stepped foot inside. That day was the last time I was even remotely close to him. At least until yesterday." He took a full gulp of coffee, hissed between his teeth. His eyes remained fixed on the fire.

Eric should say something—anything—but words had left his brain long ago. Rather, a cold fury began to build.

Alexander must have been in the mood to talk because the room filled with his voice again. "I never got to say good-bye. That's the hardest part, you know?"

Eric didn't know, but he understood Alexander didn't need words right now. He needed something Eric couldn't provide—at least right then. So, he simply nodded an acknowledgement.

"In San Francisco, at the hospital, after the Wynter family arrived, I was banished from Charles' room. Literally hauled out by three huge guys. It was easy to do in 1981. That despicable family packed up Charles, boarded their private plane, and came back here. Rebecca and I followed." He paused to take a deep breath. "Three horrible days on Greyhound buses. I was grief-stricken, but I'd never lost anyone before. When we got here, I wasn't allowed to set foot on the grounds, and Rebecca disappeared. Just inside that front gate, Alice Wynter called me the devil incarnate. Said I'd never see Charles or Rebecca again. She'd make sure of it. I told her I'd one day walk back through that gate as the new owner of this estate and I'd have a sledgehammer in my hand." He fixed his eyes on the table surface, the blue emitting so much ice he could frost over hell. "She said it would be over her dead body. Guess at least that part is true. She's dead and here I am." He downed the last of his coffee in one gulp and let the mug hit the tabletop, hard.

Eric sat back and inhaled deeply. What to feel first? Awe at the man's emotional control? Anger at how he'd been shut out? Confusion as to what happened then with Rebecca? He unclenched his fists, marks left in his flesh from nails biting into his palms. No wonder Alexander wanted this house and was so pissed at Marston's attitude. The guy was just another in a long line of homophobic assholes. Some things never change.

"Are you … " Eric shouldn't have started that question, the one in his mind flashing like a Las Vegas billboard.

"I'm negative."

The man understood his non-question. Anyone who lived through that time would.

"So was Rebecca. We'd always used condoms—or at least ninety-nine percent of the time. We checked our health status immediately … once we knew what Charles had and things went to complete shit. After that I tested often. I'll never forget that seventh year when they said I was finally all clear. Relieved, but it saddened me that—"

"Charles got the unlucky draw." His belly tightened, suddenly wanting to hit something. "I'm sorry for what the Wynters did. I had no idea." Such inadequate words …

Alexander stretched his neck as if moving on. "It was a hard time, but the social climate is better now."

"We're still not there."

Those sharp blue eyes settled on him. "No. I suppose we're not."

Eric bent forward, putting his elbows on his knees. "My family accepted me as I am. My mother asked me if I was going to ask Mary Brickman to my ninth-grade dance. I told her I'd rather go with Daniel, my best friend at the time."

"Brave."

"He was my first." He shrugged. "I never thought I had to pick sides. Men. Women. Why limit yourself to only fifty percent of the population?'

Alexander blew a breath. "Then you are unusual."

Pivotal moments were something Eric was very, very good at identifying, like the one now presented by Alexander's deeply personal sharing. Faced with a fork in this strange road he'd been asked to travel, he'd chosen right when he'd pushed for more. Fortune favors the bold.

"I guess we both are." He placed his hand over Alexander's, and holy-motherfucking-hallelujah-guardian-angel-on-high, the man didn't yank his fingers away. "I'm glad you got your revenge. Getting this house."

Alexander's lips twitched upward. "I got revenge. Now every time Marston visits his mother's grave, or sees the trees, the house, the headstones ... he will know they belong to me." The steel in Alexander's eyes returned, obliterating the pain he'd seen when Alexander had been retelling his story. This was the Alexander he knew.

"Remember the Christmas scavenger hunt he sent us on?" Rebecca's soft voice drifted into the room. She pushed off the doorway, and Alexander broke contact with him. She laid Alexander's jacket over the farmhouse table. "We'd find a clue and then that would lead to another until we got to our presents? He loved giving us things."

She'd been listening? Eric wondered how she felt about all this.

"Charles amused himself so easily." Alexander reached to his jacket, pulled out a piece of paper in the pocket, and handed it to Rebecca.

She scanned it, her mouth stretching into another sad smile. Her gaze lifted and turned to Eric, and light returned in her eyes. "I'll bet you there are more hidden letters. I could help you look."

So, Rebecca wanted to stay, too. He wasn't sure how to feel about that. She was pleasant enough, but ... his expertise wrested control from his ridiculous schoolboy jealousy. *I got this*. He knew exactly how and where to start. "You ever notice how many paintings in this house include birds?" he asked.

Alexander's smile was all he needed. Hell, yes, he was going to help this man settle a few scores.

15

"This is where you found it?" Alexander held his chin and stared at the nondescript brown paper backing of the Tobias Stranover.

"Yep." Eric studied the framing. "The curator at the Dia Foundation would kill for this."

"He can have it." He could give a rat's ass about the artwork. The real treasure, found taped to the back of this pheasant painting, crinkled between his fingers. The words rang in his ears as if Charles' voice spoke straight from heaven.

Charles Durham Wynter Note Number 217 or thereabouts.
Bluebirds, cardinals, the vicious peacock. Everyone loves the beautiful birds. Yet it's the females that do the heavy lifting, and have you seen a female cardinal? Those brown feathers look like they bathed in a mud puddle. Don't you agree? Say something if you're going to go sneaking about looking for my hidden letters.

His stomach churned. The nostalgia was getting to him—that or the mold and dust they'd inhaled for hours. At least

Eric had found something. *He* had sat in the library seeking long lost love letters, flipping through pages of old books like a historian. His phone buzzed in his pocket for the nineteenth time that day. He'd kill for forty-eight hours in one day.

"Check on Rebecca, will you? She should be sleeping." He'd ordered her to take a long hot bath while he kept going. She was then to take a nap.

He lifted his phone. "I've got to take this."

"Alexander?" Ryan's voice was edged in panic. "How soon can you get back to D.C.?"

"Hold on." He held the phone away from his ear. "Eric, we'll go out to dinner … in town. If she's awake, tell Rebecca." He strode to the front of the house to deal with whatever had Ryan in a snit.

"What's going on?"

"Remember Michael Headler?"

"How could I forget?" To think he'd wasted countless hours on trying to reform that abuser. "Don't tell me Seraphina is giving up on him, too?"

"She will now. He's here with an attorney, crying about sexual abuse. He named us specifically, Alexander. Told this attorney you run a secret sex club called Accendos."

Irritation bubbled up. He didn't have time for this. "Not the first time someone's tried that stunt."

"Yes, but this attorney is wearing the $600 shoes. Headler is well funded, which means only one thing."

"Someone is using him to get to us." He sighed. "I'll make some calls."

"Do you want to tell Carson or shall I?"

Shit. The club's attorney wasn't going to like this. More than likely his head would explode after learning the former abuser of Carson's now-wife wanted to sue *them* for sexual abuse. "I'll do it. And get ready for some furniture throwing."

Ryan chuckled nervously. "Already battening down the hatches. So, when do we expect you?"

"There have been some developments here, and I need to attend to them. Tell Carson he can handle the legal counter-attack. That should spare some of the furniture. Tell opposing counsel I'll be back when I get back. I won't be summoned anywhere by the likes of Michael Headler." Or miss the chance to lock in Rebecca. A nice dinner and spectacular sex didn't equal reconciliation. Somewhere between this morning's kitchen confession to Eric and finding this last letter, he'd made up his mind. He was taking Rebecca home with him.

He killed the call and scrolled through his contacts. This was going to take a while, and if he was going to introduce Rebecca to Accendos, things needed to be buttoned up.

16

———

"Hey, you're going to throw out your back." Eric grasped the plastic sack Rebecca wrestled into an honest-to-God Little Red Wagon. He'd seen her from the parlor window, stomping around in a pair of old Hunters. "Didn't you get ordered to nap?"

She laughed and dusted off her hands. "I'm willing to take the punishment."

And, didn't his dick do a little dance inside his pants at that? "I don't blame you."

"I thought you'd feel that way." She tipped her head. "Want to help me fill Charles' bird feeders?" She swept her hand across the land. "If there are any left. We can talk then."

It seems all he'd done since he'd gotten here was talk, but okay. "I'd never leave a damsel to haul—" he peered at the bag. "—$78 worth of sunflower seeds around. Holy Christ, they better be handpicked and organic for that price."

She laughed. "Come on. We'll start with the castle."

"The what?"

"He named them all. You'll see."

"You know this place well." He grasped the handle of the wagon and followed her along the fence line.

"I do. My parents were friends with Raymond and Alice." She paused to look him in the eye. "In both economic status and beliefs." A delicate scoff left her throat. "I lived here after they died."

"I'm sorry?"

"Me, too."

Twenty minutes later, they'd filled two bird feeders, including the Castle, which looked like a gray wedding cake mounted on a dilapidated wooden post. She was a relatively open book, volunteering story after story about running around with Charles and his friends instead of learning how to play tennis and pour tea, much to the dismay of Alice Wynter.

"Alice really called you a floozy?" He returned her laughter.

"Hand to God. It made me laugh then, too. You have family, Eric?" She lifted a scoop filled with black seeds, dumped them into a wrought iron and cedar fly-through feeder and handed it to him.

"My father died when I was too young to remember him. My mother remarried, but she died when I was in college."

"I'm sorry." Her gray eyes, a stormy blue if you really looked, warmed toward him. "Are you married?"

Married? *Hells no.* "Too busy traveling around." He hooked the birdfeeder back on its perch.

"Ah, a gypsy like me. Well, you haven't missed much." She narrowed her eyes at him, as if studying him. "You've been a good friend to Alexander. He needed someone not close to this situation who could help him with this—" she waved her arm. "—house dismantling."

"It's what I do."

"You're also in love with him."

Fishing, was she? His insides immediately threw up a brick wall. "I don't fall in love."

She raised her eyebrows. "Never?"

He shrugged.

"Well, I do. Consider yourself warned." She made that delicate titter again. "I think you have Alexander's best interests at heart, however."

Okay, now was the time to be as direct as she was proving to be. "Are you in love with him?"

If she was surprised by that question, her face didn't show it. "I can't not love Alexander. He's the single most important man in my life."

"Then why were you separated?"

She didn't answer, rather turned to the birdseed bag.

He may have overplayed his cards with that one. "I apologize. I shouldn't have asked that."

"No, it's fine. Truth is, it's complicated."

"Truth often is."

She straightened and lifted a full pitcher of seeds. "The Wynters threatened to destroy Alexander. I made sure those threats weren't made real. But I'm not really interested in the past." He eyes clouded in thought. "I'm more of a future-oriented girl."

"With Alexander."

"I honestly don't know. Since you've known him for the last few years, tell me something. Did he never find anyone? I've asked, but I think he believes it's impolite to tell me about past lovers. I mean, have you and he …"

Ah, he was familiar with this interviewing technique. He'd used it himself a time or two. Let a question trail off, expecting the other would fill in the blank. "I've seen him with others, but I don't think he's ever loved." That was as truthful as he could say, and he had no idea how much she knew about his life back in D.C. He was sworn to secrecy, as all members of Alexander's circle were, but even absent the knowledge about his secret BDSM world, how could she not know of Alexander's deep need for dominance?

"That makes me sad, actually." She turned, and he followed her, pulling that little wagon meant for an eight-year old to a tall, cylinder, feeder tucked under a tree branch.

She lifted it off the hook and turned to him. "I'm surprised to hear no one snatched him up by now. To be alone that long is terrible."

Join the club. "Yeah, I've wondered that about him for seven years. Now, I think I know why." He gazed at the memorial. "Once you've touched magic, little compares."

She cocked her head. "Magic. My word exactly. Alexander, Charles, and I defied the usual relationship, but then he told you that this morning."

"Alexander's life is unusual. Thank God."

"Yes, thank the goddess."

Her smile was guileless and warm, a nice contrast in his usual world full of pretenders. No wonder Alexander had been drawn to her—if this was who she was back then. People often change to suit circumstance.

As she poured the seeds into the feeder, he studied the full length of her. Her high society upbringing was evident in her elegant carriage, the way she handled a bulky scoop like it was an escargot fork. She was pretty, not stunning, or cute, or sultry. No, "pretty" fit her perfectly. Also, "provocative." Why the hell was he assigning adjectives to her anyway?

"I gather you three were close." He wanted more from her.

She snapped on the feeder top and handed it to him. "The three of us were interlocking pieces that formed a whole. Back then it was so easy to love— physically, emotionally, spiritually. We were young and romantic and, oh, so naive."

Her grey eyes stormed and, yeah, Eric could see how

Alexander would be captivated. All that sunset red hair framing a face with so much life ... When was the last time he was with a woman? At that yacht party during his stay in Barcelona two years ago?

He hung the feeder. "It would be good for Alexander to have love again."

"Why, Eric Morrison, you're a romantic after all."

Or a wuss where Alexander was concerned. "Perhaps."

She dusted off her hands. "Then, I'm right about you. You are good for him." She stepped closer. "Can I confide in you? I'm concerned about him. The past is stuck to him like old wallpaper or something. He's still so angry."

"He has every right to be. What about you?"

She paused to take a deep breath. "I spent some horrid days on Greyhound buses terrified to fall asleep because I was so worried about Alexander. The Wynters let me in for the funeral, and I now know it was meant to be cruel to him, to see that everyone in his life was behind that gate—" she tipped her head to the front entrance of the estate "—and he couldn't be. It was the last time I saw him until now."

Eric wasn't a violent man, but hearing this? How could the man not be bitter about the past? "They hated him."

"No. They were afraid of him." A bird rustled out of the tree at that exact moment, and for one brief second this "signs" thing she believed in felt very real. She leveled those pale gray eyes on him. "You see all that power he exudes? Well, he's always had it. He didn't need money, a Patek Phillipe on his wrist, or a Mercedes. Everyone who met him just knew. He had a certain inherent ... "

"Gravitas?" He didn't know where the word came from, but Rebecca's gray eyes sparked recognition.

There was that smile again. "Exactly. He couldn't be influenced and those kind of people scare others who are so concerned about appearances. Like the Wynters. But even they recognized his … " She trailed off again.

"Substance?"

They stared at one another for a few seconds as if they'd just discovered uranium. Alexander was remarkable, but everyone knew that. Now he and Rebecca were on the inside on how he became that way. Well, more her than him, but he'd take whatever scrap he could get.

"That doesn't mean he's invincible, however," he said.

"No one is."

Alexander didn't need to be like Teflon, though. Perhaps Rebecca knew nothing about the Alexander of today. "He has something that the Wynters don't. He has friends. You have no idea the number of people who would go to the mattresses for that man."

"You included?"

"More than." He'd not thought of having to defend Alexander before, but, shit yes, he would. Would he have to where she was concerned? He still didn't trust her completely. "So where does that leave us?"

"Friends. United in helping Alexander."

Friends? He pursed his lips a little, and the word rattled around in his brain. He liked her, despite his suspicions, so why was he hesitating? He could keep an eye on her, and jealousy was for small people. If he wanted to play in the big leagues, for that was Alexander's world, he needed to get with the program. Besides, true love was a myth. He'd hoped merely to become a friend with benefits where Alexander was concerned.

"Okay, then." He picked up the wagon handle, circled her shoulder and turned her toward the house. "We should get back inside. Alexander wants to take us to dinner." More birds squawked overhead. "So, Charles was into birds, huh?"

"He loved them. He was an eighty-year-old ornithologist inside that cute boy exterior."

"Alexander has quite an extensive garden at his home in D.C. Lots of birds there. Has he asked you to go home with him yet?"

She stilled. "No."

The shock on her face was a surprise. How could she not expect that? He could see that next step a mile away. "He's going to ask you, and, when you do go—" because she *would* "—consider me your navigator."

"Will I need one?"

"Most definitely. You should know something about his home. Once there, you'll never want to leave. But, his life is … large."

"Okay, then. Navigator." She held out her hand and he took it. Warmth seeped into his palm on contact.

Yeah, he liked her.

"Speaking of the man," she whispered. She lifted their hands together in a wave as Alexander crested the hill. "Hi. The bird feeders needed us."

Alexander smiled down at the two of them. "Guess who's playing at the Grafton tonight." His rich voice carried on the wind. "Wolfstone."

Her lips parted, and she spun toward Eric. "You like Irish music?"

Oh, please, no. He plastered a smile on his face. "Who doesn't?"

"Then it's a sign." She hooked her arm in his and pulled him closer. Shit, she smelled good, too. Okay, he officially had a new friend, united in helping Alexander get over someone dead for forty years. Yay, him.

17

Irish music wasn't so bad, especially when you got to watch Alexander Rockingham in jeans and boots move in time with the bagpipes, guitar, and drums. He twirled Rebecca and her long red hair fanned out like a belly dancer's scarf. The two of them made Irish music sexy and damned if his feet didn't start to tap in time with the rousing beat.

"Care to take a turn?" An honest-to-God Irish accent broke his train of thought. He eyed a Rubenesque woman with flaming crimson hair, a sharp contrast to Rebecca's more golden-rose tone.

"You're gonna break it if you keep chair dancing like that." She nodded her head toward his seat.

Was there anything more humiliating than to be caught chair dancing at forty-eight years old?

"I'm a terrible dancer," he said.

"With a face like yours, who cares?" She grasped his arm and, holy mother, she righted him with no effort at all. A few seconds later, he was in the middle of a sweaty crowd being pushed and pulled by the enthusiastic woman in some semblance of a dance.

"You're pretty good, Eric," Rebecca called as Alexander expertly unwound her in a twirl.

"Oh, yeah, I'm Nureyev."

"Who's that?" his dance partner asked.

To demonstrate, he spun her—right into a red-faced man with remnants of a bow tie hanging around his neck.

"Oh, look, it's a woman." He lifted her up into a bear hug.

By the way she laughed, he wasn't going to have to morph into Superman and rescue her. He was better off at the bar anyway.

After dodging other dancers, he crammed himself into a space between guys whose butts looked as if they'd molded to the stools. His hands curled around the sticky brass bar and raised his hand to catch the bartender's attention. "You got a Macallan?"

"You'll have to do with Johnnie Walker."

Of course, he would. "Fine."

Despite his better judgment, he leaned against the tacky bar top and let his attention drift back to the dance floor. Alexander had some moves and was using all of them on Rebecca, who was no slouch in the dance department. They likely grew up with cotillions and private dance lessons. The music transitioned to a lively jig. Yep. Alexander could dance that, too. The man would look stunning in a kilt.

Two men holding hands raised them into the air and moved their feet as if attempting to channel Michael Flatley. One of them laughed, leaned over and smacked the other on the lips. To think there was as a time when that couldn't have happened. As that thought crossed his mind, the guy who'd taken over his redheaded dance partner tumbled against the bar next to him, jostling one of the stool jockeys.

"Beer. Anything that's wet." From the way his words slurred, the man didn't need any more alcohol. "That girl's going to be the death of some guy." He jutted his chin toward the redhead who had found another victim—actually two—as she joined two, openly gay, men.

"She's enthusiastic." He lifted his Johnnie Walker to his lips.

The man slouched further against the bar. "Well, at least it's better than those two. Jesus, I fucking hate the North. It's why our country's going to pot."

Whatever. Eric proceeded to ignore the man. He didn't have time for homophobic assholes.

"Faggots."

Maybe he did have time. "What did you say?" Eric squared himself to the man.

"Those guys." He lifted his beer to his lips. "That's what's wrong with today's world. Girls turning into boys. Boys turning into girls." He took a long swallow.

"The Greyhound station is down the street. Hop on one."

The guy had the audacity to appear injured. "What's your problem, man?"

He should not do this. He should *not* but he was so tired of this whole homophobic game. Fuck, he was tired of watching Alexander dance with Rebecca without him. He placed his hand on the drunk's shoulder and squeezed. "You don't know what you're missing."

The guy at first froze as if not understanding, but then lurched backward as if burned. He had his fist up and out next, which was Eric's fault for taunting him but, whatever … He easily blocked the guy's wimpy-ass half-punch. The would-be brawler staggered into one of the servers, who upended an oval tray filled with glasses, sending the shattered pieces toward the bartender. Eric grasped the collar of the drunk's jacket and yanked him upright.

The guy tried to spin and landed right against Alexander, whose large hands curled around the man's lapels. Alexander's eyes, as cold and hard as he'd ever seen them, jerked the man to standing. By the look on his face, Eric expected a feral growl to rumble in Alexander's throat, but instead, he spoke slowly and quietly. "You didn't mean to offend my friend, did you?"

Drunk, homophobic asshole shook his head, eyes wide with alarm.

"Good." He handed the man off to the bartender who'd rounded the bar in no time, spitting out apologies.

Alexander straightened to his full height and fixed that hard gaze on Eric. "You all right?"

Eric swiped his hand through his hair. "They all want to cop a feel."

He laughed and slapped him on the shoulder. "Come on, let's get drunk."

"I didn't know you did that kind of thing."

"When an Irish band is playing, it's mandatory." He jerked his head in the direction of their table. "Come on. I'm buying."

Two hours later, Eric wasn't sure Alexander could be considered "drunk" given he'd switched to ice water a while ago, but his loose smile and tapping foot showed something was happening inside the man. He, however, floated pleasantly on a cloud of beer, and music, and dance, and the pride that Alexander had broken up a fight for him. It had been unnecessary, but felt good as hell that Alexander threw some of his white knight chivalry his way. Since then, they had fallen into an easy comradery, like two regular guys, watching his woman dance circles around the other people on the dance floor.

"I love watching her move. Always have." Alexander leaned his elbows on the table and peered over at him. "We used to frequent this little burlesque club in San Francisco. Rebecca even took the stage once or twice."

"I can see it."

"She was spectacular."

"She is."

He turned his body to face his. "You like her."

"She's hard not to like."

Alexander returned his attention to the dance floor where Rebecca had her arm hooked into another woman's and was spinning her. "You've been a calming force here. I appreciate it."

His chest swelled a little at that. Maybe he had done something right after all. "I'm here for whatever you need." Work, play or the need to flog something or someone—he was one hundred percent available.

"I'm taking Rebecca to Washington with me. If she'll go."

Hell, yeah, he'd called that one.

He faced Eric again. "I haven't told her the extent of what she'll find there yet, but I plan on showing her everything."

He sobered instantly and his belly responded with a stupid fluttering. This was his chance, wasn't it? "Want some help?"

Alexander's blue eyes bored into him. "Interested in women?"

"I've been known to appreciate the stronger sex." He glanced at Rebecca who showed no signs of leaving the dance floor.

Alexander took a sip of his water. "You know about her, Charles, and me, and the way I live my life."

"I appreciate the way you live your life."

Alexander smiled, tapped his finger against the glass. "How much have you had to drink?"

"Not much. Two beers. A few sips of Johnnie Walker until … " He cocked his head toward the bar.

Alexander smiled. "Good. Care to help me with something tonight?"

"What do you need me to do?"

"Follow my lead. The second you want to stop, you do."

Alexander rose, and the screech of the wood chair legs sent a thrill of anticipation through Eric's gut. Was Alexander suggesting what he thought? If helping involved sex …

"The second I think Rebecca is a 'no', it's a hard no."

"Of course."

"Beyond what you've already submitted, any details about you I need to know?"

Submitted? *Oooh.* He'd completed reams of questionnaires about limits, preferences, health conditions, and a multi-page NDA, merely to step foot inside Alexander's home-slash-club, Accendos. Fuck, yeah, he might be right about Alexander's intentions.

"Nothing new," Eric said. "I'm a bi-switch." He wasn't someone who had to be on top or the bottom. He just needed to be where he needed to be. Right now? Tell him when and where.

"Let's go back. Start a fire." Alexander moved to Rebecca, Eric's new friend, who might be a whole lot more, because please let Alexander's words be a metaphor. Eric was good at starting fires. No burning of priceless antiques required.

Alexander circled her waist and spoke into her ear. Her lashes flicked up, and she turned her head and smiled at Eric. Dare he believe his imagination could be right for one fricking night? Dare he think Alexander wanted him to join them? His cock was going to make it hard to walk to the car.

18

Rebecca pulled her coat tighter around her. When they reached the estate, they'd paused outside Alexander's Mercedes, stopped by the clarity of the night sky. The three of them had halted their progress across the drive at the same time. Alexander pulled her so her back leaned against him. His large fingers were entwined in hers, and together they traced an invisible outline in the sky.

"Which one is that?" he asked.

"Cassiopeia," Her breath, a tiny puff of vapor, clouded her vision for a second.

"You've always loved the stars."

"It's how I know everything is going to be all right."

Eric looked over at her. His eyes glinted with ambient light from the house. "In the Mojave desert, there appear to be more stars than darkness. It made me think of a Longfellow poem. 'Silently, one by one, in the infinite meadows of heaven, Blossomed the lovely stars, the forget-me-nots of the angels'."

"That's beautiful."

She took in the man's profile, the strong jaw, the stubble along his chin. He was quite handsome in a casual, elegant way. She guessed him in his forties, where maturity had settled in but not age. How could he still be single? Then again, tonight, when Eric had watched them dance, those hazel green eyes tracked Alexander's every movement. What had Eric said earlier? *"Once you've had magic—or perhaps even the thought of it— it's hard to settle for less."* She, more than most, understood that once introduced to Alexander, it was hard to see anyone else.

Alexander's arm's tightened around her. "I'm afraid there aren't many stars to be found in D.C., but there are other things to see. Eric knows all about them."

Eric turned his face up to the night sky. "Oh, yes."

She leaned against the strong man whose arms banded her tightly to him. A shiver moved through her body when she felt him harden against the small of her back. The thought her proximity caused that reaction soothed her ego a bit—something she'd not had much of lately.

"You're cold." Alexander's voice rumbled through her torso.

More like turned on. "A little." She gazed up at his eyes, still so blue even under moonlight.

"I promised you a fire. Let's go inside."

Alexander sprawled in an armchair he'd pulled in front of the snapping fire. Rebecca knelt on the floor by him, her arms draped over his knees. She'd grown woozy from the warmth of the fire, his fingers playing with her hair, the one Guinness she managed to consume tonight, the feeling that everything was right with the world. She could not remember the last time her muscles had relaxed this much and all seemed right with the world, and in the Wynter house of all places? She shouldn't even be here.

Eric stomped in, an arm full of logs. Alexander's fingers, which had been wound in her hair, tightened when she tried to rise to help him.

"Let him," he whispered. "I rather like him handling wood."

Oh. Her pussy clenched a little at the blatant innuendo. She stared at Eric's broad back and muscular ass. Yes, handsome indeed. She shifted on her legs as if that would ease the ache Alexander started in the car. Being this close to him, feeling his hard muscles, smelling him, awoke her latent sex drive with a vengeance.

Eric threw a log on the two already consumed by flames. Men and their need to play with fire. After poking at the logs, he lowered himself to the chair nearest them. His hair had fallen across his forehead and his eyelids drooped ever so slightly, giving him that rogue pirate look.

The hand Alexander had threaded in her hair stilled. "How do you feel about a foot massage?"

"I'd be happy to." She reached for his boot but his hold on her hair tightened.

"No, Eric will give you one."

Her gaze shot up to Eric's face. His lips twitched upward. "Which one first?" He'd posed the question to Alexander.

"The right."

Eric scooted down to the floor and held out his palm, his lips inched up in a half smile. She placed her foot in his hand. He rid her of the sock immediately. Oh crap. She hadn't had a pedicure in ages, that thought immediately cast aside because, oh, his fingers knew their way around. He cradled her foot in one hand while the thumb of his other pressed into her arch. When his fingers moved to her toes, pulling gently and kneading the tiny joints, she sighed and let her head fall back. Alexander's fingers combed through her hair, the pulls on the individual strands making her scalp tingle.

"Your hands are magic." If men only knew how much giving a decent foot rub or hair brushing would buy them. She sighed. "Mmm, you two could open a spa."

Alexander chuckled. "Missed being doted on by two men?"

"Yes, actually."

"Then I have a proposal for you." Alexander released her hair and the slight creak of the chair made her lift her head from his thigh. He'd leaned back, placed his hands on each armrest. "Two actually. One involves Eric."

"A proposal?" She'd been half kidding, but she knew better than to kid this man, even if she hadn't spent much time with him over the last four decades. She twisted, careful not to pull her foot free, to peer up at his blue eyes. "You have my attention."

"Proposal one." He gathered her face in his hands. "Come back to Washington with me. See my life. See what I can offer you."

Offer her? Eric had been right, and she wasn't quite sure what to do with that. "Washington?"

"Tomorrow."

"That soon?" It would be good to leave this place, but not return to Philadelphia? She had deadlines on two articles, an apartment with one aloe plant, and eventually, she'd run out of clothes given how few she'd brought with her. The practicalities of life stacked up in her mind like those burning logs in the fireplace.

"Do you have anything urgent you need to attend to? You've been away for a few days yet you haven't made any calls."

No, she hadn't. She was pitiful, wasn't she? It was embarrassing really, how she could never keep friends for long, how she never let herself stay in one place too long. Like Eric.

"And the other proposal?" She might as well learn of his other plans.

He resettled both his hands on the armchair, his face firming with intention. "As for the other. Rise and move up here."

She swallowed, but smiled at Eric as she withdrew her foot. There was no question where "up here" meant. She should be embarrassed, hesitate, do something, but her body moved her as if invisible hands guided her to straddle Alexander's lap. His familiar hardness filled the space between her legs, and didn't that turn her warm, every-thing's-all-right mood, to full-on sexual need? *Slow it down, girl.*

His eyes softened and his hands moved to her waist. "I have so much I want to show you, starting with how much my life has to offer."

Her impatience with his teasing and half information about his life grew. "Like what?"

"There's much to tell you, but here are the cliff notes. I run an international BDSM network. My house is both a home to me and a private membership club, called Accendos. It's an extended family, open 24 -7 to anyone who needs it."

Her spine snapped straight. Wait. What did he say? "Back up. A BDSM club?" She glanced at Eric who had scooted closer. He slowly nodded, all signs of a smirk gone.

She turned back to stare in Alexander's blue eyes, half expecting them to crinkle with amusement as if this was all a joke. They were as hard and icy as ever. "Oh. You really do. That's definitely ... different." What else would she say?

"Shocked?"

Was she? "Not at all." She took a deep breath. "I should

have guessed you were still active. You command a room, always have. Washington, D.C. would fit you."

"It's a place of great power, supposedly the seat of justice, but they get it so wrong sometimes. I took on steering things behind the scenes."

"Are you CIA, too?"

He and Eric laughed at the same time, which annoyed her. "No. I'm an ordinary citizen with a great deal of money and patience. I'm not interested in politics, international affairs, or war games. I'm interested in giving people the freedom to live the life they wish with clearly spelled out do-no-harm principles."

She swallowed. "Oh. So, it's like a club ... only a home where everyone plays." This news should make her heart hammer in her chest, instead all the remaining blood supply in her body pooled in one heated spot—very far south of her chest.

She could see him in a BDSM club. Alexander standing tall in a room lit only with red lights. He'd be in all black, those icy blue eyes glittering with intention as he pulled back a flogger. She'd had the privilege of seeing him like that.

His gaze locked on her face. "It doesn't matter whether they play or read the Encyclopedia Britannica. It's there for people who don't feel accepted anywhere else."

Her eyes misted with some unnamed emotion. Pride, she supposed. "I knew you'd do it. I knew you'd use your life better than anyone."

He brushed hair that had fallen into her face. "So, come to Washington to see for yourself. Or don't. The offer is open."

She nodded, unable to speak. Eric was now on his knees to the side of the armchair, as if waiting for a command. The angles in his face were more pronounced in the firelight. She was curiously tempted to run her finger along his jawline. She shifted a little on Alexander's lap, her clit mashing against his cock. Alexander's hips lifted a fraction and that's when thoughts clicked into place. Alexander's life was large, Eric had said. She'd need a navigator.

Holy shit.

The proposal ...

They wanted to ...

Her gaze bounced from Alexander to Eric and back to Alexander.

"So, about the second offer. Ready to hear it?" Alexander rumbled. His blue eyes were a radioactive seduction, and she might as well say yes now because around him there was no other answer. Then there was the way her hips had started to roll on his lap, tiny movements that had every nerve ending between her legs starting to fire.

Think.

No, don't think.

Feel. Her belly danced at the memory of his offers from the past. "I'm ready to hear." She wasn't, but her body curiously itched to fall to the ground to join Eric.

Alexander's blue eyes held her in place.

The wicked man pulled her closer so her crotch mashed against his cock that she really, really wanted to free from behind that zipper.

"Eric, come here. Closer." His voice held pure command. Eric rose and stood by the chair next to them, a clear erection pushing against his jeans. Alexander cocked his head. "Interested?"

One word that held so much meaning.

The man's lips twitched upward. "At your disposal."

Alexander's eyes, the blue impossibly deepening, returned to her. "You said you missed being doted on by two men." His rich voice made her quake a little on the inside, the good kind of shake that made her legs crave to spread open. Or maybe it was the way his hips had begun to move under her. "Remember, this is your call. It's always up to you."

She knew what "it" was full well. Few words were necessary when feeling a cock muscling against her pussy and seeing another straining the limits of Eric's tight-fitting jeans to her left. The question was "it" something she could do again? Her body screamed for the pure sensation, the possibility of getting lost in flesh, and love, and attention ... none of which she'd had for years. She'd gotten used to being invisible. Her brain, however, would not stop trying to mess her up. Lots of, "Are you crazy?" and, "You're not in your youth anymore, lady," clamped a lid on her complete enthusiasm. Alexander's large hand spanned her waist. His hold stopped her hip rolling dead in its tracks.

"What is that? That sudden tension? There's no shame in any answer you give." He'd stopped his small grinding motion, a signal he was letting her off the hook? Always such a gentleman.

"I haven't felt anything *but* shame for a very long time." Her voice cracked. For decades, she'd drifted between being fine and a low melancholy. The sharp stab of regret deflated any elevated mood she might have clung to for a few hours. "And, I'm tired of it."

Alexander lifted her hand and placed it on Eric's erection. "Say 'no,' Rebecca, if you'd rather not. It's your call."

He always said that, even before consent was a big deal like it was now. She didn't want this kindness, this gentle get-out-of-jail-free-card that he offered up. She wanted ... what?

She wanted to be taken—hard.

So say no? *Like hell.*

"I say, yes." She curled her fingers to run them up and down Eric's trapped shaft, and he groaned. Courage was never her strong suit, but her fear of losing this moment trumped any answer other than "yes." Her hips rolled freely now, her clit seeking the cock underneath her with a vengeance. Wanting, needing, craving to be mashed hard against Alexander's pelvis as he invaded her body with that hard cock. Taken? How about she wanted to be *impaled*.

Alexander fisted her hair and yanked her head backward. A gasp left her throat. He buried his face in her neck and suckled the tender skin there. "Don't stop touching him. No matter what I'm doing to you," he said against her skin. His hand slid down to capture her breast and thumb a nipple through the thin fabric of her shirt. She wanted her blouse *off*.

She arched her back into his kneading palm. "Yes, sir."

"Eric can come to Accendos with us if he'd like."

Alexander's grip on her hair eased up enough for her to glance at Eric. His nostrils flared, whether from the ongoing tease of her hand or Alexander's invitation, she couldn't say. He hissed between his teeth as her fingernails gently scored repetitive tracks from his tight balls to the wet spot of fabric delineating the head of his cock. "I'd like."

Alexander hooked his fingers through the gap between her shirt buttons and yanked her blouse open. Fabric tore and buttons skittered away, but she couldn't have cared less. He drove his fingers into her bra and yanked her breasts so they hung over the underwire, making them protrude straight out. His teeth clasped onto a nipple and he bit down.

"Ah." The sound from her throat was guttural. She ground on Alexander's lap, her body going rogue on her. It was as if Alexander held the puppet strings to her body and drove her lust for him. He sucked and licked until her nipple was a hard peak. He moved to the other breast and she struggled to keep her fingers playing Eric's cock. The man's hips now pitched forward toward her and there were just too many clothes, too many barriers. Eric hissed and sighed openly, and one hand fell to the back of the chair as if needing to steady himself.

Alexander released her hair, his lips releasing her breast. He brought his mouth close to hers. "Only you, Rebecca, could turn this house into a place where I want to take both of you." He pulled back and placed his hands on the armrests once more. "Now, stand and take off your clothes. Slowly." He raised his gaze to Eric who openly panted. "Eric, do the same."

19

Firelight did wonderful things to bare skin. Shadows played in muscle angles, like the curve under Rebecca's breasts hanging heavy and the deep crevices in Eric's hips angling to a V that disappeared into his jeans. The gold strands in Rebecca's hair lit up, and her nipples darkened to berry— nipples he was going to clamp and tether to him by a long chain once they were sheltered by the walls of Accendos. For now, with nothing but his bare hands and intentions, he was going to reclaim her in the very room where she'd let him go.

"Wider." He took one step closer and drank in the sight of her submission displayed by open knees, straight spine and downcast eyes. He'd known her like that nearly forty years ago, and some things don't change. Her inner lips, now visible to him, glistened in the low amber light. The moonstone necklace, the only thing he'd allowed her to keep on, glinted in the firelight and rose and fell with her breath. She could easily stop this entire scene. Instead, her lips parted on a sigh as Eric, standing behind her, yanked her hair into a ponytail.

The man had proved quick with his hands, and Alexander

took note of his large palms and long fingers that he imagined itched to do more. Eric had followed his orders without hesitation so far, but before Eric participated more fully, there were formalities to attend to.

He'd start with Eric. "Safeword?"

"Red."

"Rebecca?" When she didn't answer, he crouched down, cupped her face. "You're shaking."

"It's been a while." Her eyes darted up. "That doesn't mean I don't want you to … "

"To what?" He ran his finger up the seam of her groin, gathering the moisture there. "Your body seems to want something very much." He lifted his finger to her lips, ran her own juices over her bottom lip. She captured his forefinger between her lips, the little brat, and a deep sound escaped his throat at the warm, wet sensation of her tongue.

Her body wanted this, but the mind often caught up later. He pulled his finger free and arched an eyebrow. "Say it. Directly."

"Red."

"Red," he repeated. "Anything else?"

"I want both of you to fuck me."

All right. Mind caught up. Alexander granted her a smile. "Then, my sweet, Rebecca, you have the right to earn that." He stood. "If it pleases me."

She swallowed, a delicious trepidation filling those gray eyes. He was going to fuck this woman all right. As for Eric, he'd see. Having regained some ground with Rebecca, he wasn't in a sharing mood. He'd be delighted, however, to edge Eric all night.

His gaze slid to Eric. "Take off the rest of your clothes." Meeting his eyes, the man's lips tugged up into an amused smile.

Not a hint of discomfort colored the man's face or body—

and he had quite the body. Lean but with muscles that bunched as he toed off his shoes and lowered his jeans and boxers to the floor. Nice cock, too. Too bad he didn't have a harness with him to truss that thing up, make Eric beg to be released as he watched him take Rebecca over and over. He'd invited the man in. He'd decide what "in" meant as they went along.

Alexander stood and stared down at Rebecca. "Undo my jeans."

She lifted her small hands and fumbled with the button of his jeans. He rather enjoyed watching her fumble as she clasped her bottom lip between her teeth. She slowly lowered his zipper, her eyes widening with the realization he wore nothing under his jeans, and then put her hands back to her thighs. *Very good.*

With his jeans undone, his cock threatened to crawl out on its own. "You want this?"

She spread her knees more as if posing an invitation. "Yes."

"Take out my cock."

The soft skin of her hand felt oh so fucking good as she drew him out. The hunger in her eyes made him thicken, and when her pink tongue darted out to taste her lip, his erection was entirely in the game. He'd like nothing more than to thrust inside her mouth, hard and brutal, feel her flesh surround him, hear her cry out at the invasion.

"Eric, hold her hair again."

Eric's lips inched up sideways. He'd handle that smirk at some point. He was large everywhere. He knew how he sized up against others. One thrust into that tight ass Eric presented might fuck that grin right off him. He tucked away that thought for later. The man's eagerness definitely begged for prolonged edging.

He returned his attention to Rebecca. "Open your mouth."

Her lips parted and that heaven-blessed mouth found the crown of his cock. He hissed and fed more of him to her, inch by inch, reveling in the slick heat of her mouth. He never thought he'd have her again like this, on her knees, taking his cock down her throat. Her wicked tongue worked over every vein as she applied a delicious pressure with her cheeks. The good girl kept her eyes on him. God, her mouth was tight. He could come so easily. He'd honed his sexual discipline until he rarely had to think about slowing down anymore, except now. With this woman, with this mouth, the control he'd maintained for decades was in danger of cracking.

Saliva ran down the sides of her chin, and her breath drew in and out through her nose, heavy and wet-sounding.

Eric shifted on his feet and his cock danced in the air. Those long fingers fisted her hair mercilessly, holding her in place—for him. Jesus, yes, he could come from just watching these two.

"Stop."

Rebecca knelt back. Wet ran down her chin.

He trailed a fingertip down one cheek. "Mo rúnsearc, your mouth pleased me very much."

Her eyes softened, and her lips inched up in a half smile. "Want more?" She ran her tongue over her top lip.

The little brat that he'd once known and loved hadn't travelled very far, despite her circling the globe many times.

He wanted to do so many things to this woman. Bury himself inside her. Be surrounded by her flesh. Torture her. Fuck her. Bind her. Spank her. Make her wait. Make her come. Make Eric watch. She liked being watched. She liked the thought two men could take her over and over. That little captive fantasy might be something he could arrange.

"Maybe." He tucked himself back into his jeans. "Let her go."

Her face fell, and she drew in a stuttered breath. He stepped around both of them, and Rebecca's hands fell to the carpet as soon as Eric let go of her hair.

His eyes flicked toward Eric for one nanosecond. "That ottoman, flush against the sofa."

"Yes, sir."

He savored watching all those muscles gliding over bone as Eric moved. Both of them goaded his lust and inflamed his imagination with various carnal possibilities, but he wasn't about to let these two, or his overwhelming lust, make him careless. Alexander drew out two condoms he'd stowed in his jeans when they'd first arrived. It was a habit of his, having condoms at all times in case anyone needed one. That was his life. Making sure everyone was safe and abiding by rules.

Eric murmured, "Always prepared." His eyes shone with anticipation.

He smiled at Eric. It was anything but sweet. "I've yet to determine if we'll need both of these." The man's eyes flared slightly as his meaning settled in.

"Of course, sir."

He yanked his sweater and undershirt over his head but left on his jeans, undone.

He crooked his finger at Rebecca. "Come here." He pointed to the positioned ottoman. Her eyes grew wide but she crawled to him.

"Present yourself." Without needing anything more than that, she bent at the waist over the ottoman. He trailed fingers over that glorious ass, round and high, a perfect upside-down heart. With no warning, he drove a finger deep into her pussy.

"Ah," she cried out.

"Shameless. So dripping wet and hot for me. Or, perhaps for Eric?"

"You. Always you."

When she clenched her muscles around his finger, he laid a hand over her neck.

"Tell me what you missed the most. Me fucking you in the pussy or in the ass?"

She breathed heavily. "Yes."

Had she always tested his control this much? Probably. "You've been good. Holding in all that passion."

"Not good," she breathed.

Without retreating his finger, he palmed her cheek with the other hand, and pushed a thumb between her ass cheek to find that tight back hole. "When was the last time you were taken in the ass?"

She swallowed so hard, her head bobbed up a little. "A very long time."

"Pity." He drew his hand back and swatted the fleshiest part of her ass. "We could have—"

"But you still can—"

He slapped her ass, not sparing any of his strength and her whole body lurched forward, her hands tight fists under her shoulders.

He purposefully lowered his voice. "I know I can. Too bad I don't have the Contessa with me." He'd ensure his favorite flogger was taken out of storage and cleaned before they got back to D.C.

She gasped. "You still have it? Sorry."

"I'm going to flog you long and hard with it when we get to D.C. This will have to do for now." He landed a series of blows with his other hand until she was gasping, her ass reddened, his finger still lodged deep inside her cunt. He was most definitely getting this woman to Accendos.

He glanced up to find Eric fisting himself, eyes rapt on Rebecca.

"Hands by your side. That cock's mine tonight."

Eric dropped his hold—fast. "Yes. Sir."

The list of things he wished he had with him grew. A butt plug, lube, nipple clamps, cock harness, cuffs, all topped the list. He'd take his time testing every inch of that man's skin with a violet wand. He'd open up Rebecca slowly with a series of butt plugs, stretch her to be taken by him and then perhaps Eric. The dam had been broken. Time to reclaim all the lost ground.

20

In his fantasies, Eric had always wondered if Alexander had any hair on his chest. Wonder no more. At the sight of that wiry salt and pepper dusting the man's muscular pecs, he wanted to drop to his knees and beg to touch him. It wouldn't have helped. For now, Alexander remained focused on the woman in the room. He'd almost given up hope this moment would ever come. He could be patient a little longer. He'd bide his time and endure the painful hard-on that jutted straight up from his groin, leaking and jerking in the air as if possessed by a life of its own. He'd wait for an opening, which might never come, but he'd try anyway.

"Arms behind you," the man growled.

Rebecca boxed her arms behind her. Alexander grasped his sweater and swiftly knotted the sleeves around Rebecca's arms. Eric had witnessed Alexander's rougher side before. That polish, that smooth exterior, wasn't just a presentation to the world. It was real. It just wasn't all of him. He'd seen Alexander bring men to tears under his single-tail whip in less than twenty minutes. He'd watched him edge a woman with a vibrator until her sobs were nothing by soundless grimaces. But this? He'd not witnessed the singularly focused intensity he now displayed. This woman called something up in Alexander, and Eric would be damned if he knew what. Sure, she was pretty, and kind, and submissive, and—*fuck* —female.

"Eric, stand with your back against the wall. You'll watch me play with her."

Rebecca's throat moved in a long swallow. Alexander returned to spanking her, mercilessly. Jesus, he wanted to be on the other end of those hands—strong, merciless, even cruel. He could take it for her. Perhaps he'd say something.

What was he thinking? When it came to Alexander Rockingham, obedience was the only way to stick around, long term.

Eric's head rolled back against the wall, his cock screaming for relief. The head of his cock wept, the skin stretched so taut it hurt. The slow slide of pre-cum produced a maddening tickle. His hands bunched into tight fists. He would not touch an inch of his skin unless Alexander deigned it so.

Alexander righted Rebecca, and freed her arms, letting his sweater fall in whisper of expensive cashmere meeting carpet. He turned to face Eric and pulled Rebecca into his chest. She immediately moved her mouth to his nipple. Her pink tongue flicked the nub. Alexander chuckled and yanked her back.

"There she is. Greedy. Shameless. Mine." He cupped her chin and took her mouth in full possession. She groaned.

The history of these two was going to kill him. They played as if they'd been at this for decades.

Alexander broke the kiss, turned his head and locked eyes with him. Eric flattened his palms against the wall. Had he said something aloud? Maybe it'd force a punishment. Hell, force anything. He was tired of blending into the woodwork.

"Rebecca." Alexander turned his attention to him—finally. "Go to Eric."

She gave him a soft smile and moved to stand in front of Eric. "Hello," she mouthed.

He cocked his head in answer.

Alexander ran his palm down her hair. "She's beautiful, yes?" He circled his large hands to palm each breast.

"Yes." His voice was as rough as if he'd been screaming at the top of his lungs for hours—or over here dying of sexual frustration.

Alexander grasped her shoulders and turned her so Eric stared down at the back of her head. "Two men," he said. "That's what you want."

Eric didn't know if she ever answered because his brain slammed shut when her ass met the top of his thighs and trapped his cock at the small of her back. At least someone was touching him.

"Don't you dare come." Alexander smiled at her and then raised his gaze to him. "Either one of you."

Eric gritted his teeth and gave a tight nod of his head.

21

Choked moans bubbled up in Eric's throat as she ground against him like a cat in heat, needing to rub herself against a hard body.

"You teasing him, mo rúnsearc?" Alexander tweaked her nipples.

Rebecca ground against Eric in response. That thick steel digging into her spine felt so good. She knew Alexander was more responsible for his erection, but she could enjoy it, too.

"I don't mind," Eric gritted out. "Anyone this beautiful should never feel anything but worship." His lips fell to nuzzle the top of her head.

She twisted her neck to peer up at him. He did not say that. Pretty words from a pretty face. No, he was more rugged than that, though his green eyes shone with firelight. Why was she assessing his looks? Maybe because his cock was pressed hard and hot against her, and she really, really needed someone in this room to impale her with one soon.

Alexander chuckled at her writhing. "That's right, move your body all over his. Let him feel that skin, get close to that ass of yours he can't have."

For one long minute, he regarded her body, from toes to head. His detached, dominant stance never failed to turn her into a puddle of brazen need.

He kicked open her legs, and she gasped. Now open to the air, her clit throbbed. A slight breeze across it could make her come, but she wouldn't. Not until he allowed it.

He pressed against her, which in turn sank her further against Eric. Eric bent his knees, and his cock slipped between her legs but didn't breach. No one was getting what they wanted, except for Alexander.

Alexander lowered his head as if to kiss her but instead moved his face over her shoulder. Wet sucking sounds filled her ear as he took Eric's mouth, and she squeezed her thighs together to capture his cock, giving him more sensation. A long groan from Eric rumbled through her body.

Alexander broke his kiss and then glanced down at Rebecca. Her hands rested on his rib cage, on all that hard muscle. Another unfair advantage of men. No matter their age, those muscles, if used, remained.

She let her hands drift down to a cock she knew well—so well. Grasping the root of his erection, she pulled upward until the flared head crossed her fingers. He grasped her both wrists and tutted at her. "Bad brat." He yanked her arms upward until she touched Eric's hair.

"Hold on to his neck."

Eric's mouth latched on to her skin under her ear, as she dug her fingers into his hair at the base of his neck.

Alexander's mouth took her breast. His fingers slipped down to rub circles around her clit, but not nearly close enough. Every time she undulated, trying to get some relief, he moved his fingers. The man knew his way around a body.

How many hours did they tease her breasts, her pussy, her neck? Between Alexander's machinations and Eric's mouth kissing and nibbling her neck while his cock slid torturously along her slick seam, she descended into an erotic fugue of aching longing and lost all concept of time.

She gasped as Alexander bent down and scooped up her legs.

"Oh, please." A beg fell from her lips. "Please, fuck me."

"No."

"Please, please." She pitched her hips forward. Eric's pants filled her ear as their bodies moved against one another. Her skin was slick with sweat, and her clit throbbed in frustration. "I'll do anything."

"I know you will. Tell me why I should give you any part of this." He pitched his hips forward so his cock at least met her crotch.

"Because I've paid enough." She could barely understand what she was saying, but she must have used the magic words. Alexander pulled her forward enough that Eric's cock, no longer trapped by her thighs, resumed its imprisonment against the small of her back. Alexander lined up his cock and drove into her in one harsh thrust, pressing her violently into Eric. Finally. She was so wet, so slick, nothing stopped him from fully seating himself inside her. There was nothing—nothing—that could feel better than this. To be filled with Alexander, his hands harshly digging into the meat of her ass, was as close to heaven as she'd ever get.

A slight worry arose she might be hurting Eric with her fingers digging into his neck, his cock once again trapped against her back being pushed and pulled. But as Alexander's hands held her up, taking some weight off Eric, he continued to grind against her back.

Thank you Goddess for all that yoga she'd kept up, as her legs begged to be split wider, her spine bent more. She lowered her gaze. She loved watching his cock disappear into her and slide back out wet with her juice. Alexander had been right. She was shameless, and he was the only man who'd ever loved her for it.

He fucked her long and slow not letting her come until she begged without words, ancient, wailing sounds breaking from her throat. Still, he didn't let her come or allow Eric any relief. Eric finally sagged against the wall, and Alexander had no choice but to let them both sink down into a puddle of frustrated flesh.

Alexander's voice broke through as soon as she caught her breath. "Now we go to bed where I'm going to take you again—and you will service Eric."

22

This morning Rebecca had woken, sandwiched between two hard male bodies in a king-sized bed in a room she didn't recognize. She'd been drained—beyond spent from being taken by Alexander several times. In the night, they'd gone through both condoms. She didn't need birth control, not anymore, but Alexander had made Eric roll them on him. Watching that—twice— had built her need to an impossible level.

She had worked over Eric's cock with her hand. He hadn't been allowed to come inside her—or Alexander—who she suspected was Eric's preference. Rather, she'd been allowed to fist him to completion, carnal relief crossing his face. Only then was she allowed to come.

Alexander was a sadist. That wasn't something she'd known before, and she wasn't quite sure what to do with that information. She wasn't afraid of him. Intimidated, perhaps, but not scared because he'd never do anything to harm her. Sure, he'd reduce her to nothing more than a pleasure hound, but she was safe—at least for now.

Or, at least until she walked into this coffee shop.

She was right to come here. She'd had to. In a way it was an errand, as she'd explained to Alexander. She hadn't lied. She'd merely left some things out.

With a long deep breath, Rebecca swung open the door and stepped inside. Marston didn't stand when he spotted her.

She didn't wait for his invitation and sat down in the chair opposite him.

"Coffee?" he asked.

"I'm fine. What do you want?"

A waitress set a cup of coffee before her and two creams, precisely what she would have ordered—if she had the stomach for any more caffeine. "Let me know if you need anything else." The woman smiled down at her.

Rebecca eyed Marston. "You knew I'd show."

"You're a good girl, Anne." The arrogant bastard brought his coffee mug to his lips. "Though I'm rather surprised to find you here at all. Imagine seeing your car parked in front—"

"It's Rebecca, and my car is new. How did you know it was mine?"

"Plates are easy to run. So, you are reverting to your old name."

She shrugged. "Why do you care?" Sure, he'd been the one to suggest it so many years ago. Now, sitting in this coffee shop, staring at Marston, she wondered how he'd ever managed to convince her of anything. In fact, why had she bothered coming here? She'd almost expunged him from her life.

"I texted you as a courtesy in case you cared to stop by before I sold. I didn't expect you to show up without so much as a return message, well ... " He lifted his spoon and dipped it into his coffee. "So. You and Alexander. Again. Seems you forgot we had a deal."

"Thirty-eight years ago."

"I didn't realize promises had expiration dates." He stirred his coffee in lazy circles.

"Why did you sell to him if you're holding on to that old grudge?"

"He tricked me. I didn't know it was him. Though why I was surprised, I'll never know."

"Can't you just let things go? Everyone else has."

"Is that how you would characterize Alexander? Letting it go? I found him pawing through Charles' room."

Oh, shit. Marston and Alexander had seen each other? Had they talked? Why hadn't he told her he'd seen the man? Did they compare notes? No, he would have said something if he'd know about her past with Marston. Alexander likely dismissed a Marston sighting as he did so many things that didn't suit him—shovel it under the priceless oriental carpet and carry on as he wished. That's what the man did. It's what made him so formidable.

"It's his house now." She curled her hand around the coffee mug to absorb some of its warmth. "He's going back to Washington soon so you can drop it. Since you brought up our deal, you were supposed to leave him alone if I did what you asked. I more than kept my side of our bargain."

He arched an eyebrow, shook off drops of coffee from the spoon and set it delicately on the napkin beside it. "So how did he take the news ... of our deal?"

Ah, so he'd expected her to tell him about their past. They'd agreed never to speak to anyone about it. Why bring it up now? He wanted to rattle her, that's why. Her heart bounced up to her throat. She needed to say something before ...

"Unless you didn't tell him," he said.

Great, her hesitation proved his suspicions. What she said next meant everything. Marston sat there like a bulldog waiting for at a chance for another opportunity to wound a foe, like sharing with Alexander the real reasons she had to let him go. If Alexander hadn't been so steeped in the dismantling of that house and finding letters and wooing her back—for that was *definitely* what he was doing—he might have found out a great deal about her past with Marston. He had learned her pen name, Anne Broadmoor, that first night over dinner with Eric. At some point, he would learn more. She'd come clean with him first, if she could find the right time.

She straightened in her seat. "Secrets aren't kept from Alexander long."

He lifted his spoon again and dipped it back into his coffee, that annoying clank-clank-clank of metal against ceramic grating on her nerves. "Then he took the news better than I thought. I'm still standing."

Stir, stir went his little spoon. She wanted to hurl it across the room.

"You going with him?" He glared at her.

"None of your business." Why hadn't she severed all communication with Marston before? Why hadn't she blocked his number? To think she'd once felt bad for him, having such horrible parents. Had she really thought Marston would change once his mother died? Get some clarity on how resentment can eat you alive? Then again, look at Alexander. Neither of them had let go of the past.

She reached down for her purse. "Our business is over."

"Uh, uh, uh, Rebecca. You should be careful there."

His smug face made her skin crawl. That was it. She was going to Washington with Alexander.

She stood and a long screech of the chair leg caused several patrons to glance at them. "No, you should be careful. Alexander isn't that penniless college student anymore."

"I'm not afraid of Alexander Rockingham."

"You should be."

In her hurry, her chair bumped the chair of the person behind her. "Pardon me."

So what if people saw her with Marston? She could always make up some story about running into him. Regardless, it was time for them to move forward, to leave this place.

On the drive home she rehearsed what she'd say. She'd beg if necessary. She was going to Washington.

When she got back to the house, Alexander and Eric were bent over a set of papers that looked like builder's plans, curling at the edges.

Eric looked up as soon as she stepped inside the dining room. "Rebecca. Look at this. I found the original house plans in the attic. Did you know there are secret passages in this house?"

Yes, she did know. Charles had told her the day he'd died because he'd foreseen she might need them. She used them once, during a more desperate time in this house, trying to hide from Marston, Alice, and their incessant talk about Alexander and what he'd wrought. Urgent anxiety churned in her chest. She needed to tell Alexander the truth—about Marston and why she really disappeared. She would. She *would* ... just ... the timing was wrong.

She breathed hard. "Oh? That's cool. Alexander, does your house in Washington have secret passages?"

He looked at her curiously.

"I'd like to go. Soon." Away from here. Away from this house. Away from Marston. Away from the past before Alexander found out any more. She'd figure out a way to come clean. She only needed to buy some time.

His face broke into a smile.

"Eric, you'll come with us, right?" she asked quickly.

Eric gave Alexander an unreadable glance. She prayed he would go. Strength in numbers and all that.

"Of course he'll come with us," Alexander said. "When you're done, Eric, we'll all go together."

Shit. That meant at least a few more days in a fricking house that she hoped never to step foot in again.

23

"Good. Yes. I'm leaving keys for you with the Chester Management Company. Guard them with your life." Eric propped his phone to his ear using his shoulder as he signed the delivery truck manifest. "Thanks, Marilyn. Coming to Connecticut a week before Thanksgiving? I owe you."

"I know how you can repay me," his flirty assistant replied.

He chuckled. "See you back in London."

"When?"

Good question. There was no way he was going to miss that private jet back to D.C. that was taking Alexander, Rebecca, and by some grace of God, him, tomorrow.

"See you, M. I'll be in touch soon."

After killing the call, he took one long, last look at the rolling hills, still green in the chilly weather. His breath clouded in front of him. The temperature had dropped at least twenty degrees since he'd arrived.

Eric had never worked so hard or so fast as he had the last three days, putting out a 911 to his network to get help. Now, with every painting and portrait crated, every jade egg nestled in jewelry bags in more crates lined with paper cuttings, and other miscellaneous sculptures, he was ready to stop breathing in antique wood scents and the beginnings of mold.

Alexander seemed in no hurry, and continued to search for notes and scraps of paper with Charles' handwriting. Was it wrong Eric was glad they hadn't found more? Sleeping every night in the same bed as Alexander and Rebecca was crowded enough.

At first, he'd expected her to bolt. The way she fidgeted, eyed the door, he recognized the wanderlust in her eyes. When you've been on the road as much as he and Rebecca had, staying in one place grew uncomfortable. He itched to move himself. He'd not been in one place for more than a week in … forever.

He turned to go back into the house and came face to face with Rebecca, sitting in a cast iron chair, a thick blanket wrapped around her.

"Hi." She laughed. "You looked so deep in thought I didn't want to interrupt. I needed some fresh air."

He understood. "I'm glad we're leaving tomorrow. Who knew a house could hold so much dust?"

"Or memories," he bit out. "Alexander still nose deep in some chest in the attic?"

She frowned at his bitter tone. She didn't deserve his restlessness.

"Sorry for my … mood. Just tired." He plopped down into a cast iron outdoor chair that would make any 1970's household proud.

She reached for his hand. "You've been working too hard." She ran her thumb over his skin, like a lover. "Want to watch the stars again with me tonight?"

They were lovers and stargazers together, which was the damndest thing. He'd never have imagined he'd feel this close to this elf queen. Alexander had remained a little distant, even remote at times, but she was always there, open arms and heart. She was a rare wild child inside a rather cultivated veneer. He'd not guessed it three days ago.

"Sure." He gave her a wink.

She sucked in a long breath. "So I hate to bring this up, but it might be the last time we're alone together before we head out. We need to talk about Alexander."

The chair scraped on the concrete as he leaned forward.

She pulled her hand back and twisted her fingers in her lap. "I'm worried about him. He's not moving on."

"That scene where we were tied together last night wasn't moving on?" His cock got hard remembering the way her hair smelled, the way Alexander breathed on his neck. It turns out you give Alexander an inch and he took a proverbial mile—out of your hide.

She didn't return his chortle. "He brought up delaying this morning."

"He needs to leave." They all did. Enough of emptying trunks and scanning old books hoping to find a voice from the past. "Washington is a better environment for all of us, I think."

"I agree. I told him I wanted to see Accendos. Hoped that helped."

He moved to still her twisting fingers. "Worried about Accendos? It sounds scarier than it really is." He cocked his head. "Unless you're in the Library."

She arched an eyebrow at him.

"It's the main play space area. Well, maybe the dungeon is scarier."

She laughed. "Stop teasing."

"I'm not. He hasn't filled you in?"

"He said it was better to see."

"Okay, well, he has a dungeon in one of the lower levels. You'll see."

Her eyes widened. "Oh. He is serious then about this international network he's got going on."

"You have no idea." By her shocked face, that wasn't the right thing to say. He captured both of her hands. "It'll be fine. I promise."

"No matter what happens when we get to D.C., promise me we'll stay friends? Promise we won't be at odds with each other even when it gets hard. That we'll be a team. For him." Worry laced her words.

Did she think he'd bail? Or try to push her out? Well, he did have that thought a few days ago, but now? "Where is this coming from?"

Her fingers went to her throat, to touch that moonstone pendant she always wore. "Just nervous, I guess. I'm used to being in new places, but this one is personal." She eyed him, her face flushing. Was that shyness?

"People will welcome you with open arms."

Her teeth caught her bottom lip. "It's not that. I want to make sure this is going to work for you, too."

Well, didn't that come out of the blue? He sucked in a long breath. Just last week, he'd been pining for Alexander from afar, and now he was on the inside with not only him but a woman he rather enjoyed being pressed against flesh to flesh. If she was what Alexander wanted, and it kept him from being pitched to the outer circle again? He was all in, and the sex was amazing. He'd never intentionally hurt her. But leave? Yeah, truth is, he might. He was more of a have-amazing-sex-that-ended-in-an-Uber-ride-home kind of guy.

"Rebecca, you are the most intriguing woman. You're lovely, clever, and, while faithfulness hasn't been my strong suit, I believe in—"

"Destiny? Sorry, go on."

"I was going to say being open." He laughed. "I don't mind having a different future than I envisioned for myself. I'd like nothing more than to show Alexander a different future than —" he waved his hand toward the crumbling brick wall behind him. "—this place."

"Good. Then we're on the same page? The man has lived with besting the Wynters for so long he doesn't know what else there is."

"We'll show him."

She squeezed his hand. "Then, you'll stay with us."

This was really important to her, wasn't it? "I can only make that promise on one condition."

She pouted, looking rather cute he noted. She hadn't expected to be challenged—something beautiful people often believed.

"Promise me you won't abandon ship again, not without telling him what's really going on," he said.

"Yes, I promise." She smiled broadly. "I was right. You do love him."

Yeah, he did love Alexander. As for this woman? He liked her a whole helluva lot. As for love? He didn't move quite as fast as these two did. He'd just have to see.

He rose and brought her with him. "Let's go wrest the man away from the past. There's one room we haven't christened yet."

"Oh?" She arched her eyebrows.

"Alice's bed."

She giggled but then stilled. "You mean it."

"I never joke about revenge."

"Justice," she whispered and then tore her hands away. She darted away from him. "Race you."

24

An hour after landing, and one denied orgasm on Alexander's private jet, thank you very much, the car moved through an iron gate not dissimilar to the Wynters'. It was the house, however, that made Rebecca's jaw go slack. House? How about a lavish, cream-colored Federal style mansion surrounded by boxwoods, grassy lawn and trees with trunks so thick she'd not be able to wrap her arms around them? Alexander had said he'd done well, a true understatement if ever she'd heard one.

A man with an idling leaf blower tipped his hat toward the car as they pulled up. Two men dressed in black suits scurried down wide stone steps toward the trunk lid that popped open as soon as the car stopped moving. She nearly laughed at their scurrying as it reminded her of those old fashioned gas station attendants who used to come running when a car pulled up to a fuel pump.

Alexander held out his palm, which she took. "Home at last."

Home, huh? "Oh, really?" She flipped her hand as she stepped out of the car. "This is all you've got?"

Eric leaned down, his breath a comforting warmth against her ear. "Don't let the façade fool you. There are several more floors than what you can see from the outside."

"Oh, just a few?" she tittered nervously.

A woman in a crimson sheath dress and black wrap appeared through the grand set of double, white doors and stepped down the front steps. Rebecca felt a moment of fear the woman might slip on in those sky-high heels, but the woman descended with the ease of a runway model. Model, indeed. Rebecca drew her hands down her rumpled tee-shirt under her jeans jacket, donned more for travel comfort than style.

Alexander's hand tightened around her palm. "Rebecca, this is Sarah."

"Hello, Rebecca, I'm delighted to finally meet you."

This was Sarah? Alexander had told her his right hand in running Accendos was a woman, but he had not prepared her for *this* woman. She took Sarah's outstretched hand, her fingers meeting a dozen cool rings loaded with gemstones and diamonds. Sarah's dark hair shone in the sunshine, and her skin reminded Rebecca of a pearl—flawless and glowing.

"The Tribunal is assembling, though Jonathan is stuck in traffic." Sarah smiled at Rebecca. "We live and die by it in this town. Hello, Eric." Sarah's dark eyes shone as she addressed him.

Happiness. That's what she saw in Sarah. *Please let that be a sign.*

"Mistress Sarah." Eric dipped his chin, and his cheeks warmed with color. Had they been together? *Great.* She'd been here for two minutes and already a little green monster had appeared.

Alexander swung one side of the double doors open, and Rebecca blinked. Her chest squeezed as she met a familiar set of blue eyes set in a lined face. She yanked her hand free from Alexander.

"Carina?" She hesitated for one brief second, not believing her eyes. She stepped inside, into her old friend's outstretched arms. She pulled back so she could see her lips. "But, how?" God, did she remember any of her rudimentary sign language?

Carina lifted her hands and signed. *I can hear a little now.* She glanced up at Alexander and her smile widened. She pointed at Alexander and her ears.

"Cochlear implants," Alexander said. "She can hear sound but it's not well articulated."

"A gift," Carina said aloud.

A flood of too many emotions—nostalgia, regret, love— nearly swamped her. The man truly had made good use of his life, a sharp contrast to her own. Rebecca grasped her old friend's hand. "You have no idea how happy I am to see you."

Carina squeezed her palm. "Me, too. It's been too long." She cupped the side of Rebecca's face. "Beautiful as ever."

Her eyes pricked. The last time she'd seen Carina Rose, the woman strutted across a stage and held over a hundred people's attention like putty in her boa-wielding hands.

"So you know … " How could she ask about this? "You know about Alexander's new life?"

"Of course. Remember. San Francisco." Carina winked. Carina had seen much of her, Alexander, and Charles' life back then. "Then, when I moved here, well … " she shrugged.

Rebecca twisted to peer up at Alexander, who had pressed against her back. "You stayed in touch after all these years … " How could she not have known? Alexander didn't leave people behind, unlike her. Rebecca fought to not double over at that twang in her belly. She'd written to Carina in the early days of being back on the East Coast, but as with so many things in her life, she let the space between them grow until there was nothing but space. No letters, no calls.

"Alexander," Sarah's voice interrupted. "The Tribunal is assembling. It's urgent." She lifted her cell phone, and Alexander's eyes clouded.

"Can't wait?"

"I'm afraid not." She turned to Rebecca. "I'm sorry to pull him away so soon. I had hoped the other council members' wives could be here to welcome you, but it will have to be another time. They are all anxious to meet you."

Behind her, Alexander's large hands engulfed Rebecca's shoulders. "You'll want to know some of the other women who frequent Accendos."

A vision of an Amish sewing circle entered her head. It was sweet of him, but unnecessary. She'd not been someone who had many girlfriends, except for the one who now held her hand.

"My granddaughter, Samantha, is married to a council member … " Carina pointed at her heart. "Wonderful man. And, a second grandchild is on the way." She lifted up two fingers.

My how the past and future collide. Rebecca laughed and her shoulders relaxed. "I can't wait to meet everyone, especially Samantha."

Before she could ask the million questions bursting in her mind, Alexander cleared his throat. "Why don't you two ladies go to the gardens? Catch up. Duty calls for me." He kissed her on the crown of her head. "Eric, take them there? I'll be no more than thirty minutes."

"My pleasure."

"And, just the garden." He ground seriousness into his words. Her mind spun with what might lay inside these walls, but first, her friend.

Eric nodded once. "Of course."

Carina hooked her hand into Rebecca's arm. Her smile was like a warm blanket thrown across her shoulders when she hadn't even realized she'd been cold. The universe had provided the ultimate gift. Not only did she reconnect with Alexander, have Eric as an ally, but she now had an old friend who could help her figure out how to tell Alexander what really happened that terrible summer of 1981. Because Carina knew. She knew everything.

25

Sarah kept up with his long strides toward the Tribunal Council chambers. He really didn't want to start out this way.

"How was Connecticut?" Sarah asked.

Always checking up on him. "It worked. House has been secured. Rebecca helped. Eric, as well."

She smiled. "Eric has been dying to 'help' you for years."

"So I've learned."

"How long will Rebecca stay?"

"Forever." The vehemence in his voice surprised even him. "Or until she wishes to leave." Truth was, they hadn't discussed it, but he'd be damned if she waltzed out of his life without a damn good reason this time.

"I see. And Eric? I mean, making him a full member so quickly ... "

Heard about him, had she? He'd directed Ryan to start the membership process. The man deserved it.

"You know my story involving Charles and Rebecca. Well, we're feeling our way." If he couldn't trust Sarah, he couldn't trust anyone.

She paused in front of the closed chamber doors, and cocked her head. "Not like you."

She always did go straight to the heart of the matter. Her sense of fairness and attention to rules and protocol made her a perfect candidate to take over for him once he retired. If he could ever empty his desk of requests and matters requiring his attention.

"Let's say Rebecca brings out the explorer in me."

"Rebecca or Eric?"

He laughed. "Does it matter?"

"Well, I'm happy for you." She turned to open the door, but then turned back as if remembering something. "By the way, how did you finally find her?"

"I didn't. She found me. She had a feeling and acted on it. She had a hunch that I bought the place and just arrived."

"Oh."

The surprise on her face was to be expected. He, himself, almost couldn't believe how his luck had turned—first with the house sale and then reuniting with Rebecca.

"Well, I'm glad you were ... found."

Found. He supposed that was the right word. Now that she was back in his life, he wondered how he'd let thirty-eight years go by without tracking her down. Never again. He pushed open the Chamber door, and the other Council members stood.

"I have fifteen minutes." He meant it.

～

Rebecca stood at the top of a flagstone terrace. "Alexander never did do anything in half measures."

"You should see it in spring," Carina said.

She couldn't imagine. Before her, acres of landscaping unfolded, the garden interrupted only by flagstone paths that spidered out from the bottom of a broad back terrace. Dark green holly trees were peppered with bright red berries. Neatly trimmed boxwoods and pansies still bright with color lined paths. Firethorn shrubs thick with clusters of orange berries and Japanese maples blended to create a perfect fall palate. It was like looking at an artist's paint tray. A flutter of wings followed by an annoyed chirp sent her gaze to the sky.

"That's a big cardinal."

Eric's laughter behind her soothed her. "They're well fed." He took one step down as if urging her from her trance. "I told you Alexander supports half the birds of the Western hemisphere."

That thought warmed her. An ode to Charles, perhaps?

The three of them passed a fountain with a life-sized Greek statue in its center and, at Carina's urging, headed straight for the center path. Determined to take in as much of the earthy, cold air as possible, Rebecca breathed deep as she and Carina strolled, arm and arm. She had never been so grateful as she was in that moment to be with someone familiar, cloaked in that comfortable silence that only very old friends can manage.

A young woman with short blond hair magically appeared with coats and blankets to place on a cast iron bench under a bare dogwood tree as if she'd divined that's where they'd end up.

"Thank you, Carrie," Eric said. He must have been meandering a respectful distance behind them. He shrugged at the question Rebecca wore on her face. "You'll find Alexander doesn't suffer discomfort unless it's requested."

As she settled on the bench, she turned to Carina. "Okay, first thing, how do you still look twenty-eight?" She envied the woman's high cheekbones and almond eyes that kept her face as smooth and beautiful as a diamond despite the fact she had to be in her 70s.

Carina scoffed and waved her hand.

"Like Alexander. 'The Picture of Dorian Gray' syndrome." Eric looked up from his phone. "Aging painting in a closet somewhere. I hope you two ladies don't mind. I have my own duties calling." He lifted his mobile.

"We're fine here." Carina patted her hand. "And we have a lot to catch up on."

"We do."

After Eric disappeared down the pathway, Carina turned to her. "That man is handsome. If only I were younger ... " she laughed a little.

"He's mine." She sucked in a quick breath. "Oh, that came out so bad." This was her friend, and who was she to lay claim to anyone?

Carina's eyes crinkled in a smile. "Ah, so you are back."

"Maybe. I don't know. Alexander's life seems to have ... expanded."

"Oh, yes."

Rebecca squared herself to Carina. "What about you? Still dancing?"

"A little. At my granddaughter's dance studio. Today the girls now are more circus than dance. Flying through the air." She twirled her fingers in the cold. "Remember when I dragged you up on stage at that tiny little club so long ago?"

She smiled at the memory of feeling that free, to jump on a stage and not care if she was any good. No rules, no expectations. Carina's kindness had saved her back then. She, the wise and seasoned dancer in a questionable world, and Rebecca, the newbie living off the faith that anyone she encountered was good. How wrong she'd been.

"I do, though my dancing days are pretty much over."

Carina scoffed. "Never."

"I write. Freelance."

"Ah."

They sat for more minutes, not speaking. Then Carina said the words she'd hoped to hear. "I kept your secret."

Rebecca took in a stuttered breath. "Thank you. I never told him about … " She couldn't say the words aloud. Sadness threatened to rise. Today already was overwhelming her.

"Will you? He's different from San Francisco," Carina signed. "Understand?"

Rebecca nodded that she understood what she'd conveyed. "He's guarded. Still angry." She signed the word anger. Then, patted her chest over her heart.

"He missed you. He still looks at you the same. Besotted."

A half-laugh escaped her lips. "I'm not sure I want to jeopardize that again." She rubbed her forehead. "When he finds out the whole story about why I had to leave him … "

"Do you see Marston anymore?"

God, she even hated hearing that name. "I try not to."

Carina scowled. "Good. I never met the man but I don't like him."

"You're not the only one."

"Care for a little advice after all this time? Come clean with Alexander. Get to know this version of him. He's wiser."

This Alexander was different, but then again, so was she. Her fingers ached from twisting them so hard. "I don't know. He'll hate me."

"That man doesn't know how to hate. He loves people all the way. Even through their faults."

Oh, but the mistake she'd made forty years ago wasn't just a fault. The depth of Alexander's convictions and his demand for honesty were unflagging—even after all this time. She'd undo everything if she didn't explain the details of the deal she'd had to make with the Wynters to keep them all safe. She could also undo everything if she *did* tell him. Then, there was a failed marriage and a miscarriage she'd yet to broach with him. Pain that no one should have to go through …

Carina tapped her hand and then signed. "I lost my Sergio too soon. Now that you've found one another, sink into it. Enjoy it. Don't deprive yourself. You are at the age where you shouldn't deny yourself what you want." She lifted her chin at that last statement. "Speaking about someone who knows herself. My granddaughter." She stood and held out her arms as a woman with a baby on her hip ducked under the low-hanging branches.

Rebecca blinked at seeing the baby. For some reason, she hadn't thought children would be part of Alexander's world. Why not? Because she'd given up on that aspect of life?

Samantha broke into a huge smile seeing them but then grunted a little when her baby yanked on a long lock of her long chestnut hair. "Ow, easy there, big guy." She extracted her hair from the muffin-shaped fist. "He's got his daddy's eyes but my strength."

Carina cooed at the little cherub and kissed him on the forehead.

Samantha turned the squirming bundle to face out. "He wants to move today. Hi, I'm Sam, and, this is little Alexander."

Oh. Named after grown-up Alexander? A twang of jealousy thrummed through her whole body so suddenly she was nearly knocked off her feet. This was no little green monster. This was the big, hairy, green Godzilla that arose. *Get a grip.* Her time for children was long past and pining for what couldn't be was ridiculous.

Rebecca shook off her momentary stun. "I'm Rebecca. What a beautiful baby." She touched his arm. "Hello, you." Little Alexander was all chubby legs and arms in a sailor suit and tiny peacoat, with the largest blue-green eyes she'd ever seen on a baby.

He raised his chubby arms as if wanting to hug her. Green Godzilla melted into a puddle of instant, gooey love. "Oh, may I?" Her eyes shot to Samantha, whose cheeks were rosy with color.

"Please do. My arms are killing me." She grunted a little as she pushed the squirming warm body into Rebecca's arms.

Rebecca buried her face into the downy hair on his head. Mmm, baby powder was such a beautiful scent. The baby grasped onto a fistful of her hair and giggled. "Well, aren't you a little monkey?" She found herself rocking back and forth. What was it about holding a baby that made people start moving?

Samantha smoothed down the collar of the little sailor suit, and he stuck his fist in his mouth—or tried to. "We don't normally allow children here, not unless it's a specific function, but Alex loves to meet people and it's PG day."

"What's PG day?"

"That's what we call no s-e-x in the garden on Wednesdays when the gardeners are wielding power tools. Alexander is a stickler for safety. The garden is off-limits to adult activities if you know what I mean. We're allowed to bring children only on Wednesdays, and only outside."

"Even in winter?" She couldn't imagine anyone wanting to do anything outside that was remotely sexual this time of year.

"You'd be amazed. Some people are into it."

Rebecca gave up. She'd never figure out this place. Babies. Motherhood. A private home that doubled as a BDSM international network—that still made her smile in amusement. How had Alexander worked all this out, while she had worked out nothing?

Samantha tickled him under his chin and he giggled. She glanced up at Rebecca. "I'm having another in about four months." She flushed a bright red.

This woman was five months pregnant? She could model in maternity ads.

Samantha's face cracked into a brilliant smile. "A girl. I can't wait until Derek holds his daughter the first time. Total mush."

At that moment, Rebecca could see the resemblance between grandmother and granddaughter. They bathed you in a certain kind of warm energy that only a mother had.

"Well, I'm sorry to share baby and dash, but Derek texted and had the car brought around. He's almost done." Samantha folded little Alexander into her arms and winced when he took renewed possession of her hair. "Come on, Alex, I think it's time for your nap."

"Nnnooo."

"That was his first word. Imagine that." Samantha laughed as she managed to extract her hair from his fist once more. "Rebecca, I'm sure we'll see more of each other soon. The other girls are dying to meet you."

Rebecca tucked a lock of Alex's hair behind his tiny crescent ear. "I was very happy to meet you both." The baby truly was adorable. The little cherub smiled but then buried his face in his mother's hair.

"We can walk you inside," Carina said to her.

"Oh, don't bother. I think I'll sit out here for a bit more." She had a feeling this would be the last of her quiet time at this place for a while. She hugged Carina goodbye with promises of seeing her again soon.

The woman pulled back and placed her hands on either side of her face. "You call me soon. I take you dancing."

She laughed a little at that. "I'd like that."

"And tell him. It's time." The vowels were a little slippery but that didn't matter. Those two words cut into her heart. Carina was right. She'd tell him—someday. For now, she'd take her friend's other advice. She'd enjoy herself, even if the scent of baby powder clung to her hands and the jealousy monster now warred with the secret that lived inside her like an unlaunched grenade. Maybe Alexander would forgive her after all. She could only hope.

26

Alexander drummed his fingers on the note Tony had slipped him. They'd been at this for over thirty minutes, and he itched to get back to Rebecca and Eric. This Headler lawsuit against him and Accendos was a sham anyway. "What does he really want?"

"I don't give a flying fuck what Michael Headler wants." Carson's collar might burst open any second from the tension in his neck. "We don't negotiate with terrorists."

Alexander had to give Carson credit for not calling the man who once abused his wife something worse.

"He wants his dignity back." All eyes turned to Mark who usually said the least in these Tribunal Council meetings. He lifted one shoulder in a half shrug. "Rule number one of war. Let the enemy save face."

"I have some things I can do with his face."

"How much money does he want?" Alexander asked.

Carson's brow knit together. "You're not seriously considering paying this guy off." He slipped a piece of paper into the center of the table. "He wants a formal, public apology. Oh, and $5 million."

Ryan snatched it up. "Is that all?"

Alexander had enough of this pussyfooting around. "Tell him I'll meet with him."

All eyes in the room trained on him. Ryan, Jonathan, Mark, Derek, and Sarah had been uncharacteristically quiet and allowed Carson to do most of the talking, or in his case, shouting.

It was Sarah who broke the silence. "Generous of you."

"I'm feeling generous today. Tell him I want him in my office, Tuesday after Thanksgiving."

Ryan nodded once. "Consider it done. And Marston? Are we expecting anything from him?"

Again, all eyes turned to him. They knew all about the Wynter family so why would they be surprised to hear Marston's name? Long ago he'd filled them in. They needed to know in case the Wynters had a mind to go after them—if they'd ever learned about his chosen family, that is.

"What I don't understand is why he'd continue to bother," Sarah said. "I mean, forty years, Alexander. It's not like you've been trying to do anything to him."

Derek laughed. "Except buy the ancestral home."

"He doesn't care about that house."

"What does he care about?" Mark asked.

"I don't know. And, you know what?" He rose. "I don't care. Meeting adjourned."

Ryan scratched his five o'clock shadow. "One last thing. We're making Eric Morrison a full member?"

"Yes." Eric deserved this reward for his recent service.

"I suppose you'd want Rebecca Beaumont to become one as well."

He hadn't thought of that, which was not his style. Perhaps he had been a little lax of late. "Good thinking. Yes. The usual paperwork. Oh, and her legal name was changed to Anne Broadmoor. Found that out in Connecticut." He rapped the table with his knuckles and spun toward the door.

He only got ten feet away from the chamber when he rounded the hallway and plowed straight into Eric, who stared down at his phone. It slipped from his grasp and landed with a muted thunk on the carpet.

"Whoa. Sorry. Wasn't looking where I was going."

Alexander swiped his phone off the floor and handed it to him. He glanced down at the man's crotch, a hard-on the size of Texas pressing against the jeans fabric. "Must be some message."

The man's lips lifted into a smile. "It is. That blue and white painting? It's the original. The one missing for the last few decades." He arched his eyebrows and adjusted himself. "Finding something like this gets me hard every time."

Alexander laughed and slapped him on the shoulder. "Eric, you are one of a kind."

"Bet you say that to all the girls."

"Where's Rebecca?"

"Gardens."

"Good. Care to help me introduce her to Accendos?"

"Like … ." He waggled his eyebrows.

"Yes. Like." He steered him to his destination. Work could wait. Time for Rebecca's full tour.

27

"It must take an army to dust this place." Rebecca gaped at the long hallway lined with paintings set in huge, ornate frames. A tall army given the height of the ceilings, too.

Alexander chuckled slightly. The crinkles around his eyes were quickly becoming her second favorite part of his anatomy. He did seem happy to be back home. Home? How about his compound.

"So, that's the first floor." His large palm on the small of her back seeped more warmth into her body. She hadn't realized how chilled she'd grown sitting in the garden despite the blankets supplied by Carrie. "There's more."

Of course, there was. She glanced over her shoulder and rolled her eyes at Eric, who had been trailing behind them. He gave her a wink, and she got the secret message. His "navigator" offer the other day was pure prophesy.

For the last hour, she'd fought the sensory overload by concentrating on the minutiae—the velvet cushions, thick carpets, little lights over paintings, scrolled iron railings and the people, oh, so many people. Alexander occasionally stopped to introduce her to an Accendos "member" or a "staff member," the distinction apparently making a difference as he pointed it out every time. What did it matter? They all nearly genuflected when they encountered him in the endless, absurd, maze of hallways and rooms that had names. Names!

The "Yankee room" filled with Americana furniture and battle scene paintings could have doubled as a gentlemen's club. The "submissive's lounge" complete with crystal chandeliers hanging over black, velvet-covered couches against a soothing backdrop of cream and gold belonged in a photo spread. The "Kyoto" room with its sparse oriental theme presented nothing but a low square teak table and a mural of a Japanese pagoda and cherry trees in full bloom for "times when you need a little less stimulation" as Alexander described its use.

She was going to spend a lot of time in that last one. She knew it.

He took her hand and placed it back into the crook of his elbow. "Did you enjoy your time with Carina? Meeting Samantha?"

"I did, but how did you know Samantha was here?"

"Carrie."

Eric smiled at her. "Carrie is the bomb. She knows everything that goes on here."

She'd have to remember Alexander had a spy.

"Carrie is the lead submissive assistant," Alexander said. "It's her job to make sure anyone who self identifies in that category is taken care of."

"Everyone? Wow." Because she'd seen at least a dozen people already since the two of them had retrieved her from the garden. "Samantha's son is named after you, isn't he?" Well, that barreled in with zero sense of timing, didn't it?

Alexander's blue eyes twinkled. "So they tell me. You'll meet his father, Derek, soon. He's like a son to me."

She wasn't used to such humility, and obvious delight, from Alexander, but then perhaps Carina was right. He had changed, and a few days in Connecticut at a place that held so much pain for both of them probably wasn't enough for her to see how different he'd grown. "I have to tell you when you first mentioned other women, I pictured an Amish sewing circle."

Eric laughed. "Not on a Wednesday. Fridays are sewing. Saturdays are for churning the butter."

Alexander's lips lifted on one side. "You'll want some people to talk to other than me."

She circled Eric's arm. "That's what Eric's for."

"I hope I'm useful for more than that. I do my best work not talking, after all."

"True. Wouldn't you agree, Alexander?"

He murmured and smiled. Not a resounding acknowledgment toward a man who clearly loved him, she thought. She'd bring that up with him later, that is if she didn't get hopelessly lost in the corridors, never to be found again.

Alexander held open a door into yet another hallway. She stepped through but stopped short at a muffled crack that emitted from the other side of two large oak doors outfitted with cast iron handles.

Alexander touched her arm. "Would you like to see your room?"

Her what? The cracks built up to a rhythm, waking up her clit with a vengeance. "My room?" *Concentrate.* Focus on the grain of the wood paneling—or something.

"You'll have a place of your own so long as you'd like it. However, you're welcome to stay with me."

"Yes, you," she said quickly. Being alone in this house would feel odd, like she was at a hotel or something.

"Eric, I've arranged for you to have a private room, though you are welcome to stay with me, as well."

A wail emitted behind those doors, and yeah, that orgasm he'd denied her on the private jet to Washington? It wanted out. She pointed to the doors. "What's in there?"

"The Library. Or at least it was a library. We call it that for sentimental reasons."

Eric leaned down and whispered in her ear. "It is a place of great learning."

Ah, the famed Library he had mentioned. Alexander grasped the door handle. "Would you like to see?"

"Yes, please."

He pulled open the door. Two men dressed all in black who'd been standing before the entrance doors stepped aside and bowed to Alexander as if he was a king. They parted like the red sea to let them enter, and she came face to face with … *Okay.* "Not a reading library."

Eric's, warm, low, chuckle sounded on her right and her vision sharpened.

Spanking benches were scattered throughout the center of the room, and to her left, a web contraption was occupied by a man wearing nothing but a series of black straps. A woman wearing a black, burnout-velvet, catsuit Rebecca couldn't have pulled off when she had a seventeen-year-old body let alone one in her fifties, tightened his bonds. Two St. Andrew's crosses, one occupied by a red-headed woman secured to the saltire, took up the far wall to the right. Scenes she'd imagined—and oh, how she had over the years—lay before her in living, vivid color, the sounds of flesh against flesh and scents of human sweat, oranges and leather surrounding her.

A flash of fire to her right had her stepping backward. Eric's chest met her back.

"Fireplay," he whispered in her ear.

"This is the only place it can happen due to those." Alexander pointed to the ceiling. "See those sprinklers?"

She nodded. She wasn't worried about fire. Rising curiosity replaced her earlier feeling of being overwhelmed. Fireplay wasn't something she'd seen in any of the dingy basement spaces she'd been to decades ago.

"This is nothing like those dirty clubs in San Francisco." Oh, she'd said that aloud from the way Alexander's eyes crinkled in amusement. She, Charles, and Alexander had kept to themselves. They'd find a corner and try not to get too close to the harder impact scenes.

"Charles loved those," he said, all mirth dying from his eyes. Yes, he'd loved hearing the slaps, the hits, the thuds. One particular torture scene she'd witnessed had her crying so hard Alexander had whisked her out despite Charles wanting to stay. Until that second she'd forgotten about how Charles almost had a death wish.

No tears today, however. Instead of the chill she'd felt for the last half hour, her skin warmed as quickly as if she'd sunk into a hot tub.

Alexander and Eric flanked her, like bodyguards, as she found her legs moving her inside.

She jumped at a loud crack of leather meeting flesh. A woman on one of the spanking benches clutched at black straps at the base. A dark-haired man, with biceps flexing, brought a belt down on her backside once more. This time she wailed, but a slight arch of her back showed she was leaning into it—not away from it. Rebecca understood that craving, the need to meet the pain, all too well. The dull craving between her legs sharpened.

She swiveled her head, lured by a man's long groan near them. He leaned against a long ladder like the ones found only in ancient libraries when shelves ran from floor to cathedral ceiling. He was blindfolded and his hands curled around rungs above his head. He hadn't been cuffed to them, rather appeared to be holding himself there willingly. A woman half his size ran her long red nails over his bare chest. "There, there," she cooed. His mouth dropped to an "O" when her fingers reached his sizable erection. She cupped his balls and twisted a little. A moan escaped his full lips.

Rebecca's neck prickled with heat. She pulled at her t-shirt to get a little air between her skin and clothes. Her skirt, her bra, her t-shirt, were suddenly too tight. She wanted them off.

"Would you like to leave?" Alexander breathed in her ear.

Leave? Not on your life. She swallowed and shook her head slowly, but before she walked further, Alexander grasped her arm and spun her to face him.

"Go ahead," he said. "Look around, but not too close, mo rúnsearc." He took her hand.

She smiled at him and squeezed his large palm. He didn't allow her to let go of him.

She walked slowly, Alexander on one side, Eric on the other. Together they kept a respectable distance from the scenes. A nude man leaned against a second tall library ladder as a woman, in a long red chiffon gown, sucked him off with abandon. He hissed between his teeth as her head bobbed, short blond curls waving with the motion. One hand curled into a rung high above his head, the other on the back of her head as if feeding himself to her mouth. "Open that throat, Lina."

Her own scalp instantly tingled as the man's fingers grasped a handful of Lina's hair and he began bucking against her face. "More," he growled.

The woman's kneeling stance fell further open, and her

whole body lowered, her neck stretching to take him deeper. As the woman served her Master, for that was certainly the roles at play, Rebecca's own throat longed to stretch, her mouth watering.

Her breath grew faster, her gut tingling with something … want, need, longing, yearning … all of it. An arm went around her waist to her hands to still them. She'd been rubbing her fingers over Alexander's knuckles. She leaned against his chest, and his nose nuzzled her hair. His subtle spicy cologne mixed with the scent of musk, sweat and an unidentified perfume.

They stood like that for long minutes, in the center of the room, as if they also were on display.

Alexander's erection pressed against her belly, and his hand fell to her hip. She'd been shamelessly grinding herself back into him. She was a little dizzy from panting so hard.

"Do you like to watch?" he growled in her ear.

"Yes."

"Do you want to do more than watch?"

God, yes. She swallowed and nodded.

"Tony?"

A huge man stepped forward. "Yes, sir."

Where the hell had he come from? Her body pressed further against Alexander.

"This is Rebecca. And, you know Eric. We're about to engage in some play."

"Oh. Why does he—" she started.

"No one engages in any sexual activity or a BDSM scene here without a witness to your consent."

"I consent." She answered quickly. She batted away the thought they hadn't had a witness in Connecticut.

Eric nodded once toward Tony. "As do I."

"Safeword?" Tony's face must be made of steel. No smile, no hint of amusement played in those dark, unreadable eyes.

"Red is fine," Rebecca said.

"Red. And, you Mr. Morrison?"

Eric's lips lifted into a sly smile. "Ladies choice. Red."

"Master Rockingham, consent witnessed." He gave a single nod and stepped backward.

No sooner had he done so than Rebecca was off her feet and tumbling backward into Alexander's lap. He'd sat in a chair and taken her with him. With no hesitation he grasped her knees, yanked her legs open, her skirt bunching at the waist. *Oh.* She'd been forced to straddle him, backward. The fact she could watch the scenes, and they could watch her, was not lost on her. Her soaked panties, for they were drenched, were on display for anyone who chose to see. No one was looking. No one in this entire room noticed anyone other than who they were with.

Eric's thigh pressed against her. He'd sat on the arm of the chair. She looked around to find Alexander had hooked his arm around the man's waist. She hadn't noticed how much larger Alexander was than Eric until she saw Alexander could reach around the man to the front of Eric's pants. His hand cupped Eric's crotch, stroked him.

"Keep your eyes on that woman," Alexander growled. "Her name is Lina. See how she takes what he offers." Was Alexander's command for her or Eric? She couldn't tell. She didn't care because his other hand circled around her, and his finger had no trouble breaching her elastic so his middle finger could thrust inside her. A long, loud breath flew up and out of her throat at the invasion, how easily and decisively he drove forward.

She grasped Eric's thigh with one hand, her other hand finding the chair's armrest. She could so easily pitch forward and ride his finger like a cock. If she could move forward a fraction of an inch that long digit would mash against her clit. Every time she tried, his arm tightened and held her in place.

"Just take it." His voice rumbled through her back and down her limbs.

Lina widened her knees even more, almost in a full split. She groaned as the man mashed his pelvis against her face. He pulled back and an audible breath in floated to her ears. Was that her own breath or Lina's?

Eric moaned next to her. She didn't dare rip her eyes from the scene in front of her, but Eric's thigh quivered next to her, and in her periphery, she could tell his cock was getting a workout from Alexander's hands.

Alexander's erection was a steel beam that ran up her ass crack. Alexander moved his hips ever so slightly against her. She ground herself backward as his finger finally, thank the goddess, began to fuck her. She swallowed rapidly as her orgasm built. Alexander's finger, the man viciously throat fucking Lina's mouth, Eric openly groaning next to her, all added to the carnal environment she sank into as if entering a parallel universe.

"Take her hand." Alexander's voice broke through her pants.

Eric grasped Rebecca's fingers and raised them to his lips, soft lips she now wanted to kiss. He sucked a finger into the heat of his mouth, his tongue swirling around the tip. She gulped air as Alexander's thumb flicked her clit, almost in perfect rhythm with Eric's tongue.

"When you come, mo rúnsearc, let me hear it."

"I can … "

"Yes."

His permission would have been enough for her to let go, but it was the completed circle — her finger in Eric's mouth, Alexander's finger inside — that launched her into a new territory of pleasure. Her vision blurred until all the scenes in the Library morphed into writhing masses of color and sound. Only Alexander's arm banded around her thigh kept her on his lap. She released, the wet sounds of Alexander's working hand joining her small moans.

Eric's body leaned against her in a slump. His pants had become unbuttoned at some point, and his cock thrust from the placket, glistening and spent while his breaths labored hot and quick. They glanced at each other and simultaneously let out a relieved chortle.

"Welcome to the Accendos Library," Eric panted.

The rumble of Alexander's return laughter cleared her head. She twisted to look at him. "What can I do for you?"

He flicked his gaze to the floor and back up to settle on her.

"Eric, kneel on the floor next to me," Alexander said.

He obeyed.

"Now, you. Kneel in front of me," he said to her.

She sank to her knees and twisted to face him. Alexander's large hands curled around the ends of the chair's arms and his steely blue eyes twinkled down at her. "I always did like this look on you. Pure expectation, wanting to see what I might like, what I might not. And, yes, you have permission to touch me."

Her belly danced as she unbuttoned his pants and drew him out. She could be decisive, too. She didn't wait for his permission to wet her lips and take his broad head into her mouth. He didn't stop her, letting out a long hiss at the same time as a long, male groan behind her signaled that Lina's Master had climaxed. Rebecca nearly came again at the sound coupled with the feeling of so much flesh filling her mouth. She clung to her senses, however, and kept her own cresting pleasure at bay, because from this moment forward she'd not come again until he was involved. The final piece of independence she'd clung to vanished. In her heart, on her knees in this strange and beautiful place, she'd handed herself over completely to a man she hoped never again to part from, despite the past clinging in the back of her mind like a parasite.

Eric was right. Alexander's life was large, and she wanted in.

28

Insomnia wasn't Eric's thing, except for tonight. He knew why. He was by himself in a bed while Alexander and Rebecca lay down the hallway, together, without him. *Fuck.* So close and yet so far? He thought they were home free when they'd had dinner together in a private room. Then, there were the after-dinner drinks and a slow rise by Alexander signaling it was time to end the evening. Then Tony, who he was growing to dislike openly, magically appeared and said, "this way." Eric was led to this bedroom and left alone. A-fucking-lone. He was spending the fucking night, down the hall from a man who—could he even think it —might have used him to get closer to Rebecca.

Had she used him to get to Alexander?

Why was it so bloody hot in here? *Because you're thinking of Alexander, idiot.* And, maybe a little bit about Rebecca. Every fantasy he'd ever had was unleashed this past week. That's what Alexander did. Eric could drown in the amount of porn filling his head, this time with a woman included. For him, it wasn't unheard of, but it'd been years since he'd done so. Their little Library encounter only solidified that deal. Did Rebecca have to be so kind, sweet, sultry—and so adventurous? No wonder Alexander loved her, and damn, the man did love her. That was so obvious.

He threw off the covers.

Alexander didn't use people, he reasoned. Rebecca had been open and honest with him. He hadn't been used. Then why the fuck did it feel like it? He was too hot ... that's all. It should not have bothered him. He was often uncomfortable, sleeping wherever, whenever he could between jobs, on floors, in tents.

A sharp crack made him sit up. A slice of light cut across the floor, and a woman's silhouette filled the door.

"Are you asleep?" Rebecca had come to his room. She probably needed to chat. Well, he was in no mood to help her navigate.

"No," he growled.

"Good." The thick oriental carpet muffled her footsteps. Her hand felt down his arm to his hand. "Come on."

"To?"

"To bed."

"But—"

"He told me to come get you." She dropped her hold on his hand. "Unless you don't want to."

His legs hit the ground, and he stood. All his mental garbage for the last thirty minutes was for nothing, perhaps? Good. "No, no, of course ... "

Her delicate hand recaptured his. Out in the hallway, torchiere lamps at the baseboards lit up as they passed. God forbid people had trouble finding their bedrooms. He was only in his boxers, and the cooler air of the hallway felt fantastic against his overheated skin.

They stopped at the end of the hall before a door that looked like any other. Well, what had he expected? Carved lions in the wood? A soldier with a spear standing guard outside? Actually, yes. Ever since Rebecca brought up South Africa, that's all he could think about now. Going on safari with them, seeing the last known wild areas where elephants, giraffes, and lions fucked with abandon, and people stopped their vehicles and didn't dare disturb them if they lay across the road. His imagination really needed a vacation.

She opened the door and pulled him inside. Alexander stood at a bay window in an enormous room. He turned, one hand in the pocket of his loose trousers and the other holding a tumbler of dark liquid. His shirt sleeves were rolled up. The entire row of buttons up the front of his shirt were undone revealing considerable abs for a man who'd just turned sixty. He wanted to drop to his knees at the sight, as he had every night this past week.

"There you are," Alexander said in that smooth deep voice.

Drop? How about dive for the floor? "Here I am."

"Good. Nightcap?"

Eric shook his head.

Rebecca crawled up onto the bed and settled herself against the headboard. She dipped her feet under the covers. "I call the middle."

She was such a girl. At least until she wasn't, like in the throes of abandon.

Alexander swallowed the last of his drink and then strode to the side of the bed. He eased off his watch and placed it in a tray. He tugged off his shirt, then his trousers, both of which he draped over an old fashioned valet stand. He stood there as if waiting for Eric.

Eric shook himself. He'd been standing there—staring. "You have a painting aging in a closet somewhere, don't you?"

Alexander chuckled at his Dorian Grey reference. "If I do, I'll let you auction it off."

Eric smirked. "I'd keep it." He forced his body to move to the bed. They'd slept together in Connecticut. Why was this different? How about because they were at Accendos, the home Alexander had made for himself. It all felt so intimate, personal, rather than the last few days where they'd had a fall-asleep-together-after-sex arrangement rather than something planned.

Alexander eased into the bed behind Rebecca, the two of them instantly cradling one another as if they did this every night.

This was his moment to lay claim to his place versus merely fitting in wherever they landed after sex. He'd been too slow before, like at that art auction the first time he'd met Alexander and let the man walk away. Not this time. Jesus, he might earn a lashing for this, but he was taking his shot. He eased down alongside Alexander's back. He needed to feel all that strength and power, skin to skin.

Alexander lifted his head.

"Permission?" Eric asked too late. Alexander's low chuckle in response warmed him to the core.

"Granted." The man settled his head back onto the pillow.

Eric circled his arm around the man's chest, and his heart nearly punched out of his ribcage when Alexander laid his hand over his and then moved their stacked arms to hug Rebecca.

She moaned a little and his cock nearly punched a hole in Alexander's back. Alexander adjusted and captured his hardness between his legs. Holy Christ. He hadn't been allowed to be inside the man—and somehow, he knew he wouldn't. As for him? Alexander could take him body and soul, ram that cock deep inside his ass for hours if he desired. For now, he'd take this vanilla, lovey-dovey contact, something he'd never been good at.

"It didn't feel right, did it?" Rebecca asked. "To not be together?"

Okay, definitely not used. He wasn't sure how any of this was going to work, but those thoughts weren't anywhere near his brain. Actually, nothing was happening in his brain.

"Tomorrow, we'll see the rest of Accendos," Alexander said.

The rest? His cock thickened more because *more* was Alexander's specialty.

29

Alexander stretched his legs under the sheet and met cool air, a sharp contrast to the heat blazing on the other side of him. *Eric.* Of the three of them, who knew he'd be the one who liked to snuggle up like a rabbit in winter. By the size of the guy's erection pressed into his back, he also was a morning person—at least in one arena.

He pushed backward and Eric shifted so he could roll to his back. "Where's Rebecca?

"Taking a shower."

Alexander eased up to rest his back against the headboard. "She been in there long?"

Eric rose up on elbows, his back arching and the globes of his ass—also quite the package—rose under the sheet. "You know women. How they can spend thirty minutes under scalding hot water, I'll never know."

He chuckled. "Surprised you're not in there with her." He wasn't really, but he'd seen the way Eric eyed her.

Eric ran his eyes down the length of Alexander. "I'd rather be out here."

He looked the guy over, all tousled hair and sleepy eyes. No wonder women fell at their feet for him. Men, too, from what he'd witnessed. His own cock woke up with a start at thinking how he'd denied the guy even a fraction of himself. He enjoyed denial. He wouldn't mind something else, either.

Alexander snapped the sheet down and resettled his hips. He sent one arm behind his head, the other reached for his cock. "Any reason why?"

Eric eyed Alexander's hand running up and down his length and swallowed. "You."

Starting the day with a strong release? Have at it. He let his hand drop to his side. "All yours."

Wasting no time, Eric kicked off the sheet fully and scooted closer. He gripped Alexander's cock with enough strength to earn a hiss from between his teeth. He did love a confident handling. Eric ran his thumb over his broad head and wet his lips. When he sucked Alexander's cock into the back of his throat, no hesitation or resistance, he fought a moan. As Eric drew him out, he proved he had a wicked tongue by flicking up the length of his underside. He swallowed him whole again.

"Good mouth," he growled.

Eric rumbled an appreciation and the vibration ran through his cock into his balls and down his legs. Alexander widened his legs, and Eric settled himself between them. The man picked up signals well, another thing he'd made a mental note of. When Eric's hand drifted to his own cock, Alexander grasped handfuls of the guy's hair.

"Hands," Alexander barked, and Eric placed his wayward hand on Alexander's thigh. That was better. Later, *he'd* decide what to do with the guy's cock.

The man sucked cock like a pro. In appreciation, Alexander didn't hold back and unloaded down Eric's throat when he felt like it—which thanks to a mouth as hot as Hades—was about ten tongue-strokes in. The man not only took it all but cleaned up after himself, licking and sucking every last drop.

Alexander pushed himself further up the bed while Eric settled back on his knees, his eyes gazing directly into his, the brave soul. If Eric were Alexander's sub, he'd have an issue with such directness. Instead, he rather enjoyed the man's green eyes shining at him with such confidence, despite the smirk—which he really would handle. He hadn't taken a man in a while. Maybe it was time to end that streak.

"Good morning." Rebecca leaned against the doorframe, her wet hair twisted into a long braid. "Mind if I join you?" She dropped her towel.

∼

Rebecca squirmed underneath him, his cock buried root deep in her. She mewled like a kitten, the sound lighting him up more than a shot of the finest whiskey. "Have you ever thought about Eric being inside you?"

She visibly swallowed. "Yes."

He turned to look at Eric, lying beside them on the bed. His cock, a vicious purple, pointed northward. "Have you ever thought of me being inside you?"

Eric's eyes fired. "Every second since I met you."

He laughed. "Now there's an answer." He glanced down. His laughter didn't decrease that erection of his one bit. He had made the man watch as he took Rebecca to the edge. He really was a sadistic son of a bitch, though Eric's psych profile, which he'd been studying of late, showed how much he craved exactly that.

Alexander pulled his cock out of Rebecca and leaned

back. He stared down at her as she nodded her head enthusiastically.

He chuckled. "I haven't asked you anything yet."

"Yes. Whatever it is."

He'd been holding her at the brink. He wanted her first orgasm this morning to blow the roof off, and he knew exactly what she needed for that—denial until writhing in near pain.

"Eric." He dipped his head toward Rebecca and made room for him. "Make her come. With your mouth."

There was a term Alexander particularly hated—an eager beaver. He now understood the sentiment, however, as Eric was between Rebecca's legs in two seconds. He also bent over, putting that perfect ass on display and in offering.

Alexander rested his hand on the man's back. Eric could offer, but he'd decide when and where. Instead, Alexander yanked open the man's knees and earned a long, groan from him—from anticipation, perhaps—and settled himself between them. He then leaned over him, trapping his own cock against Eric's ass crack. He pressed down, and Eric flexed. The man had some glute muscles.

He growled in Eric's ear. "When I say."

Eric nodded and relaxed that squeeze that had felt amazing, but unrequested and Alexander's tolerance for topping was nil. He pulled back and placed his hand on Eric's neck.

"Make her come."

Eric's head dipped and Alexander knew exactly when his mouth latched onto Rebecca's flesh. She cried out and a needy groan rumbled from Eric. He let the man service her for long minutes, keeping his hand on the man's neck. He ran his fingers along the cords of muscle there, the ends of the man's hair teasing his skin. The younger man had taken care of himself, and while Alexander found other qualities more important than looks, he took a long moment to appreciate the guy's physique. Smooth, tanned skin glided over taut muscles as he worked Rebecca's pussy over with his mouth. The man's whole body seemed to get into the act, slight undulations and movements that had Alexander itching to touch—and touch later, he would.

Rebecca didn't take long to pitch into an orgasm, evidenced by her back bowing, her hands clasping at Eric's head. Between the wet flesh sounds, Eric's grunts and Rebecca's high-pitched whimpers, his own cock wept with need.

Grabbing a fistful of Eric's hair, he urged the man to back off. It was his turn. "Lie on top of her. Do not penetrate." The man climbed up Rebecca's body and Alexander wasted no time positioning himself so he could push Eric's body further into her, trapping his cock against her belly. The man's neck fell into Rebecca's neck, smearing wet on her skin. For Rebecca's sake, Alexander, his front now covering Eric's body, was careful to keep most of his weight off them, his arms and shoulders muscles knotting with strain. He could hold himself here for an hour if it meant he could feel all that male muscle under him, see Rebecca's face twist in pleasure.

He bent his neck so he could take her mouth. By the way her long moans vibrated against his lips, Eric's pelvis was hitting the right spot.

Alexander grasped a fistful of Rebecca's glorious hair and tilted her head so he could take her mouth deeper, the position forcing Eric to bury his face in her neck. All that hard male flesh felt good underneath him. Coupled with Rebecca's soft lips and mewls in his mouth, his body filled with a serenity he hadn't felt for far, far too long. An overwhelming need to keep them close, to keep them here, followed with a conviction he could no longer ignore. They were his.

"Come for me again," he said into her mouth. "Both of you."

Eager? Hell, she cried out against his lips and Eric latched onto the side of her neck as Alexander felt him shudder underneath him. The two of them earned those orgasms. They deserved everything for taking what he dished out. Hell, he wished he could spend the day in this room because he was just getting started.

30

"But I can still do it. Maybe you need two people on site?" Rebecca's hand grew a little numb from clutching her phone to her ear all morning. She's waited too long to call the editor of her best client, Travel & Style magazine. She'd waited too long to call *anyone* until now.

"I'm sorry, Anne. We needed copy yesterday. You were MIA and I had to get someone rolling on this. Already Style and People and a dozen others have writers on the ground feeding their web pages with this debut. Everyone's been waiting for those bungalows over the water to show up in the Caribbean, though why they haven't cropped up every-where before now, I'll never know."

"I decided to take a little vacation." Rebecca chewed the side of her fingernail. She'd have loved to cover that story. Who wouldn't want to spend a few nights under a thatched hut, staring at pretty fish under the glass floor?

This wasn't good, not good at all. Her stomach roiled with nerves.

"Well, good for you. You deserve it. Listen, if anything

comes up, I'll be sure to call you again first. Just answer your phone, okay?"

She ended the call, determined to stay glued to her phone for the rest of her life. That Caribbean resort debut was the second assignment she'd discovered she'd lost, all because she was playing tourist herself—or rather playing love slave captured by two pirates.

Here she thought life was just swimming along fine. Bills were paid automatically through her checking account, and her mail had been forwarded to her. Even her aloe plant was being watered by a neighbor. If she didn't return to Philadelphia for six months, everything would be fine—*not*.

Instead, for the last two days, she'd been in Alexander's room, nude most of the time, coming her head off—or not—depending on Alexander's mood. Eric, too. The man's appetite hadn't waned one bit in forty years. And, all the while she was losing jobs and, it seemed, her way.

At least she'd missed Marston's texts wanting to know if she'd meet again. It was their pattern. She'd disappear. He'd find her. And, now? The mystery of her being anywhere near Alexander would be too much for him. Those calls and texts she'd continue to ignore.

She turned a corner and nearly plowed over two young women. One gasped and stepped backward. She flushed pink, her big brown eyes blinking. "Oh, sorry, ma'am."

Ma'am? "I'm fine." She clasped her arm to reassure her. The girl coyly dipped her head before grasping the arm of her equally beautiful friend. Her long blonde hair flowed and swayed like waves of gold down her back as she sashayed down the hallway with her friend in four-inch heels, because that's just what women wore here. Four-fricking-inch heels were everywhere, all on women who'd probably put themselves through law school—by modeling high fashion, of course—

because everyone here also had high powered careers. They worked for think tanks, nonprofits changing the world, and members of the U.S. Congress—or *were* members of Congress.

She adjusted her plain, knit sweater. For the tenth time, she silently questioned Alexander. How could he want to be with her when all this gorgeous, *younger* female flesh floated in and out of Accendos like it was a casting call for a talent agency?

She didn't have time for these distractions. She had two articles already researched and placed with Coastal magazine —if she would sit her butt in the chair and write them even though their deadline wasn't until after Thanksgiving. That would get her enough money to last until year's end, which was fast approaching.

She peered down at her phone. She had contacts—lots of them. Who should she call? Would make her feel she had something to say, didn't care what she looked like, or how young she wasn't, because vacation was over. Once the holidays were here, according to Eric, she had to get ready to face *all* of Club Accendos. "All" apparently was hundreds of people. Great, more BPs as she named the "beautiful people" scurrying about, playing, laughing, looking so relaxed, looking like they belonged here.

She continued down the hallway she'd found herself in. She always thought better moving. She turned the corner and came face to face with an archway that led to a conservatory. She swiveled her head to peer back up the hallway. Where the hell was she?

"Miss Beaumont, may I help you?" A man in a black suit stepped forward.

How did he know her name? "I'm fine. Just thinking." She just needed a minute to retrace her steps.

He nodded once and continued along his way.

She was being stupidly rebellious to brush off his directions. It's just Accendos had so many staff—all of whom knew her name. Miss Beaumont this. Miss Beaumont that. She couldn't take a deep breath without someone running over to "help" her as if she was some decrepit senior citizen.

She studied the carpeting. *Get a grip. Everything is okay.*

Rebecca ran the mantra she'd had to adopt in recent days in her head over and over. She took in a long, cleansing breath and pushed air from her lungs, an attempt to exit any negative feelings.

I am loved. I am fine.

She honed in on details around her. On either side of the arch, tall potted palms in ornate brass planters waved slightly under vents overhead—marked by ornate brass grates. Tall, stained glass windows of milky white, blue and green lined the room and allowed muted sunshine to stream inside. White scrolled iron benches were scattered among ceramic pots and long rectangular plant holders overflowing with flowering vines and tall ficus trees.

"Of course, he has a winter garden, too."

"I believe if the city would allow it, he'd have a bird aviary, as well."

Rebecca startled and turned. Sarah rose from a chaise in the corner, setting a heavy, ancient-looking book down as she delicately swung her legs over the edge to stand. She smoothed down a black pencil skirt and strode forward. "Hello, Rebecca. Welcome to the Palm Garden."

Of course it had a name.

"It's beautiful." It was, and she really needed to start seeing what was right instead of what was wrong. "Sorry to disturb you." She indicated the book that curiously looked like a law reference book. "Catching up on some reading?"

"The Rise and Fall of Machiavelli. I read it once a year to remind myself of certain … things."

"Oh. Good plan." What else does one say to a woman who

helped run a BDSM club and studied Italian political philosophers? That she herself preferred People Magazine?

Sarah's cocked her head. "You look lost."

"I am." She half laughed. "It's silly, really, but I seem to keep losing my way." She swiveled her head as if her gaze might land on something familiar.

"Easy to do here." She hooked her arm around Rebecca's and began leading her out the archway. "Where can I take you?"

"If you could just point me in the direction of Alexander's office, I'd be grateful."

"I'll do one better. I'll show you."

And that's how she ended up being delivered like a lost sheep to Alexander's office. He'd laughed at hearing she'd gotten lost—again. She didn't return his mirth, but instead went to work. With work, she could ignore the niggling feeling that she might never find her way around Accendos—and that perhaps it was a sign she didn't belong here.

31

Clarisse, Alexander's assistant, clicked across the hardwood floor to Alexander's desk. Rebecca shifted on her hips so she could see through the archway of her office nook into his office. Clarisse did what she always did, smiled at Alexander, handed him a thick stack of folders and stood there in her perfect pencil skirt to see what else he might need.

How was she to get any work done like this?

I am grateful. I am fine. I am loved. I love.

She took in a long, cleansing breath and pushed air from her lungs. *Let it go.*

Clarisse, in all her leggy, willowy, young, blondness, bent over his desk. He stared at the folder, to the exact point where she pointed. Her pencil skirt stretched over her ass. He kept his eyes downcast but still, the woman was *bent over in a pencil skirt.*

I am fine. I am loved.

His low rumbling voice murmured something. Paper rustled under his hands. His executive chair creaked under his shifting weight.

I am ... in desperate need of a walk.

Rebecca slapped the laptop shut and rose. She ran her hands down her batik peasant skirt, comfortable and cheerful, but not a pencil skirt. Maybe she'd head out to a mall or wherever the hell they sell those tight-fitting skirts in this town, and from the looks of Sarah and Clarisse's wardrobes alone, they sold a lot of them.

She rounded the corner from her nook to his office. "Hi, I'm going to take a walk. I hear there are some nice shops on Wisconsin Avenue." She ran her hands down her plain white cotton t-shirt. "I could use a change of clothes."

His blue eyes lifted to her and her heart nearly stopped. Had he always done that to her? *Yes.*

"Don't be silly. Sarah is coming back this afternoon with her wardrobe selections for you."

Oh, right. Sarah had mentioned that when she deposited Rebecca with Alexander. That was one answer why Sarah always looked so put together. D.C.'s most desired wardrobe consultant extraordinaire was to outfit her because every need Rebecca had could be met inside these walls.

"I need to get out. Come with me? You're working too much." She perched herself on his desk.

He raked his gaze up and down her torso. His large hands reached around her waist and pulled. Papers, an old-fashioned desk blotter, and a stapler, were pushed off to the side as he slid her to the center of the desk. Parting her knees, he moved in closer.

"What's going on?" Those steely blue eyes honed in on her like a laser.

"Oh, nothing."

"Mmm-hmm." His hand moved down to her thighs, his thumbs rubbing small circles on the inside of her legs. "You're worried about Thanksgiving."

Oh, right. The guy could see into her mind, her desires, her fricking soul. "Really, a hundred people are coming?"

"114." His eyes lit up as if this was a good thing.

"That many, huh?"

"If you'd rather not ... "

"No. You do this every year. People expect it. You're not canceling because of me."

"I wouldn't cancel. I will let it go on, and you and I can go somewhere else. Easy."

"Easy." Yes, everything was so easy for Alexander, except not. He lived a strange dichotomy. If he wasn't driving her and Eric mad with lust, he worked—constantly.

"I don't remember you loving large groups," she said.

"I don't, but I don't like the thought of someone I care about not having a place to go."

Did he have to be so perfect? She put her hands on either side of his neck. She loved the warmth there, and it usually calmed her to feel him under her hands. "No. I will be fine." She grasped his wrist. "Let's go outside. It's nice out, not too cold, and the sun's out."

He removed her handhold on his wrist, turned her palm up and laid a chaste kiss in the center. "In a bit. I'll meet you. You're perfectly safe in the garden."

Safe. He meant walled in. Before she was "so safe," she'd never felt unsafe. It was as if some amorphous threat existed she needed to worry about—something she'd never been aware of before. It was creeping her out.

He cocked his head. "An hour. I was away for a long time and the work piled up."

She shrugged and attempted to jump down but he held her fast.

"Rebecca. No one is more important to me right now than you. Know that. I have people counting on me, however. People like us."

Us. People who lived and loved so freely it scared others

witless, made them seem less controllable, and oh how people loved to control others. Like the Wynters.

"If you need to go out, I understand. Find Eric. Just don't leave without telling me." His eyes were too serious.

She leaned down and pressed a kiss to Alexander's lips. "I'll leave you to your work."

"Yes, work." His hand moved up her thighs, fingers crept around the elastic of her imported lace thong, courtesy of his vast network of minions who scooted up and down hallways at all hours of the day and night. *Oh.* He'd yanked them so hard, they ripped.

She gasped, a gush of fluid gathering between her legs. *Traitor.* Her body that hadn't responded sexually to anyone in so long reacted to his touch like a bolt of lightning splitting a tree in two.

He stood. "I have critical work to do here, first." He leaned over, pushing her back to the desk surface. "Open." Her knees widened without a nanosecond hesitation.

His hand circled the front of her neck and her belly curled in pleasure. Cold metal touched the outside of her thigh followed by the clip of fabric being cut. He'd used scissors. The zing of his zipper was next, his broad palm keeping that pressure against her throat, and then that long slow glide of his cock stretching her, filling her up to her furthest point.

"Now what will you do?" he rasped.

"Wait for your permission." No need to be much more specific anymore. Their dynamic was established. He took. She gave. He decided when she deserved that mind-blowing ecstasy that would rack her body with spasms inside and out. The order of their agreement held such peace. It was everything else around it that was the problem.

Her shoulders relaxed, her legs went limp as he fucked her hard and long. When he did release her to climax, all thoughts of pencil skirts and walks had vanished. She was nothing but a receptacle for his pleasure, which gave her everything she needed—at least in that moment. As she was coming down, her skirt pulled into place, reality came crashing back.

"One hour." He pecked the end of her nose with his lips. "See you in the garden."

It's okay. I'm loved. It's all going to be all right. I think.

Guess she was taking that walk—in the garden, however, because that's where he wanted her. How bad would it be if she walked out the front door? Be alone for a bit?

32

Alexander picked up Rebecca's hand and kissed it. "I'm going to leave you ladies to discuss hemlines and fabrics. Rebecca, I'll be in my office if you need me." He pecked her on the top of her head. Of course, he'd be in his office. She had not gotten very far in her attempt to leave, as Carrie came bursting forward with news about this "meeting" with Sarah.

God, she was in a bad mood today—for nothing.

Rebecca crossed the threshold into Sarah's private room, another perk she'd recently learned of that was given to all the Accendos Tribunal Members. Everyone had a massive, personal, bedroom suite assigned for their use.

Sarah's had a bay window, trees swaying in a breeze outside, and a king-sized bed similar to Alexander's, though a beautiful blue fabric sheathed the tall bedposts.

Sarah stepped back and examined the length of Rebecca, starting at her black ballet flats and ending at her hair pulled back into a careless ponytail. A chill ran through her entire body, as if the woman had undressed her. "Yes." Sarah nodded. "You are quite beautiful."

Her smile was like dawn breaking, bathing her in approval. Her insides loosened a little, as if an army of fists around her internal organs uncurled.

Rebecca lowered her gaze. "Thank you … Mistress Sarah." Was she to use her first name?

"No need for that with me."

Rebecca looked up. Sarah's perfect cheeks warmed with color. "Let's be friends."

"I'd love that." She hadn't made many female friends in the past, but Sarah was someone who understood that you could have two men and not be a freak. It would be nice to have someone who approved of her situation but didn't want to strap her to a St. Andrew's Cross for mind-numbing pleasure. Eric was wonderful, but the threat of sex was always there, and she'd never really put aside her belief that Eric was there for access to Alexander—not her. Plus, perhaps Sarah could shed some light on Alexander's life—or nonlife. She'd begun to worry that his world was nothing but sex and work.

"That's a beautiful necklace." Sarah dipped her head toward her décolletage.

Rebecca's hand rose, her fingers finding the small moonstone pendant as it had nearly every day of her life since Alexander first clasped it around her neck. "Thank you. It was a gift from Alexander a long time ago."

"It suits you."

Sarah's eyes held something, a sadness, perhaps? Was she interested in him? *No.* Rebecca had learned from Alexander that Sarah had her own men, not unlike Rebecca's situation. It was an odd thought, really, that she had two men in her life today when a few weeks ago she'd had no one. Her new life was such violent change from the way she'd lived the past few years. Perhaps that's what provoked these odd jealousy moments that alternated with a need to flee. Her previously quiet life had been under her control, while she controlled nothing about her present situation. Her emotions regularly got the best of her. Neither the jealousy or the urge to flee were like her. She'd prided herself on being chill, in fact.

"So, now, for your wardrobe." Sarah snapped into a professional mode, jarring Rebecca a little. She moved to the bed piled high with more clothes than Rebecca owned.

"Oh. That's a lot of dresses." Garments were laid out in long rows—reds, blues, blacks, some with pleats, some with lace and others so sheer she wondered why anyone would wear it at all since you'd be bearing your underwear to the world. Oh, look, a stack of sheer panties and bras were stacked on that chair in the corner.

"I normally would measure you first, discuss what you like, but I took a chance from our first meeting. You're a size eight?"

"How could you tell?"

"Professional habit. Measuring people in my mind. By the way, my Steffan and Laurent send their apologies for not coming over yet. They had to go to New York for some meetings on Steffan's nonprofit, but I promise they'll make it up to you."

My Steffan and Laurent. As casually as if reciting a grocery list, Alexander had told her Sarah was married to a fellow Dominant, and they had a third man who was "collared" to them. "I look forward to meeting them." Questions she wanted to ask rose up like a tide, half to get a handle on how all that worked and half because Sarah might have advice for her sudden, new "situation."

Sarah lifted a gold dress with an empire waist and Fortuny pleats. "So, let's start with the Christmas Masquerade Ball. Alexander requested—"

"The Christmas ball?"

"He didn't tell you?"

Here she'd been thinking of some pantsuits and a casual dress or two, but a gown? "A ball," she repeated as if she had a stuttering issue.

"More like a Christmas party that gives everyone an excuse to get dressed up and act mysterious behind masks. Now, you tell me if any suit you. Don't spare my feelings. This is about you, not me." She held the gold dress up to her and frowned. "Wrong color." She dropped it on the bed.

"You're being so generous."

"We help each other here. Everyone has a talent and we lend it to each other." She lifted three more dresses but seemed not to like them, either.

"Then I might be out of my league."

"No league. Just family at Accendos." She cocked her head at Rebecca as if she didn't understand.

"It's quite a big family."

"Thousands, actually." Sarah snapped a forest green dress to get some static cling to release, and Rebecca shuddered. Thousands? There were more people?

"Rebecca? Perhaps we should sit and talk for a bit. You look quite stunned." She snapped her fingers. "Slave ... "

A woman appeared, darting out from under a cricket table and crawling like a spider. Rebecca cried out. Where the hell had she come from? Rebecca's knees hit the back of a chair, and she shot her arm out to steady herself.

"Rebecca. Sit." Sarah's voice broke through her momentary panic, and she found herself sitting in a large overstuffed chair, her eyes furiously blinking and her head shifting from Sarah to the dark-haired girl. She knelt in the center of the room, head downcast, fully nude except for a series of thin chains wrapped around her body. Rebecca's heart punched at her insides and her legs began to shake.

Sarah had her hand on the back of her neck, and Rebecca was then staring at the carpeting. "Breathe." Sarah's hand circled caresses over her back as Rebecca took in lungfuls of air. She'd almost fainted? What an idiot. What was going on? This was ridiculous. She'd accompanied a caravan from London to Algiers on a story about relief workers. She'd slept in a tent in North Africa to write about the last of the Bedouin tribes. She'd hiked—and gotten lost, damnit—in *Nepal*, but made her way out.

"Slave. Water."

Rebecca gulped air as she raised her gaze. The young girl unfolded herself from her crouch and scooted over to a table. Water rushed into a glass. Sarah took it from the woman and handed it to Rebecca. She wrapped both hands around the glass, the cool temperature clearing her head a bit. She took a sip.

"Leave us." Sarah's voice was clipped, direct.

The girl scooted forward, and Rebecca shrank into the chair as if being affronted by something alien, foreign. The girl quickly kissed the back of Sarah's hand and scooted backward on hands and knees and out the door.

Sarah's hand hadn't left Rebecca's back, an invisible tether holding her in place. "Take a minute. Desiree scared you."

She could say that. "I'm just getting used to the dynamics here." Like people jumping out of shadows asking if they could help. Like being presented with twenty-five ball gowns to try on for a thousand-person ball. Like Alexander taking her on his desk. It was all so … surreal.

"We can do this another time."

"No, please. I don't want you to have gone to this trouble for no reason." She stood and placed the glass of water on a coaster. "I like that blue one." She strode to the bed and fingered a midnight blue silk dress. "This is pretty." She could not catch her breath.

"Rebecca." Sarah's voice was firm, so like Alexander.

Her gaze shot up to the woman, finding more warmth in her face than she'd expected.

"Shall I call Alexander?" Sarah strode over to her.

"No. Please. I'm fine." That edge of panic in her voice was humiliating.

Sarah's brows furrowed.

"I mean. He's working and … You don't have to worry about me. I'll adjust."

"It's not about adjusting. It's about being honest. It's wonderful you and Alexander found one another again but you're allowed to take your time."

"I understand things," Rebecca said. " I've been around … this before." Except for this ball gown thing, and the slave thing and the constant barrage of people and parties and … She fingered the diaphanous silk. *Focus on the details.* The midnight blue gown was pretty with gold stars embroidered into a tulle overlay.

"Yes, I know. I hope you don't mind that Alexander told me years ago about you and Charles," Sarah said. "He needed someone to talk to."

He gaze darted up. Sarah knew? Everyone here seemed to know everything about Rebecca, and she knew nothing about them. Did they know she'd been so awful to him once? Her heart thudded in her chest. "I'm glad. Sometimes people forget he has needs, too."

Sarah cocked her head and smiled. "You do understand him."

"I love him." The truth blurted out.

"I believe you."

"Do you mind if I try on this one?" She lifted the star dress, not wanting any of them, but her questions had dried up. The timing wasn't right.

"It will look stunning against your red hair."

Sarah eased her into the dress, and with a zip of a side zipper, she was encased in a tighter bodice than she'd expected, though the gossamer overlay floated around her.

"Good eyes, Rebecca. You complete this dress. It's like it was made for you." Sarah steered her to a full-body mirror.

"Oh, I love it." She did. She smoothed her hands down the front of the dress. From the outside, she looked radiant. Her hips were wide, but her stomach was flat. A few wrinkles lined her eyes, but her skin had remained clear from her sunscreen habit. She knew when men looked at her, their eyes lingered. Inside, though, she didn't feel this beautiful, and certainly not someone who should be with a man who seemed to contribute so much to the world.

She turned away from the mirror. "May I ask you a question, Sarah? How did you meet Alexander?"

"In a club. He saved my life."

"Oh." That was quite a bombshell. Everyone here was so … direct. "I understand he does that."

"More often than you know. How is Eric getting along?" Sarah asked.

Another direct question, but one welcomed. "Thank you for asking about him." He needed someone watching out for him, someone powerful like Sarah. Alexander's cavalier approach to him concerned her. 'He seems … fine." *Fine.* Such a weak word.

"Everyone here is important."

She may be stepping over a line here, but she was worried about him. "He cares for Alexander though I don't think Alexander sees it."

Sarah smiled. "Alexander has so many people who want to be with him, sometimes he can't see what's right in front of him."

Rebecca drew in a long breath. "Thank you for that. I haven't wanted to say anything. Or even think it … "

"Because that would be speaking badly about your Master."

Her master? Sarah was right. "I didn't mean to—"

"Rebecca, you may come to me anytime. Tell me anything. I'll keep your secrets."

That was the problem. She already had too many secrets.

Sarah looked at her in the mirror. "Many people are intimidated by Alexander, and sometimes he misses their true intention. It's important to be straight with him at all times."

"I am."

"Good. Pass it on to Eric. I mean, if you will be continuing with him."

Her heart hitched at the mere thought. "I don't want him to go away."

Sarah placed her hand on Rebecca's arm. "Then tell Alexander. Otherwise, I think he'd keep you all to himself." She chuckled a little.

In that second, with her words, Rebecca's desires crystallized. She did want Eric in her life. She wanted Alexander, too. What she wasn't sure about was this place. She'd been happier at the Wynter estate, as bizarre as that thought was. But she had a chance to choose—again. God love the Universe for giving her that gift.

"His life is complex," Rebecca found herself saying.

"Yes. He has many people counting on him."

"I hope he takes some time for himself, however."

"I'm sure you can help him with that." Sarah winked at her in the mirror.

A soft knock on the door sounded.

"Enter," Sarah called.

That creepy Desiree was back. At least she wasn't doing that spider crawl move straight out of a horror movie. She held out an envelope, which Sarah took and read.

"Oh, Alexander sends his apologies. He's been called into a meeting that might last a few hours."

Of course, he had.

"I'd like to wear this dress," she found herself saying. This was Alexander's life. She'd adjust—maybe.

33

"There you are." Eric sidled up to Rebecca, who stared out the window over the terrace leading to the gardens. "Thinking of going out? Feeding the birds?"

"No need to feed them. He has *staff*." She turned to him, an adorable scowl on her face. He chuckled. He'd been waiting for this moment. How do you prepare someone for the extent of Alexander's life? You don't.

"What?" She crossed her arms. "I'm fine. I just tried on fourteen ball gowns when I wasn't drinking champagne. I'm feeling sorry for myself over nothing. I get to do that once a month. It's good for the soul."

"Oh?" He tugged her to him, her arms still crossed. "I know something else that's good for the soul."

"If it involves calling up a nail technician or having a personal stylist come measure me, I'll revise my rules on never getting violent."

"I wouldn't dream of pampering you, Princess High Maintenance. I mean, my god, you expect to be fed every day."

She let out a half-laugh. "I know I sound terrible. Awful.

Alexander was supposed to meet me and now he can't." She lifted a note.

"You're the worst. Come for your spanking."

She stepped back two steps. "What?"

"Kidding. You're just bored. Restless."

Her lips parted and her arms dropped. *Bingo.*

"You're used to flying about, meeting deadlines, then rewarding yourself with bouts of self-care because you've earned it. Deprivation balanced out by indulgence. I'm familiar with the pattern."

She let out a long sigh. "You're right." The furrows between her eyes smoothed. *Double bingo.*

"You're also jealous."

And, the forehead lines were back. She scoffed and waved her hand dismissively. "I don't know what you're talking about."

She may be the Elf Queen On High around here, Alexander's soul mate, or whatever else she believed in, but she had to learn something. Alexander was a hot commodity and always would be. "Alexander's life guarantees he's surrounded by people all the time. You're going to have to get used to it."

She swallowed. The truth never was easy.

"Consider me your truth-teller, along with your navigator," he added.

"How do you do it? I mean, be so casual about this sharing thing."

Eric shrugged. "I'm a realist. Getting ten percent of Alexander equals more care, acceptance, and love, than most people get in a lifetime."

She forcibly sighed. Resignation, perhaps?

Her eyes softened. "If you ever leave me, Eric Morrison, I will hunt you down—"

"I thought you didn't do violent." Eric tugged her to into a half hug. "Come on. I have an idea. Let's run away together."

He'd been kidding, but her eyes sparkled and her lips, an unhappy line until then, curved up. She'd do it. "At least to the District line. There's life outside these walls, you know." He recognized that wild look in her eye, and didn't that raise alarm bells? The zoo animals pacing their cages wore the same look.

"Oh!" She snapped her fingers and pulled her phone from her pocket. Before he could puzzle out that all that batik fabric had pockets, she furiously swiped at her phone screen. "Thank the goddess. They're open." She looked up at him, the storm clearing from her eyes. "When's the last time you got to do your favorite yoga move?"

"This morning." He held out his arms. "What? You think this body is achieved by Sumo wrestling alone?"

"Eric, I think I might love you." She pulled him toward the stairway leading down to the front entrance.

He winked at her. "That's what all of Alexander's women say."

She mock punched him. "Careful. I've also done Krav Maga."

He'd tuck that away for future reference, because this woman had a temper under all that pretty. He liked it. Alexander's world had no room for the jealous types, but also no room for pushovers. She was going to be fine—with his help. Guess this friend thing was going to work out after all.

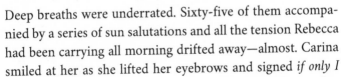

Deep breaths were underrated. Sixty-five of them accompanied by a series of sun salutations and all the tension Rebecca had been carrying all morning drifted away—almost. Carina smiled at her as she lifted her eyebrows and signed *if only I was younger* and pointed at Eric whose bent position gave her a fantastic view of his perfect butt. Rebecca rolled her lips together to suppress a slight laugh.

Samantha's studio had floor to ceiling mirrors up lit by fairy lights lining the edges of the floor and twenty-four-foot ceilings. It gave her a terrific view of every other woman in the class staring at Eric like he was fresh meat. He was the only man in the class, and she was half sure that brunette, who'd immediately claimed the mat next to him when they'd arrived, would take a bite any second.

She couldn't blame any of their roving eyes. Eric was quite the package.

He also was smart, having been annoyingly spot-on about her jealousy. She was ordinarily good at identifying her inner feelings. How did she miss this about herself? She wasn't a teenager, for Pete's sake. Eric circumnavigated Alexander's life so calmly and gracefully despite being in love with the man—who seemed oblivious to his feelings—and being forced to share him.

She stretched into a downward facing dog and spat a strand of hair from her face so she could see Eric—her navigator, her truth-teller. Damnit. The man had perfect form, all that lean muscle stretching and bunching at the same time, and she got to be with him *and* Alexander. A jolt of gratitude filled her. Couldn't what was offered be enough? For the last twenty years, an ostracized Bedouin in the desert had a better love life than hers. Men's gazes might find her, but they didn't linger long.

She lowered into a plank, let her hips hit the mat, and then arched her back into cobra. God, her back needed this. Moving into child's pose next, she inhaled the rubbery lavender scent from the mat under her and made a decision. She would not display ungrateful irritation again. She had friends, and whenever that totally uncalled for ingratitude rose up, she'd come here—to this gorgeous space with a piece of airy flute music softly playing in the background, a wash of amber, and flattering light bathing them. A gorgeous man who'd been a great friend to her was by her side, and he seemed to like being there. She had everything if she'd notice it. *I am loved. I am grateful.*

Her heart pinged an odd beat inside her chest as Eric sighed. She turned her head, rested her cheek on the mat. He'd also dropped into child's pose. Her belly tightened at the sight of the muscle cut in his thighs, his capable arms and hands stretched out. A greedy ferocity of feels for the man rose up—sensual, erotic, devotional, possessive. Okay, she was going to have to work on this possessive thing.

The instructor, a beautiful dark-haired and exceptionally limber woman by the name of Gabrielle (of course her name was beautiful, too) pushed out a long breath and lowered her arms. She then pressed her palms together and bowed. "Namaste."

Rebecca and the rest of the class sat back on their heels, folded their hands at their heart chakra and returned the salutation.

The brunette next to Eric jumped to her feet as soon as he made a motion to stand.

"You're really limber," she said to him. "I'm Barbie. Come to this class often?" She held out her hand.

She did not just introduce herself as a doll. A rude laugh burst out of Rebecca's throat, and caught the woman's attention for a nanosecond—but only that short because Eric took her outstretched hand.

He gave her one of his polite smiles, thank God. "Visiting. Rebecca and I both." He held out his other hand to her, and Rebecca scooted into him, forcing his outstretched arm to encircle her.

"Oh."

She had to give Barbie credit for recovering quickly,

casting her eyes down and bobbing her head in resignation.

Rebecca had to stop this. "It was nice to meet you, Barbie," she said quickly. She typically was a gracious person but something was off inside her, and she was going to punch it down if it killed her. The other students rolled up yoga mats and chatted as they slowly made their way through the curtain leading to the dressing room.

"Hey, there's another class in a few minutes. Want to stay and do another? That one was rather … tame."

"Still tense?" He placed his hands on her shoulders and kneaded. Oh, man. He was not making it easy to kick that possessive, jealous thing.

Carina touched her arm. "I need to go pick up Alexander."

Rebecca's heart jumped, and her fist flew to her sternum at hearing the name. *Oh, the baby.* She let out a relieved breath and hugged her friend. "Thanks for letting us drop in again. It's what I needed."

Carina cupped her cheek. "Call me. We'll go out to coffee."

She squeezed the woman's hand. "I'd love that."

Carina left the two of them alone in the studio.

Eric's eyes slanted down at her "What was that? That sudden jolt of fear when you heard Alexander's name?"

She waved her hand at him and turned away. "Nothing. I might have neglected to tell Carrie we were leaving."

Eric stopped short. "Tell me you didn't."

"Yeah." She reached down to roll up the mat she'd borrowed from the studio. "I did."

He crossed his arms. "Okay, out with it. What's going on?"

She blinked at him. Was she that Captain Obvious to him? The man's uncanny perception around her both soothed and irritated her. "Let's not talk about it."

"At Accendos, we—"

"Talk. All the time." Lord, did she know. "I wanted a little space from Accendos, that's all. I wanted a moment where I didn't feel like I was punching a time clock, okay?"

"And Alexander? What's doing there?"

"It's nothing. Alexander is perfect. And, cagey." That last word she said under her breath.

"Guarded," Eric offered.

"Stubborn." She stuck her nose in the vinyl mat trying to capture the lavender scent again so she could have some sense of the centeredness she'd felt just five minutes before. This conversation was a buzz-kill.

Eric lowered her mat from her face so she'd be forced to look at him. "Dominant. Wonderful."

"Like I said, fucking perfect."

"Now you're stretching it." Alexander's voice crashed into the room.

She spun around. Alexander, a whisper of a smile on his face, pushed off the doorjamb. At least he didn't look angry.

"Been there long?" she asked.

"I heard enough." His eyes were unreadable as he strode over. "I agree with Eric. Guarded. Dominant and wonderful. I'm going with those."

"Sorry."

"I got a little tied up with work. How about dinner out?" He settled his large palms on her waist. "There's a new restaurant in town. Italian, your favorite."

"Really?" She was over-the-top giddy at the thought of going out, which should have been her first clue all was not as it should be.

"Yes. We can discuss how neither of you told me you were leaving home on the way over." His hand gripped her fingers, a stronger squeeze than she'd anticipated, and he pulled her toward the door. "Come on, Eric. You are invited, too."

Well, she wasn't a child, for God's sake. What could he do? Later, she'd realize what a foolish thought that was.

34

"Champagne doesn't exactly go with my outfit, but okay." Rebecca took a sip from the flute and stretched out her legs. The limousine had the space for it. Eric, also holding a chilled champagne flute, sat on the bench across from her and Alexander, and looked like a magazine ad for Dolce & Gabbana. She shivered a little.

"Cold?" Alexander asked.

"Not at all. Thank you for asking." Her skin had warmed from the heated seats and Alexander's hand on her knee drawing lazy circles with his thumb. She'd start her new gratitude practice by focusing on what was right, over what was wrong, like how her skirt, hastily pulled on to replace her skintight capri pants, brushed against her bare behind. She wasn't wearing panties as Alexander's request—or rather, his demand.

Not wrong. This is his world. Eric's eyes kept drifting down her body, an action that had her feeling alternatively unnerved and appreciated all at once.

Alexander's grip on her knee tightened. "Get that skirt up higher. I want that bare ass on the seat."

"But—" Words died on her tongue as cold blue eyes snapped to her face. His stare was tangible, heavy, as if she could feel the energy he radiated. She attempted to sink into the leather as she eased the fabric up and over her ass. Her skin met warm leather.

Alexander returned his gaze forward. "You two looked good together today."

"Maybe next time you'll join us?" Her breath sucked in as his hand moved up her thigh.

He roughly swiped a finger through her slit. "Mmmm." His lids hooded. "Perhaps. Scoot down, knees wide. Eric is going to get you ready."

Her heart rate went from zero to sixty. By the look on Eric's face, so had his. Ready for what? She sucked in a small breath.

"Is everything okay?" Rebecca placed her hand over Alexander's.

His glanced down so sharply, she pulled her hand back.

"Neither of you told me you were leaving today. It was disturbing."

Oh. So it was a wrong move. Sue her. "I'm sorry we left without … " Her words shriveled in her throat because now Eric stared daggers at her. Crap, she'd implicated him, as well.

Alexander's gaze drifted down the man's entire body. "Undo those pants. Cock out. I want to see it."

Yes, it had been the wrong move. Truth was—because that's what she was doing now, telling the truth even to herself—she'd done it on purpose. In an unwise petulant moment she'd actually thought *serves him right.* Looks like she was about to be served.

His eyes found hers. "Lower yourself on the seat, Rebecca. Knees wider."

Rebecca scooched down, her skirt riding even higher on her waist now.

"Grip the sides of the seat and keep them there unless I tell you otherwise."

Eric lowered himself to the carpeted floor and, on his knees, made his way to her spread legs. He made a show of unzipping his pants. Didn't the man ever get nervous around this? Clearly, not by the way his cock bobbed out, full, thick and ready for action. He made to touch her knees but then glanced up at Alexander. "May I?" Eric's lips curved to one side.

Alexander inclined his head in response, his eyes turning to enraged blue flames. "I'll handle that smirk later."

Eric licked his lips, a sliver of trepidation crossing his face. "With pleasure."

Only Eric didn't grab her knees. He scooped his hands under her legs and his fingers dug into the fleshiest part of her ass, and god help her, her hips pitched up in response. Her fingers curled around the seat edge, perspiration pricking the back of her neck. Her legs quivered. Anticipation had always been like that for her. That second before his lips met hers, when fingers moved closer to her pussy but not quite there yet, was almost the best part.

"Just what I thought." Alexander let his gaze run over her body. "Shameless."

She *was* shameless around these two men. She had the presence of mind to glance up at Tony, who was driving. If he glanced in the rearview mirror, he'd get a full view of her bared pussy, Eric on his knees with his cock out, and Alexander, face incensed and dictatorial. She almost said something like, can the privacy screen go up? But then, Eric's lips met her flesh, and Alexander moved to the other bench, away from them.

And, that was the end of talking because between Eric's mouth and Alexander's cold blue eyes bearing down on her, she was nothing but sensation, inside and out. Fear, pleasure, shame—emotions that swirled together into one lethal cocktail she was forced to drink.

Alexander brushed hair from her face. "How does it feel, Rebecca?" She mewled like a kitten, the sound lighting him up more than any shot of the finest whiskey. He checked the thin chain connected to the nipple clamps. "If you'd stop fidgeting, it wouldn't pull so hard."

He'd attached the chain to the thick leather collar he'd wrapped around Eric's neck while the two of them faced one another on hands and knees in the center of the limo floor. He'd brought the largest of his fleet on purpose, instructed Tony to drive around D.C. for a while with privacy screen up. It wasn't the first time the man had done so—or done so with a scene playing out. Tony once admitted he rather liked driving around the nation's capital, among all those black SUVs with dignitaries, BMWs with businessmen and government contractors, and pulling up to red lights, the dozens of pedestrians likely wondering who was behind all that tinted glass—and what they were doing.

Alexander let his fingers slide up and down his cock as he applied a heavy coating of lube. "Too bad I can't fuck both of you at once. Then again, I'm not sure either of you deserve it."

Eric panted and Rebecca could not stop rubbing her thighs together, already slick with her own arousal. Just applying those nipple clamps raised that needy light in her eyes. When he pushed a butt plug into her? Her moans came freely. The dildo, now lodged fully inside her, made her cream herself with no signs of stopping. She could take more than he recalled, but then, what did he know back then? He knew a hell of a lot more now.

"You holding those in for me, Rebecca?" He continued to let his fingers play up and down his cock.

"Yes, sir." She swallowed thickly.

"Too bad I don't have a clit clamp." He really needed to stock this car better now that he had two eager people whose depth of desires were surprising him. It should not have surprised him that they tested their boundaries. Leaving wasn't the issue. Their silent disappearance was the big problem.

"And, you, Eric? Holding that plug in tight?" He wiped his hands on a towel and threw it to the floor.

Eric nodded furiously. His jaw tensed, and his eyes remained trained on Rebecca. Perhaps it was a little self preservation on his part. Alexander knew the man was desperate for some penetration, and seeing a cock he may or may not be granted might make his erection, now weepy in need, grow even more painful than it appeared. Strapping that monster into that cock harness, a simple one by Alexander's standards with black straps that wrapped around the man's full length, had been quite satisfying. He'd rather enjoyed Eric's guttural sounds during the process.

Now, which one to fuck first? He'd overheard it was Rebecca's idea to leave without telling anyone. She wouldn't be rewarded for that. That's something he'd forgotten about Rebecca, her wanderlust, her need for spontaneous movement. She had been destined to become a travel writer or dancer. She certainly had the body for it, long, lean curves that he swore he'd not be parted from again—at least not until she told him she didn't want him anymore. He'd cut off his own balls before he'd be played in the meantime.

Alexander reached into the black bag he'd brought and freed his favorite flogger. The long, black braided, handle was threaded with gold. The lengthy strands were made of black elk strips—a little frayed now, but still quite serviceable.

Rebecca gasped a little at seeing the Contessa. It was his first, made by a leatherman he'd met in San Francisco. He couldn't use it to its fullest use in the limo but that wasn't the point.

"Remember this, Rebecca?"

She nodded. He'd used it on her so many years before, and at the time, it was her favorite impact play.

"Perhaps another time for you." He held her gaze.

He trailed the ends of the flogger on Eric's backside. The flanged end of the butt plug moved a little as he trembled from the sensation. Perhaps this man most desperately wanted to be flogged. Rebecca's mouth dropped open as the thin chain pulling her nipples elongated another inch. His mouth watered at seeing those berry nipples, now a deep red, extended and stretched.

He teased Eric for long minutes, until his back bowed and gooseflesh raised on his skin. The man really did have a great ass, so why was he denying himself? Alexander didn't deny himself shit.

He dropped the Contessa to the ground and placed his knees between Eric's, spread wide as if in invitation. He pulled on the butt plug and Eric groaned. He pushed it back in a little, then out and then back in, fucking him with it. Eric panted hard and fought not to move his neck. Protecting Rebecca, perhaps?

"Rebecca, eyes on me."

Her gaze shot up as Alexander rose up on his knees. He pulled the butt plug out of Eric's ass and positioned his cock at the man's entrance.

"So, since you met me?" he asked.

"Every second since." Eric's voice was hoarse, strained. "I'll do anything."

Alexander grasped handfuls of Eric's hair and pushed his cock deep into him. The man let out a long groan as he seated himself fully. His eyes locked with Rebecca's. "Think about that dildo, that butt plug, as I take him." He didn't need to add he'd deny her.

Her eyelids fell to half mast, and her pants grew louder. In desperation, perhaps? Arousal? Upset? Remorse?

Alexander banded himself to Eric "Rebecca, get closer." She awkwardly inched her knees closer so she and Eric had their faces buried in each other's necks, giving the nipple chain some slack.

Perhaps it was the male ego in him, or some unfounded thought Eric could take it, but Alexander spared none of his strength as he began to fuck Eric mercilessly. The man groaned and pushed his hips backward, meeting each thrust. The cords in his neck strained, his skin's color rising to crimson. Rebecca panted in obvious frustration, the limo's interior ambient lights reflected on the skin of her slick thighs.

Somewhere over the Memorial bridge, as the limo clunked a rhythm under its tires, he came inside Eric.

He unchained them, removed plugs, and wiped skin and faces with damp clothes. He wrapped Rebecca in a blanket to lie on the back seat, still undulating a little as she held ungranted orgasms inside her body. Eric cleaned himself up, a sly smile on his face, fully sated as Alexander had granted him a climax into his own hand.

He sat back and rapped on the privacy screen. "Home, Tony."

They'd eat in his room, not the restaurant, where he'd

eventually release Rebecca himself. *Eventually.* This woman had his heart, and truth told, Eric had begun to creep inside, too. He'd be damned, though, if he'd ever let his affections be toyed with and crushed by anyone. He would ensure today would be the last time they'd leave without telling him.

35

Rebecca leaned back in her chair and gazed over the Library. Apparently, the rich not only made problems disappear but could throw a party for over one hundred people in less than one day. What was once a playground for sexual play was now a Martha Stewart magazine spread. One hundred and fourteen people sat at round tables draped in starched white tablecloths under tree branches threaded with little white fairy lights, strings of red berries and fall leaves. Gleaming white plates edged in gold, cut crystal goblets with red and gold napkins spilling out in an origami-worthy spray, and gold and silver place settings glinted and sparkled as if brand new. They probably were. Martha would be so proud.

Alexander, at the head of the center table, had ensured she sat on his right. She had the oddest sensation of being in the eye of a whirlpool, all that people energy swirling around her. Or perhaps it was the wine.

"May I pour you more, madame?" A white-suited waiter hovered with a white wine bottle over her glass with a questioning look.

She waved him off. "No, thank you." Three glasses of

chardonnay over three hours was plenty, and she had people's names to remember. She had engaged her best reporter trick equating characteristics with their names to etch them in her mind, especially the wives of the Tribunal Council. Christiana, London, Isabella, and Samantha turned out more Vanity Fair magazine cover model than the soft-spoken seamstresses of an Amish sewing circle she'd once envisioned.

Christiana, wife to Jonathan, resembled an innocent Madonna. London, wife to Carson, looked every inch the sophisticate, like the city. Isabella, married to Marcos, had a femininity true to her lyrical name. With any luck, all that would stick.

Samantha was easy to remember, as she'd forever be etched in Rebecca's mind as the mother of little Alexander who now bounced on the lap of her Vikingesque husband, Derek. His arm was thrown over the back of his wife's chair in a protective stance, his other hand rubbing circles on their baby's back, so loving and sure. Seeing them comforted her, the conventionality of their family clear even though she understood they were also part of Club Accendos. The alternating domesticity and heady sexual energy of the group had her head spinning—even if her experiences to date, even the limo scene, were thrilling, and pleasurable, and honestly desired. She'd been oddly comforted by Alexander's vehemence about keeping her close. However, not every day can be a trip to the candy love store.

She tried not to stare too long at the baby and his huge blue-green eyes, his lids drooping a little after polishing off a baby bottle while nestled against Derek's neck. Little Alexander was so beautiful Rebecca had found her gaze drifting to him a dozen times since they'd arrived.

That could have been me. Her eyes darted to grown-up Alexander. He would have been a magnificent father, albeit a little strict in the discipline department. She could have been the counter force to that, taking their son out to the garden to watch the butterflies and count the birds.

Alexander's hand came down on hers. "Feeling all right?" His sophisticated veneer was back, a sharp contrast to yesterday's lion growling at his pride. His eyes bathed her in all the warmth missing then.

"Fine. Time for water, that's all." She lifted an etched crystal goblet to her lips and swallowed down a lump in her throat.

The screech of Alexander's chair made her straighten in her seat. He rose with his wine glass in hand, clinked it with a knife.

"Friends, family." He glanced down at her and then back up to the crowd. "Thank you for being here. Thanksgiving season is a time for gratitude, and this year I have extra blessings to be thankful for. My first gift to you during this holiday season is a short toast."

A titter ran across the room.

His lips inched up into a mellow smile. "My first blessing. Rebecca."

The sound of chairs shifting and fabric adjusting nearly knocked her off her seat. Her skin prickled. So many faces were turned toward her. What did they see? The aging travel writer? The childless woman with a tragic past? Alexander's submissive?

"I count being reconnected to you as an undeserved gift, but I promise to keep hold of it with both hands and all my heart." He reached for her fingers with his free hand, raised them to his lips and placed a chaste kiss on her knuckles. "You were my first love, and I promise my last."

Yes, they were in love. She stared up into his blue eyes, let herself sink into them. She'd never doubt he loved her, and she him. Was love enough? They'd never have a conventional life of children, a white picket fence, Sunday dinners with just the three of them. Their life together would be … She ran her gaze around the room. *This.* Every emotion possible ran up and down her spine. Every. Single. One. A thesaurus couldn't have helped her name them all. How about anxiety, aching, affection, aggravation, amusement … and that was just getting started on the A's.

"And, Eric." Alexander held his glass toward him. "You have been a special gift to me. To us."

Eric's cheeks colored, something she'd not seen happen often. He dipped his chin toward Alexander but didn't say anything. Instead he lifted his glass and took a sip. Men didn't have out-of-control emotions as she did, and she was glad Eric had been acknowledged.

"Happy Thanksgiving to each and every one of you." Alexander raised his glass in the air accompanied by lifted flutes, tumblers, and etched goblets from the one hundred and fourteen guests, creating a crystal forest.

As soon as he took his seat, a line of waiters with soldier-straight backs appeared behind each of them, and at the exact same time, like a choreographed dance, lowered plates overflowing with turkey, stuffing, mashed potatoes, green beans, and cranberry sauce. She took another sip of water and gazed at Eric, who laughed heartily with the beautiful African-American woman sitting to his left, Cindy. "Sexy as sin," was how she'd remember her. Cindy reached under the table, and Eric winced but smiled. His hand rose up, holding hers. Ah, so she'd had to cop a feel. No jealousy, she reminded herself. An impossible feat where he was concerned, but she should at least try.

Carina, who sat across from them, sent a scolding if not amused look toward Cindy. Rebecca laughed inwardly as her friend signed to her, *I'm watching them.*

You are a true friend, Rebecca signed. She then picked up her fork. She had to get some food in her stomach.

"So, Rebecca, have you gotten lost yet?" Christiana smiled sweetly at her.

"There really ought to be an Accendos app. Ow, there, big guy." Derek pulled his baby's fist free from his hair.

"Now why didn't I think of that?" Alexander retook possession of her hand.

Rebecca ripped her gaze from the baby. "That would be helpful. I've already gotten lost three times today."

"Happens all the time," Christiana said. "But someone will always show you the way."

"That's why you, my lovely, wear this." Jonathan, her husband, who sat next to her, ran his finger over the mermaid nestled at her throat. "In case anyone thinks they can spirit you away in the wrong direction."

"Not that you'd ever let her out of your sight for one second." Derek laughed into his drink as his son bounced up and down on his knee.

"That's a beautiful choker," she said to Christiana. "A mermaid?" A mother of pearl mermaid dangling between two shells hung from a choker encrusted with diamonds, sapphires and pearls. It could have been a museum piece.

"Thank you. It's my collar. My wedding present." The words were delivered with such honesty and lack of self-consciousness, Rebecca found herself sitting back against her chair.

No one blinked at the young woman's words. She studied the other women and noticed for the first time their elaborate neckwear did resemble collars. London's choker was made of pearls and diamond-encrusted filigrees that bore a pendant of a bird with rubies for eyes. Isabella wore a twist of silver metal with a diamond-encrusted ring in the center. Only Samantha didn't display one, but that may be more due to the fact little Alexander's fists kept grabbing for anything close by.

"Is that what you'd like some time, Rebecca?' Alexander whispered in her ear. All the wind left her lungs. Alexander's hand found its way to her neck, and her throat reacted with a nearly imperceptible ache. A collar. She'd never given such a thing a thought before, and now all she could think about was what something like the beautiful mermaid dancing at Christiana's neck would feel like.

She grew dizzy. Food, her stomach growled. She took a mouthful of mashed potatoes.

"So, Rebecca, I hear you're a travel writer. That must be so exciting," Christiana said.

"It can be." No need to burst anyone's bubble on what it was really like. Writing about resorts, fighting jet lag, tucking spiral-bound notebooks into her cargo pants pockets to scribble down notes on bumpy bus rides, grabbing sleep where she could. "No place is paradise," a wise editor once told her, which bore truth. Even when staying at a five-star tropical resort, battling mosquitoes, sunburn, and impossible humidity was on the menu. No one's life is perfect, she reminded herself, no matter that Christiana's hair shone like spun gold under those fairy lights and London looked tan even in the dead of winter.

"And what about you?" she asked Christiana.

"I intern for Steffan's company." She nodded toward the tall blond gentleman next to Sarah, whom she'd been introduced to. She sent a silent thanks to Christiana for saying his name. She'd forgotten already. Laurent was the name of the other man sitting next to Sarah. She noted how each took turns, turning inward to her, touching her.

Eric should be here, next to her. He'd say something in his jovial way, and whatever was swirling in her belly would settle. Maybe she'd go over to him, though he seemed quite entertained by sexy Cindy.

Christiana's voice broke into her thoughts. "I'm working on a project related to the impacts of industrial and agricultural activities combined with climate changes that threaten major alterations to the hydrological cycle."

What? "That sounds very important."

"The next war will be fought over water," she declared. It was unfair to believe a beautiful woman wouldn't also be smart and savvy, but Rebecca was not prepared for the level of articulation from the young woman. Then again, everyone here appeared quite accomplished. She'd learned London ran her own public relations firm at the ripe age of thirty-two and was married to a high powered attorney. Samantha had her studio, and Isabella, whose submissive demeanor was more pronounced than anyone else in the room, ran her own nonprofit that put green spaces in urban areas.

And what glorious accomplishments could she boast about? Articles about safaris and who had the best mojitos in Key West, Florida.

Jonathan tugged a strand of Christiana's perfect hair. "Lovely, no shop talk on a holiday."

She nodded at Rebecca. "Sorry. I'm just passionate."

All accomplished, independent, yet all collared. Her mind grew dizzy at the seeming dichotomy. "I can tell, and that's a wonderful thing."

Jonathan's arm had found its way around the back of Christiana's hair, his thumb moved up and down her arm in a subtle caress. Christiana grew still, her lids dipping slightly.

Rebecca suddenly felt like a voyeur, viewing something so intimate she felt compelled to pick up her water glass and hide her face behind it. It was hard not to stare at anyone in this place—so much beauty, so much power, so much ... everything. All the obvious, subtle dominance surrounding her made very un-Thanksgiving thoughts flood her mind. But then little Alexander's gleeful high-pitched squeal broke through. It was impossible, but she would have sworn her chair legs lifted off the floor—that she was floating, shrinking, the air constricting around her limbs as if she was being squeezed into an invisible box.

She touched Alexander's arm, and he broke off his conversation with Jonathan. "I'll be right back. Ladies room." The claustrophobic moment required a moment of escape.

I'll escort you." Alexander placed his napkin next to his plate.

"Oh, no, I can find it. Even without an app." She laughed a little, but he frowned as if he didn't believe her.

She rose and slowly made her way through the maze of tables, teetering a little on her kitten heels. Oh, yes, three glasses of wine had her head swimming. She'd merely drunk too much. Her body wasn't going all Alice-in-Wonderland on her. She wasn't shrinking and becoming invisible. *Really, I'm not.*

36

With three stalls and three sinks, the bathroom could serve a crowd, and its muted lighting put a visitor in the kindest light. She stepped into a stall, hell, more of a small room and sat. She took long, deep breaths and tried to empty her mind. The quiet, except for the faint sound of strings, was soothing. Wait, music? She peered up to find a circular speaker embedded in the teak paneled ceiling.

"Teak. On a bathroom ceiling."

"Everything all right in there?" A smooth upper crust female voice startled her.

She unrolled some toilet paper, rattled the brass holder. "Everything's fine."

She made a production of flushing the toilet and rustling her skirt, which was sooo stupid. She opened the door to find Sarah standing just inside the door. Her gaze momentarily locked on the woman's bright red pencil skirt. Another one? She stood mute for a few seconds, feeling like the country mouse who'd been transported to Oz. Sarah broke the stalemate. She smiled and strode forward in impossibly high heels with such grace Rebecca wanted to ask where she'd learned how to do that.

"Rebecca?" Sarah touched her arm, tenderly.

Her eyes began to sting with emotion.

"Uh, oh." Sarah reached for a tissue. "Holidays can be overwhelming with all that forced cheer."

"I thought no one was forced into anything here." She took the tissue and dabbed under her eyes.

Sarah laughed. "Beautiful and intelligent. No wonder Alexander wishes to keep you all to himself."

She didn't know where the sob came from, but it was as if a bomb released from her chest. She couldn't stand upright. Her muscles wouldn't obey, and her arms banded around her middle. Somehow, the back of her legs met a velvet—because of course, it was velvet—settee along the wall. Sarah had pulled her down to it.

The woman held her hand, and Rebecca lost it in an ugly, emotional, pitchy-sounding spate of sobbing until snot ran down her nose and her eyes squinched shut. More tissues found their way into her hands. When that emotional wave finally subsided, like a tide receding, she pressed wadfuls of tissues into each eye. Through the swollen slits of her lids, she stared down at smudges left on the damp issues. They resembled mini Rorschach tests. An inane giggle followed.

She was officially losing it. "I don't know where that came from. I might be a little drunk," her voice rasped. She lifted her eyes to Sarah despite the fact she probably looked like an escaped insane asylum patient. "You're always catching me falling apart."

"Not at all, Rebecca. You've been run over by a truckload of memories along with a caravan of new experiences and people in a very short period of time. You're handling yourself remarkably well."

Sure she was. She sniffed. "That's so nice of you, but I

think not, and I have no idea why I'm reacting so poorly. I'm good with new." She shrugged. After all, her job was nothing *but* new all the fricking time.

"Ah, but I imagine your job wasn't personal. Here, everything is. Care to talk?" she asked gently.

She blinked up at her. That made sense, the first thing that had that day. Was her life before so barren that a sudden influx of intimate connections, family, friends—a baby—would hurtle her into bouts of hysterical sobbing? Apparently so.

Sarah cocked her head and waited.

Oh, what the hell. "Two weeks ago, I was alone. I didn't always know what the next day would bring, but it was just me, and I'm pretty self-sufficient. Now I'm with Alexander and Eric, and I didn't think things through before agreeing to come here. I hadn't expected his life to be so ... " What? Decadent? Full?

"Big?"

"Public. Yet ... oddly private."

"He's created his own world."

And she'd traversed the world on the outside. "I thought we'd ease into things. I'm a willing participant. I asked him to bring me here because I wanted to help Alexander move on. Repay him for the years he was unhappy because of me." She beat her fist against her chest. "Because, you see, I broke his heart once." God, it felt good to say that aloud.

Her confession hung in the air for long seconds. Did Sarah suspect there was more? What she didn't say was how her present situation with Alexander felt all too familiar. She still felt lost and incapable of getting the ground under her feet.

"I know what it's like to take on the tragedy of another, Rebecca." Sarah sat back. "So, care for a little advice?"

"Please."

"You're taking on too much." She raised her hands to stop a rising protest that must have shown on her face. "Submissives do that. You can't live for another. You can only live *with* another. For you to be here, with Alexander, it's important you have something for yourself, and not get lost inside another's desires. He'd want that for you. If you don't know how to ensure that, well, sometimes it's better to be alone until you can."

"Are you saying I should leave?"

"Not at all. I'm saying you need to find yourself and your place here. At Accendos, taking care of yourself is mandatory. Sacrificing yourself for someone else's happiness, even if that someone is Alexander, isn't allowed."

"Not allowed."

"Alexander built this place to be a safe haven. That means making sure everyone is true to themselves all the time. Honesty is imperative."

The little bits she'd kept from Alexander gnawed at her insides, like her past with Marston. God, she was tired, but this little emotional breakdown? It wasn't happening again. She'd come clean with Alexander tonight. She'd tell him everything and let the chips fall where they may. And, just like that, the planet righted itself around her. Why had she waited so long? Why did she think she could get away with not telling him?

"Thank you, Sarah." She took in a stuttered breath and blew her nose, probably getting mascara all over her face. She didn't care.

"Why don't you go to your room to rest? I'll let Alexander know."

"That's a great idea." She nodded. She'd get herself together and then come down for dessert. Then, tonight, they'd talk—*really* talk.

Sarah rose. "I'll tell him. Rebecca, remember, you have friends here. Remember, you're allowed to take your time."

That made her eyes prick even more, but blessedly, Sarah didn't pry more and allowed her to sneak off.

Perhaps Sarah was right. She'd turned into someone she didn't recognize—jealous, possessive, a martyr. She'd reclaim her backbone and talk to Alexander. It was time for them to have the talk she'd been avoiding. She also had some requests, such as slowing down. Her body seemed to agree with that plan because as soon as she was through the doorway of Alexander's bedroom, his bed called. She tumbled onto the surface, taking a soft blanket draped at the end of the bed with her. Her plans to go back downstairs dissolved into a hazy dark.

37

"Sir," Tony whispered to Alexander, his body throwing a shadow over him. "Can I talk to you outside?"

"Tony, sit. Have some pumpkin pie."

"We have a bit of a problem." Worry etched deep furrows in Tony's brow. "Marston Wynter is here."

Alexander threw down his napkin and stood. "Hallway."

As soon as they strode into the hall, Sarah stepped around the corner.

"Ah, Alexander. Rebecca went to lie down. I think she's a little tired."

"Wine." Eric's voice snuck up behind him. He shrugged. "I've been watching. I can go up and see if she's okay, but is everything okay here?"

"Thanks, Eric. I'll meet you upstairs. Explain later." He turned back to Tony. "Where?"

"Main entrance hall."

Alexander didn't hold back his strides, but Tony managed to keep apace. He nodded at the Ambassador from Spain who was in the hallway, but didn't stop.

"How did he get past security?" He'd kept his voice down despite being out of earshot of anyone. Anyone who saw his face would know he was pissed as hell.

"With so many people coming and going today, he managed to get through the front gate, but we were able to intercept. He's in the entranceway with the team."

He'd been getting paranoid in his old age. Now he was glad of it. He had his personal security team, anyone available and wanting a double-pay shift, to surround the place, mostly to keep photographers at bay. That only made it doubly suspicious that Marston got inside.

"Harlan found Marston craning his neck into the windows, cigarette in hand." Tony's chest rose and fell in irritation. "When questioned he'd simply said, 'Tell Alexander I'm here.'"

Marston stood in the portico staring up at a painting, hands in his pockets, legs wide, his back to the three men in all black. His stance was casual, irritatingly calm. The man should be shaking in his overpriced and environmentally incorrect alligator shoes.

"Marston." Alexander crossed his arms.

"You do like your art." He turned. "Wherever will you hang all of Mother's? Every inch of this space seems taken up."

"What do you want?" He be damned if he'd discuss his acquisitions with him.

"I need to speak with Rebecca."

"You have no business with her." Alexander's legs carried him so close to Marston he could smell the guy's cheap aftershave.

"What the fuck are you doing here?" Ryan's voice sounded from behind.

Alexander flicked his gaze over his shoulder briefly to catch Ryan, Carson, Jonathan and Mark, filing into the room.

They'd noticed his hasty exit. They were an unnecessary show of force, but he was still glad for Marston to see them.

One side of Marston's mouth curled upward. "Is this the part where your gang threatens to take me to the basement and torture me?"

"Don't be so dramatic. I'll simply hand you over to the police. They will hold you in jail overnight for trespassing."

"Yet another unoriginal threat, but one quite familiar to you."

Yes, he had been told those exact words by Marston himself, hadn't he? Only that was decades ago, and today was today.

"Tony, throw him out." He was done wasting his time here.

Before Tony could place a hand on him, Marston, in that pompous, rich Bostonian accent spoke up again. "I'm surprised you took her in after you learned of our past together. Keeping her in a dungeon?"

"She's none of your concern." Alexander grasped the front door handle and opened it for him.

"Oh? I'd say my ex-wife is of much concern given your ... habits."

It took a minute for his words to pierce his irritation at the man showing up. When they did, Alexander let the door smash against the doorjamb.

"Oh." Marston let the syllable glide into the space for several seconds. "She never told you we were married? Typical. The woman always was full of secrets." He hung his head with a dramatic flair. "And, then there was the baby ... "

Time was a funny thing. It sped up. It slowed down. And, sometimes it hung in suspended animation—like now. Six words rattled in the space, but two lodged in his gut. *The baby.* Not "a" baby, *the*.

He had the man by the lapels. Hands grasped his arms,

and shouts joined the thunder of blood in his ears. He was pulled off Marston. All of it blurred as every ounce of rage he'd tamped down over the years erupted.

38

She didn't know exactly what woke her from a sound sleep. The door cracking open? Alexander's voice?

"Eric, give us a moment." Alexander stood in the doorway of his bedroom, face stone cold serious.

"Of course." Eric extricated himself from the bed, grabbed his shoes and skirted past the man.

Alexander took two steps inside, turned, and clicked the door shut. He hesitated a moment, his hand on the door handle for a long second, before turning back to her.

She'd eased herself from the bed covers and sat on the side for a moment. Her head ached a little, probably from the wine and the interrupted nap. She'd fallen almost immediately into a deep sleep. And, Eric? When had he arrived? She rose and slowly made her way to Alexander. "Alexander?" Her hug met a wall of concrete. His arms remained rigidly by his side as he glared down at her.

A shiver ran up her legs and back and across her scalp. His eyes were a cold fury. "I'm sorry I left the party—"

"Marston is here."

What? Her head shook back and forth quickly as if trying

to shake the words from her ears or wake up more. *Marston. Here?*

"When were you going to tell me?"

Tell him? Tell him what?

A cold bath of awareness flooded her body.

Marston *didn't*. He'd promised he wouldn't. It was part of their deal never to speak to anyone of that time, ever. She swallowed hard. Neither of them moved for long minutes. She searched his eyes but only found a deep blue nothingness, as if shutters had been pulled down.

She broke eye contact, went back to the bed, and sat praying, praying so hard. "Exactly what did Marston tell you?" She looked down at her fingers, white and blotchy from twisting them.

"Your ex-husband, the father of your *child* told me many things."

A spear of pain lanced her heart. All the breath blew so hard out of her body, her ribcage collapsed. "No." She raised her gaze to him. Those blue eyes could have lit the room on fire. "He didn't have a child."

"You going to tell me he lied? You didn't have a child? With Marston Wynter—"

"No. My baby was not his." Her hand rubbed her collarbone, her fingers catching a little on her necklace chain. "It was yours."

Oh, that bit of news registered. A flicker of shock crossed his face, but as quick as an ocean gust, it was gone again. His chest expanded in a long inhale. "Mine."

"I was pregnant, Alexander. Eighteen and pregnant with your child and—"

"And, you didn't tell me."

Tell him? She couldn't have, not after the Wynters threatened them both with so many things. Where would they go?

Another greyhound bus to another city, penniless and ... "No, Alexander ... I ..." How did she begin this?

His hand scrubbed down his face. "Keep going."

She swallowed. "I found out a day before Charles' funeral. Marston found me in the bathroom getting sick. It just came out. Then, the day we laid Charles to rest, Alice Wynter threatened me."

"Threatened to do what?"

Jesus, his voice made the air drop ten degrees.

"What do you think? That heartless ... callous woman threatened to take my child away from me." With every word, an invisible vice squeezed tighter around her heart. "They didn't do DNA back then. Alice said they would insist it was Charles', and they'd take the baby away. I'd never see him again—"

"Him."

How could one simple word—*him*—call up so much pain for so long? For thirty-eight years? Long seconds stretched between them as she tried, and failed, to read his face.

Suddenly, he started to pace with such intention, she sat back a little. "But Charles wasn't the father, unless ... " He stopped and turned to her. A muscle in his cheek twitched.

"No, you know Charles and I were never together that way. But, given everyone knew we ran away together, Alice said their word would carry more weight than mine."

"And you believed them?" His roar set her back on her hands.

She purposefully slowed her breaths. "I was going to tell you."

"When?" All traces of warmth, love, anything she knew from this man, were gone from his eyes.

"Tonight, actually." Hot tears blurred the room into an angry gold and red mass. She stood anyway. She had to keep going. "I made a deal with them. The Wynters were never to find you or hurt you in anyway, and I could keep him. But then Marston ... "

"He what?" He strode forward and grasped her biceps.

She winced, and he dropped his grip, stepped backward. Horror—that's what she saw in his face.

"He offered to marry me, legitimize the heir, as Alice called him. The family would pay for everything. If not ... " Blood thrummed in her ears as the storm kicked up in his eyes.

"And you did it?"

Was he seriously angry? At her? From some corner of her soul, she grasped onto her last shred of courage. She could use it now. "I was eighteen. Alone."

"You were never alone."

There it was again. The thought he could save anything, anyone. "Oh, I was. You don't remember things well, you know that? You could barely hold it together after Charles was whisked back to the East Coast."

"I got *us* back to the East Coast."

She shook her head. "No. I did. Where did you think the money I gave you came from? You knew we didn't have more than twenty dollars to our names, but you never asked. When the Wynters took Charles off in their private plane without us, it was Marston who gave me—*me*—the bus fare to get us back to Connecticut."

"Because of that you promised to marry him? The price for lying about my child was bus fare?"

How dare he? How could he *fucking* dare? She snapped her lips together and pointed at the door. When he didn't move, she jerked her arm again for him to get a fucking clue that he had to leave right now. She couldn't speak. The pain had made her mute. She'd bared her soul, despite the fact Marston beat her to it, and all he could see was how hurt *he'd* been.

His eyes glazed with fury. "Not leaving. It's my house, and I want it all."

"Because you always get everything you want, don't you? Snap your fingers and people come running. Well, I'm not one of your staff."

"No. You were the love of my life."

Her insides seized. *Were*. He couldn't love her anymore? She'd been afraid to tell him for exactly this reason. Certainly no love existed in this room right now. "Charles was the love of your life. It was never me."

"No. You both were, but Charles is gone." He closed the last remaining distance between them. "Where is he? The child?"

She shook her head and let all the bitterness she felt coat her words. "Lost. I miscarried." Give him the details, she told herself. He was never going to forgive her anyway. "Twelve days after the funeral, and one day after marrying Marston in that powder blue front room where I could see where Charles lay, I lost him."

Not since Charles died had she seen those blue eyes water. He turned away, his gaze dropping to the floor, shoulders slumped. She'd never, ever, in all the time she'd known him, seen his spine bend in what she registered as defeat.

His head shook from side to side. "I could have been there. I could have done so many things for you. If only ... "

"If only what, Alexander? You were twenty-one. You were shot at and spent the night in jail simply for trying to attend Charles' funeral. We couldn't have fought a family as powerful as the Wynters. We had *nothing*."

He turned and instead of fire, she saw an unsettling despair. He gently grasped her wrist, brought her hand to his chest over his heart. The pain in his eyes was so intense, it would burn her soul if she kept looking. She couldn't tear her gaze away. "We had everything." His voice was nothing more than a harsh whisper. She didn't see, as much as feel, his walls go up in an attempt to shut her out. He dropped her hand. "But you never saw it that way, did you?"

He turned and strode toward the door. Her mistake blazed like a billboard. She'd taken away his choice *and* his control over the situation—worse than death to a man like him.

"Oh, but I did," she said. "More than."

He paused, his face turned in profile. It was her last chance.

"I was responsible for everything bad that happened to us. I wrecked us," she said to his back. "Wrecked *me*, for you. I was trying to fix things, all for you."

That was something else he didn't remember well. Running away to San Francisco with a sick Charles in tow? It had been her idea. It was all her fault, beginning with their recklessness that got them discovered, to Charles' disinheritance, to the deals she agreed to that spawned Alexander's life-long pursuit to best the formidable Wynters. In the end, her poor choices had been responsible for it all, and telling him now was the worst thing she could have done. She'd hurt him then, and now she was hurting him all over again. Like amputees who have phantom pain, they would never have distance from what happened.

She collapsed, her knees burning against rough carpet, her hands slapping the ground so hard she felt a boom. She let out a wail, the one she'd been holding on to for this moment.

39

Her howl broke him. He spun and was on his knees, grabbing her, pulling her into him, so hard, he might have broken bones. Those sounds coming out of her ... cries of pure agony.

His mouth was in her hair, his hand on the side of her head pressing her against his chest and still she wailed. He'd done this. He'd been unable to stop himself. Bitterness had risen up his gorge like a bad meal, until he was incapable of holding back those cutting words.

A child. They could have had a child together, but then ... She had been alone, and he'd let it happen. He'd left her to those people.

His days of playing by the rules were over. The Wynters believed they'd seen how far he'd go for the woman going to pieces in his arms, but they hadn't.

He scooped up her body, limp as a wilted rose. She didn't fight him. He laid her on the bed and did the only thing he knew to do. He stripped her so they were skin to skin and made love to her until they were nothing but flesh molding over one another, their breath in each other's mouths, their heartbeats pounding against one another.

He took his time to make love to her. Later there'd be time enough to crush the Wynter family out of existence, for that's exactly what he was going to do. He was going to erase them.

40

Eric opened the door to Alexander's bedroom as gently as he could. He let his eyes adjust inside the dark for a long minute before moving deeper inside. He'd waited for hours on the other side of this door, his ass on the carpet, arms hugging bent knees. Only when the sounds abated—pained voices, sexual moanings, desperation—did he dare venture inside.

Light seeped under the bathroom doorway. He padded to it silently so as not to wake Alexander, though he doubted the man was asleep by the way he lay on his back soundless, motionless, hardly breathing.

Rebecca sat with her back to the tub, her laptop open, typing furiously. She didn't register him entering until he clicked the door shut behind him.

She gasped, and her hand slammed the laptop shut with a loud click. "You scared me."

"Not as much as you and Alexander are scaring me."

"I'm sorry." Her throat moved as she swallowed. "It's fine. We just had an argument. It happens, you know." She smiled at him, an obvious ploy meant for him to drop the subject.

"That why you're designing a new game plan there?" He indicated the laptop she held close to her chest.

"A game plan? How about the assignment of a lifetime?"

Sure it was. A wild need to escape rippled in her eyes. Her body, even her voice, screamed, "flight." Her fingers curled around the edges of the laptop, and her spine was ramrod straight, as if prepared to jump to her feet.

Now he needed to not spook her. "Oh?"

"Glamping in West Virginia. It's the new millennial thing. It makes them feel like they're roughing it, but not ... I need to go see."

The door cracked open, and Alexander, in nothing but boxer shorts, filled the door frame. "You're going somewhere." Not a question, it came out like a foregone conclusion.

"It's work." Her fake smile faded.

"I see." He moved to the tub and sat on the edge. "When do you need to leave?"

Rebecca's eyes widened. "Really? You don't mind?"

"You're not a prisoner here."

"I know."

"Do you?" Alexander lifted his eyes but didn't seem to see anything. He wore a mask of glazed resignation.

"What is going on here?" Eric had no business interrogating them, but this odd formality between them made every organ in his body harden. "What's happened?"

Rebecca's lips thinned to a straight line, her gaze staring at the wall behind him. "Nothing."

"Not the time, Eric." Alexander placed his elbows on his knees and looked down at the tile. "When do you leave?"

This was bad. He didn't know what their fight was about, but no way was he going to wait for some other time. "Something's—"

"Leave it." Alexander's bark made him step back. He

backed out of the room, but left the door open. His center ached at her next words as they drifted into the bedroom.

"I'm sorry." Her voice, pumped full with false good cheer, echoed slightly in the cold bathroom. "I just need to take a step back. See the stars again for my sanity. It won't be for forever. It's a work assignment. I'll be back."

No, she wouldn't.

41

He'd awakened the next morning to find her gone. Alexander fingered the note Rebecca had left on his desk.

"I know you can find me. You can do anything. If you are the man I know you to be, you'll grant me this space. I promise I'll be back. I always keep my promises, even the ones that were hard to. Remember that."

P.S. You are the love of my life. Always were and always will be. I'm leaving this with you for protection while I'm away.

Another fucking note. This one, however, he didn't want. He clutched the moonstone pendant she'd left hanging on the lamp. That was even worse than the note. He sighed and laid the gemstone face down on the desk. He couldn't stand the sight of it.

How had things deteriorated so badly? This wasn't just about what happened forty years ago. He'd let her lose her way, right under his nose. She'd gotten confused and confusion is a terrible state.

He knew firsthand. After Charles had died and Rebecca was lost to him, he grew so disoriented he couldn't have told you if it were night or day. He found himself back in San

Francisco, roaming the streets until Carina Rose took him in after he passed out outside a club. The Rouge? Was that the name? Later, his uncle found him in a bar in Kansas City attempting—and failing—to drink himself into oblivion or get beaten to death. As they drove back to D.C., he'd told his uncle the whole story, sparing no details. God bless the man, he'd said nothing as they crossed over state line after state line. He just nodded as the lights of passing trucks lit up his features. When they'd pulled into his driveway on Foxhall Road, not five miles from where Alexander now sat, he'd turned off the ignition, faced him and told him—not asked, told him—he was going to work for him. He was a newly-elected, first-time, state senator, who then proceeded to teach him the most useful tenets of his life. Don't beat anyone. *Best* them. Keep all your promises. Surround yourself with friends. Always help if you could. Don't owe anyone anything.

Alexander had built a new life on those basic ideas.

He'd amassed his fortune with one idea in mind: keep the three promises he made on the day Charles died. He'd repaid everyone who'd ever helped him—from getting Carina Rose a permanent gig in Washington D.C. to making sure when his uncle died of cancer it was in the finest cancer ward in the United States and only after exhaustive medical care. He'd helped so many other people in the following decades. The only one he hadn't helped was Rebecca. He could have been kinder to her when she confessed what truly happened decades ago. He knew how vile Alice, in particular, could be. He just had to pile on more guilt? He'd likely validated every fear she'd held about telling him. Oh, to have those few hours back ... he'd handle things better. No wonder she ran away—for that was exactly what was happening here.

Fuck.

Like *hell* he'd let her disappear again. Anger rose hard. It was not unlike grief, he supposed. It all boiled down to having to bear a contemptible injustice that originated in their past and despoiled their current happiness. His foot tapped a rhythm on the oriental under his feet. Unjust? How about despicable?

He stood, unable to sit any longer, and turned to face his gardens through the window.

Having everything and valuing nothing. He'd had nothing and valued everything. What did it get him?

Rebecca should be here, not in some Marriott in Baltimore because, hell yeah, he'd tracked her movement. Glamping in West Virginia, his ass. She was hiding from him. So, he put eyes on her, ensured she was at least safe.

He fell back into his chair and pictured all the things he could do to Marston Wynter. He snatched the phone from its cradle. He could ruin a person in a variety of subtle ways impossible to defend against. Sully their name from restaurants to the White House. Put them on banking blacklists. Hell, drop a dime to the Justice Department with suspicions of money laundering. The JD might believe something was there given that the original paperwork on some of those paintings—some rare and priceless—seemed fishy. The man likely did more than sell ivory across state lines.

What the hell was he doing? What had the man done, really? Offered to marry Rebecca? He was certain Marston had caved to pressure from Alice Wynter, for that bitch had orchestrated the whole thing. So the man kept a secret? Some tiny, goddamned, do-gooder part of him had to give the man credit for his discretion. *Fuck.* He didn't want to give the man anything.

The problem was the real person he wanted to destroy was already dead. He was sure if he held a sledgehammer right now he might be tempted to destroy the very walls that surrounded him just to exorcise this red hot anger.

He rested the phone back in its cradle. For the first time in his life, he didn't know who he wanted to be in this scenario. The destroyer of the last remaining heir to a family he no longer had the energy to despise? Or something else?

He leaned back in his chair and tapped his finger on his lips in thought, again lost in a maelstrom of options, strategic moves he could play, possibilities … How often had he done this over the years? In his mind, the remaining years of his life stretched out before him and the clarity of what he saw stunned him. Without Rebecca, he was destined to live the same year over and over again like groundhog day.

42

Eric stepped inside Alexander's office just as he hung up the phone.

"Clarisse." His rough tone froze her for a moment. Hell, it froze him.

He handed her a manila folder. "Tell Carson this is all his. I'm through managing this one."

The man turned his chair and gazed out on the gardens through the window. Alexander didn't move when Eric cleared his throat. Clarisse gathered up a few folders. Her face before she slipped through the door adjoining their offices told him everything. Alexander was not all right and that would shake anyone who knew the man.

Eric rapped on the doorframe, and Alexander finally turned his head. "Come in."

"Came by to see if you've had a chance to go over that auction list."

"Clarisse has it. I think." No emotion. "Your plan is fine. Go ahead, disperse everything as you see fit."

"Okay, five auction houses, two private sales and the rest—"

"I don't care," Alexander snapped.

Eric scrubbed his chin. The man had been tight-lipped since Rebecca left, shutting himself in his office. Meetings were held. Scenes happened all around them. Alexander had not come to bed until very late and sometimes not at all. Eric had parked his butt in Alexander's bedroom, refusing to give up the field he'd been granted. They didn't touch. They didn't speak. Eric still stayed.

Rebecca called. They sometimes talked to her together, sometimes apart. Every time Alexander hung up, he was a little bit more like granite, the air around him growing heavier.

Time to step it up. Eric set his ass on the corner of the desk. "Care to go downstairs?"

Alexander's eyes slanted toward him, his body rigid as steel. "Downstairs."

"Whichever room you choose. Any instrument. Any room. I have a pain level tolerance of eight. In case my folder didn't make that clear."

The man's chest expanded in a long inhale. "Enjoy pain, do you?" His nostrils flared.

Hell, he was pushing it right now. "Yes."

"Never say that to a sadist."

He inched his lips up in a smirk, on purpose. "That's exactly who I'd say it to." Goading the man out of this mood might not be smart, but it was all he had at the moment.

"Another time."

Eric rolled his eyes. Of course, another time. But when he returned his gaze to Alexander, something had shifted. He smirked anew for extra measure.

Alexander slowly rose from his chair. Eric swallowed the distinct feeling he was watching a lion unfold himself from resting into a battle position.

The man's steel blue eyes bore down on him. "You'll meet me in thirty minutes. Bottom level."

～

A violent shiver ran through Eric's whole body, as Alexander gathered up a single tail whip, running the length of it through those large hands, circling the leather tail over and over until it coiled in loops.

Eric was insane to do this. The man was hurting viciously, and he'd just taunted a sadist to take it out on him, but he wasn't backing out now. Alexander needed this, needed him.

He had bent Eric over that spanking bench, squirted in a hefty amount of lube into his ass with an inserter and affixed heavy thick leather cuffs to each wrist. Now, with arms over-stretched overhead, he tested the chains for the third time, yanking hard to see if there was any give—as if there would be a change from five minutes ago—and only managed to spin on his toes once more.

"You keep testing them like that I'll stretch them farther. Make you hang." With the whip coiled in one hand, he cupped Eric's balls and squeezed them. Like a wanton pussy, Eric huffed out a groan. His cock had been at full mast ever since he'd knelt outside the door, waiting for the man who was late. Very late. His knees were practically numb by the time Alexander showed up in jeans, a white linen shirt open with sleeves rolled up. He'd showered, and smelled like fresh rain and evergreen. God, he'd wanted to latch his mouth onto one of those nipples outlined through that linen fabric. Instead, he'd dropped his clothes outside after Alexander's clipped instructions to do so and crawled inside behind him like a puppy.

Alexander brought his face so close his rough unshaven chin tickled his skin. "Safeword."

"You choose."

His eyes narrowed to slits. "Don't test me."

"Wouldn't dream of it." He cried out when Alexander twisted his balls. "Winter."

Alexander's jaw tensed so hard, a muscle twitched in his cheek. He nodded, his eyes almost violet in the red lighting. His pecs and abs planed beautifully in the low red lights. He played his fingers up and down Eric's cock. "You enjoy being a brat. So like Rebecca."

"She's not here."

Alexander's lips curled up slightly. Saying that was throwing down a gauntlet, but one Eric willingly laid at his feet. He wanted Alexander to unleash on him. The man needed to discharge whatever he was holding inside.

The door cracked open, and in his periphery, he caught a woman crawling into the space.

"I invited Lina to watch. You enjoy being watched, don't you, Eric? Shared? Used?"

Shit. He'd wanted Alexander to himself. But the man would have guessed that, wouldn't he? There was no taking Alexander off guard, no room to play the man.

Lina crouched in the corner.

"Look at this spectacular cock, little pet," he called to her. He didn't take his eyes off Eric, his rough finger moving up and down his erection at a maddeningly slow pace. Eric openly panted. Cold concrete under his toes did little to cool the heat that was rising up like rocket fuel.

Eric spent his life at Accendos semi-erect just from Alexander's proximity. Now, arms overhead in the Accendos famed dungeon, his skin crackled and buzzed with adrenaline, and his cock was going to explode from Alexander's eyes narrowing to slits of intention—of need. That's what he saw there. The man *needed*. How had he not noticed that before?

"I'm all for you," he breathed. Rip his skin off his flesh. Wail on him. Whatever the man needed he was going to get from him.

"I should take you down, put you on all fours, spread your ass wide and fuck you hard."

Oh, yes, he should.

Alexander's fingers left him and his hips pitched forward as if trying to follow. His cock bumped the man's wrist, and Alexander's eyes fell down to his wayward member. He stepped backward, snapped his fingers, then pointed at Lina. The woman scooted forward on hands and knees and lay prostrate before him.

Alexander kept his eyes on Eric's face as he grasped the woman's hair and yanked her forward, putting her face in Eric's crotch.

"Fuck him with your mouth."

The woman's warm wet mouth swallowed him whole with no warning, no hesitation. He cried out at the sensation, the unwavering assault on his cock. He didn't dare break eye contact with Alexander.

In his periphery, he caught Alexander's shoulder muscles ripple under his shirt, as the slick heat of Lina's tongue and lips glided over his cock. Alexander, with eyes locked on his face, fed Lina's mouth to him in an aggressive rhythm. Holding back was going to be nearly impossible. A wet lick of sweat trailed down his back and rivers of tingles ran up and down his arms.

"You like that, Eric? Having a slave suck you off?" He let go of her hair. "Slave, you keep that mouth on his cock."

Alexander then moved behind him. The rasp of the single tail whip uncoiling mixed with the wet sucking sound at his crotch. The air changed, and he cried out at the first sharp bite of the whip tip hitting his shoulder blade. Alexander didn't wait long to land a second crack on his ass.

"You keep that cock hard, Eric. No coming."

Then he went to work on him.

For a brief second, Eric worried the ends that sparked across his skin might hit Lina in the face, but his hips shielded her, and Alexander's aim was spot on. Blows fell on his ass cheeks, the tips scoring his skin until he was sure he bled. He got lost in the sounds of the leather hitting his flesh, the wet sucking sounds from Lina, and the brush of his feet on concrete. His hips pitched forward with each crack, shoving his cock deeper into Lina's mouth. Her wet breaths sounded around his erection and, fuck, he was *not* going to be able to hold back.

"Don't you dare."

Three words from Alexander and his orgasm stalled. He focused on his breathing, the numbness forming in his arms, the fire on his back and ass, anything to keep from losing it down Lina's throat.

The devil brat applied more suction to her lips, and anger shot through his system. She wanted to make it difficult for him? Fine, but he was trying to do something here: perfect obeisance, distraction of the highest order, to put Alexander back to the man he was for at least a few hours. Eric's teeth ground together, and his eyes slanted down, trying to catch her eyes, but she kept them forward and continued that infernal sucking, licking … fuck, he was going to explode.

He unloaded with a loud hiss and *fuck. No, no, no* rattled in his brain as his hips bucked and his legs and arms thrashed as he came hard.

With a loud thunk, the single tail hit the ground. His pants filled the room and he blinked. Alexander had stopped. Eric tried to turn his head, but he couldn't. Rough hands circled his wrists. Alexander was undoing Eric's cuffs.

"No, I … I can do more." Was that his own voice in his head? He floated a little, the lights made it hard for him to focus on any shape or shadow. His depth perception was nonexistent, and he stumbled a bit.

Alexander didn't say a word as he brought his arms down, banded Eric against him so he didn't pitch straight to the floor. Chest hair hit his skin. Alexander had rid himself of his shirt at some point.

"No, you can't, but I can." Alexander's voice rasped low in his ear. The man grasped his wrists, pushed him forward and slapped his hands onto the wall. A zipper sounded. Alexander kicked open Eric's legs, yanked his hips backward so he was bent over more, and rammed his cock deep into Eric's ass. Eric let out a sharp gasp at the invasion, his whole body lighting up with pain and a fuck-hells-yes pleasure. His awareness slammed back into the room with a vengeance.

Alexander's hand grasped his hair, the other firmly holding his hips in place. He then fucked him hard until Eric's cock swelled with new arousal. Eric's hard-on bobbed in the air as Alexander pistoned his hips against his ass for a while. The man had some stamina, and Eric's cock wept in desire … and frustration.

He'd gotten what he wanted—Alexander. It should have been enough. It *should* have been.

43

Alexander gripped the phone in his hand as he stared out over his gardens, dark and shadowy under the December night sky. "How's the glamping campground? Making the Millennials happy?"

Rebecca's forced laugh crackled in his ear. "Rustic. I'll need to stay a few more days."

Of course she did. "Oh?"

"Yeah, the executive director isn't here, and I really need to talk to him."

"I see." He strained to hear her voice over the loud whoosh of wind blowing across her phone speaker. "How are the stars in West Virginia?"

"Beautiful. I'm looking up at them right now."

Sure she was—from Baltimore where he knew her to be. "Good."

Silence stretched between them.

"Well, I should go." Her voice was soft, tentative.

"Have a good evening, Rebecca."

"You, too."

The line went dead. He had a meeting to go to anyway.

44

Alexander crossed his arms. "Marston. You can't stay away from me, can you?"

The man's face reddened. "You always did have an ego."

"I should have guessed you bankrolled this witch hunt."

His face stretched into a grin, making Alexander's hands crave a whip. He knew what to do with smirks. Marston stretched his back, leaned against the chair. "Actually you bankrolled it. With the house sale, I could afford a few luxuries, such as—" He waved his hand. "Paying you a visit with a legal team." His eyes slanted as if in thought. "I especially like that irony."

Headler was funded with the fucking money that he'd paid for the Wynter estate? Alexander had to admit, it was ironic, and well played. "I don't really care."

"Sure, you don't." Michael Headler inched around Marston and sat in a chair at the Tribunal Council table—a chair usually occupied by his nephew, Ryan. Alexander silenced Ryan's rising protest with a lifted eyebrow. They had bigger things to deal with. Ryan chuffed and sat on Alexander's other side.

Alexander glared at Michael Headler, his smug face grinning from ear to ear, as Headler introduced his legal team. Two attorneys from Anson and Anson Partners had flown in from Manhattan, as if that detail, delivered by Headler, was meant to scare Alexander. If the man only knew ...

"You know my legal team." Alexander turned to his lone attorney. "Carson Drake." Carson's eyes glinted like a cobra waiting to strike. However, ever the consummate professional, he merely nodded once in the direction of the other lawyers.

Alexander set both his hands on the table. "Now, what can I do for you gentlemen?" That's when the expensive suits from Manhattan went through their case. It seemed Alexander, the Tribunal, Club Accendos and likely even the flowers outside, owed Michael Headler formal apologies, restitution for mental distress and physical harm. The demands didn't stop there. The list grew so long Alexander had to stifle a yawn at the end of it.

"Coffee?" he asked.

One of the Anson suits blinked at him.

Alexander cocked his head. "It's imported. From Columbia. Care for some?"

"No, thank you, now as I was saying ... "

Carson raised his hand in the direction of Alexander's assistant, Clarisse. "I'll have some, Clarisse." He smiled at Michael Headler. "I never could stay awake when listening to fiction. I'm a non-fiction kind of guy."

Headler snorted in derision. "You all can act—"

One of the suits laid his manicured hand over Michael's arm silencing the man. "Cutting right to it. Good. I appreciate someone who likes to get straight to the deal."

"Is that what you'd call that ... " Carson nodded in the direction of the file folders before the suits " ... a deal?"

Suit One sighed and leaned back in his chair. "Just write him a check."

Headler's nostrils flared as he glowered at his legal counsel. "A check? I want more than that. I want ... "

The man's words halted when Sarah stepped through the door. Her heels clicked across the stone floor. Michael's eyes tracked her as she circled around the table, completed a full circle to stand behind him. She placed her hand on his shoulder. "Hello, Michael."

He visibly swallowed and snarled at Alexander. "If you think trotting out Mistress Sarah is going to do anything, you'll be sadly disappointed."

"Is that what you call her?"

The man's face hardened. "You know full well ... " he trailed off when Suit Two laid a hand on his arm.

The suit leaned forward, folded his hands in front of him on the table. "I think we've established that this house—"

"Home."

"Okay. Home. Is a place of deviant and immoral sexual activity participated in by high-level public figures with deep pockets. People who wouldn't want anything to reach the press."

"Deviant." Alexander tapped his finger over his lips. "Hmmm. Someone's been holding out on me then." He let his lips lift into a smile. He hadn't lied. Everyone's version of "deviant" was different, and to him, nothing that went on within these walls would fit that category. "Well, whatever you gentlemen want to imagine goes on here, it doesn't matter." Alexander lifted his eyes to Sarah who gave him a small smile.

"I'm glad you came, Michael."

Surprise crossed the man's eyes.

"It gives us a chance to deliver the news in person. Sarah is taken, you see. She's married."

Michael's swiveled his head toward her.

Good. Let him see how much he'll miss forever. Alexander lowered his gaze to stare directly into Michael's eyes. "Married, and, more ... "

"Much more, actually." She ran her fingers over Headler's shoulders. "It's a pity really." She leaned down to whisper in his ear. "To never again feel what you know you can."

Marston blew a long breath. "Are we done with the theatrics and double entendres yet? Mr. Headler doesn't need this place or you ... Mistress Sarah."

"I rather like hearing that from you, Marston."

The man's face burned bright.

Sarah sighed dramatically. "So, Michael, I guess I should tell Seraphina that she can return to Caracas?"

Michael's head lurched up. "She's here?"

Bingo. The man still craved a Mistress—and one in particular who'd been working with him for over a year.

"In the Library." Sarah strode toward the door. "I'll let her know."

Michael straightened his jacket. "Wait."

"Michael. Don't let a little manipulation veer you off course." Marston tapped the paperwork before him. "Stick to the plan."

"Speaking of manipulation." Sarah paused in the doorway. "Coming, Michael?" She gazed at the two attorneys and whispered dramatically. "It was nothing but a lover's quarrel."

Michael's eyes darted from the attorneys to Sarah and then to Marston. He rose. "I need a minute."

"What?" Marston was up like a shot. The two attorneys leaned back in their chairs, expelling long sighs as the scene unfolded in a way they hadn't envisioned. Suit Two shook his head, an amused smile playing on his lips.

"Marston, are you okay? Do you need some water?"

Alexander asked. The man did look as if his suit might burst at the seams.

"Michael." Marston made a ridiculous finger jabbing move in the guy's direction. "You walk out that door, and you can forget it. This is our shot."

Michael glanced at the faces around the room. "I need … time."

This bogus lawsuit wasn't over. Alexander wasn't stupid, but he rather enjoyed watching Marston squirm.

Suit One laid his phone on the table, face down. His face was white, and he stared at Alexander with something akin to fear.

"Something the matter?" he asked the man.

The man swallowed. "My father says hello, Mr. Rockingham. He just, ah, … " he tapped his phone. " … texted me."

"Oh? How is George? Give him my best." He'd used his old friend's firm, Anson and Anson, a few years ago.

Suit Two's face shot to his partner's. *Now* the lawsuit was over.

In fact, the conflict of interest was so great, he had half a mind to ask the two suits how they'd been hired in the first place. He thought better of it, not wishing to extend this ridiculous circus show.

Alexander tapped the table. "Marston, Michael is going to be a while. Sure we can't get you that coffee?"

The Anson suits stood, rebuttoning their jackets. "We'll pick this up later when we have a chance to regroup."

Marston glared at Alexander. "This isn't over."

Alexander rose, straightened his jacket. "It never is, Marston. Desires ignored become obsessions."

He should know. He, too, was tired of his own obsessions, like besting the Wynters, fighting Marston at every turn. He was so fucking tired of it all.

45

Alexander blew through into the Library like a hurricane. He paused at the sight of him, and his face immediately hardened. Eric's hand was on top of Lina's head, stroking her hair. She knelt, nude, head downcast, holding a skein of rope in her hand.

The man strode to him. "What the hell are you doing?"

"Care to join us?"

Alexander scowled, spun on his heel and exited.

Eric made sure Lina was settled and then went to find him. This situation was getting ridiculous.

It took a few minutes, but he found Alexander standing on the back terrace overlooking his gardens in nothing heavier than his suit. The early December wind lifted his hair, and Alexander had his hands stuffed in his trouser pockets. His breath hung in the air before his face. He looked very much the portrait of a bull ready to charge.

Eric stepped outside, the icy air arrowing through his whole body. He didn't turn away, however. He'd fucked up with that Lina gesture. He couldn't seem to stop making the wrong move with Alexander.

He sidled up next to him. "Sorry about that. Was just trying to help."

Alexander didn't register his presence, keeping his gaze outward.

Eric swallowed, rubbed his hands over his arms ... and waited, staring at the same garden as Alexander. A sheen of white frost coated the bushes and tree branches, some of them covered in burlap sacks with twine around them as if attempting to protect them from the inevitable winter. He probably should leave, and was about to when Alexander took a long breath of the frigid air.

"I apologize. Seems you're always catching me in the throes of emotion."

"No need to apologize. I wasn't thinking." He stuffed his hands under his armpits, a vain attempt to get warmer.

"I have more than fifty Black Baccara red rose bushes in here. Rebecca's favorites. Or so I thought they were. Now I'm not so sure." Alexander inclined his head toward Eric but didn't look at him.

"Where is she now?" Alexander had told him he'd been keeping tabs on her, and she never seemed to be where she reported she was.

"Baltimore. The Harbor Inn." He hadn't hesitated in answering.

"Care to take a drive? Bring her back?"

Alexander glanced at him. "She's not coming back. I don't force anyone to be where they don't want to be. She willingly walked away from me this time."

"You're not seriously going to—"

He stopped short when Alexander rested his cold blue eyes on him. "Yes. I seriously am. For once, I'd like the person I love most in the world to choose me. She'll have to return to me of her own free will. If not, then, it was a pipe dream. I should have known the past can never be revisited."

This was such bullshit. Rebecca needed affirmation she was important to Alexander. Of course, Alexander needed that, too. They were at an impasse. Was he the only one who could see this?

Alexander stepped down the stone steps and headed into his frozen garden with his fifty rose bushes, alone.

Eric didn't follow him. Instead, he stood there, impotent and ruined forever for anyone else—and knowing exactly what he had to do next. There would be no luring Alexander to a basement dungeon. It had been a pipe dream, as Alexander had nailed so well, to think he could be with the man. Alexander's heart had room for only two people, one was dead and the one alive didn't know how good she had it.

He'd lost them both. His time here was over. He'd get past it—someday. He wasn't concerned with the tears that ran down his cheeks. Frigid air made your eyes water. Everyone knew that.

46

Eric spun his hand on the steering wheel, put the rental car into park and shut off the ignition. Rebecca sat on a picnic table, hunched over a book, her back to him. He stared at her for a few seconds. Beautiful as ever. Oblivious, too, by the way she didn't stir.

He had expected his text message to her would go unanswered. Over-the-top relief filled him when she had.

He cracked open his door. She didn't move when he lowered himself to the opposite bench. "Must be a good read."

She gasped and spun around. "Oh, God, Eric, you scared me."

He cocked his head toward the book. "War and Peace?"

She smiled and lifted the huge paperback. "J.R. Ward's latest. I like the fantasy." She twisted her body so she sat across from him. "I'm so happy to see you." She gave him one of her million dollar smiles.

Not so fast, princess. "I thought that's what I was supposed to say."

"Thanks for coming. How's Alexander?"

He eyed her. "Oh, no. You don't get to do that, Elf Queen."

Her chin pulled backward. "Excuse me?" She let out a half laugh.

"That's what I thought the first time I saw you. Elf queen from Rivendale. But you don't get to pretend you're some magical being when you're breaking the heart of a man who'd give his life for you."

She pursed her lips together. "Wow. Starting things off with a bang." She huffed and looked out over the park. "But you're overstating things."

"Bullshit. And you know it."

She twisted the side of her mouth. "You're in love with him."

"So are you. Which is why it's so odd that—" he peered around. "—we are sitting on a dirty old picnic table in a park in Baltimore."

"It's complicated."

"No. It's not."

She looked aghast and then moved to stand up.

"You are a runner," he said.

She stilled. "Excuse me?"

"You run when things get hard. It takes one to know one. " He looked down at her duffel bag, a gold A etched into the black canvas. The irony of that one wasn't lost on him. "You're disappearing again, aren't you?"

Her eyes cleared, all flirtations and pretense gone. She took in a breath and blew it out quickly. "Wouldn't it be easier if I was gone?"

"No."

"Well, that's a surprise. Alexander and I are too different now."

"That why you only ran away forty miles? Of all the exotic places you could go in the world, you chose Baltimore?"

Her lips thinned at his derisive snort. "You're right. I can go anywhere." She angrily slammed her book down on the wooden table and reached for the duffel bag.

"You don't deserve him."

She stilled. Tears flooded her eyes, like a rising river. "I know."

"Why? Because you tried to protect him? Lost his baby? Yeah, I finally got Alexander to spill. Someone had to have his back. You sure didn't."

"Jesus, Eric." She took in a stuttered breath. "This tough love thing is … "

"Tough? Give me the real reason why you're leaving him again—and by the way, you're breaking the deal we made—and I'll leave you alone."

Oh, yeah, the promise she'd made to him the day they filled all those bird feeders—never to leave without telling him. Seems she was always making deals.

"I don't want to lose myself again. He has this huge life, and he's loved and … " She stared out over the water. "He doesn't need to shrink himself for me."

"News flash. You've already shrunk him, and he needs you. Now, why don't you trust him?"

"I do. I don't trust myself."

"You know the secret to trusting yourself? It's really simple but no one seems to get it. It's keeping your own agreements with yourself. You say you won't eat that cupcake, you don't. You say you love someone, you do."

She looked at him like he was crazy, which he was a little bit on the inside since everything went to shit.

"I never said I didn't love him," she said.

"Then grow up."

The amount of steel in his voice surprised even him, but he was not going to let this woman undo Alexander. He couldn't stop the man's descent into wherever he seemed to be falling, but she could. Case closed.

"You both have got the past so shoved up your asses, you can't see each other anymore. Stop looking for the old Alexander. He's gone like Charles is. Start loving the one that's standing right in front of you."

"You're standing in front of me."

"Only because that man is too proud to come for you. I have never known Alexander to chase after anyone. It won't happen if that's what you're waiting for, but if I have to throw you over my shoulder and carry you back to Washington, I will do it."

She looked at him aghast. "Wow—you're like, really in love with him."

"There are no words big enough for what I feel for that man. You know what I do for a living. I take rich people's things and get rid of them. I see more privilege, callowness, jealousy and hate than anyone should see in a lifetime. I have seen the worst of humanity. Alexander could be one of them. But he's not. He's not because he chooses not to be. Instead he's—" Emotion choked his throat closed.

"Magic?"

He swallowed. "Yes." He closed the distance between them. "And, you're afraid to need him."

"You might be right there." Her eyes were wide and watery and still beautiful as ever.

He chuffed. "Maybe, for once, someone he loves should chase him—and that someone should be you. And, if you don't, then I was right. You don't deserve him."

A choked gurgle came out of her throat, and she knelt over her own lap, face in her hands. Her shoulders shook for long seconds. *Oh, fuck him.* He sighed and eased himself up to sit next to her. He put his arm over her shaking shoulders, and she lifted her head.

"I have no idea how to be with him. None. And I know one day it will be too much. I won't ask him to change for me. I thought it would be better to go now."

He waved his arm. "To a park forty miles away?"

She sucked in a wet breath and her cheeks inched up in a tentative smile. She shrugged.

"I'm going to ask you a very simple question." He brushed hair back over her shoulder. "What are the odds you'll regret not trying again with him?"

She swallowed hard. "Wow. You're good at this."

"Didn't you hear? I'm a genius." His face sobered. "Tell you what. I'll answer. You'd regret leaving him for the rest of your life."

"I already do."

"Then stop being a putz."

A laugh burst from her throat. "A putz?" She swiped at her cheeks.

"I can come up with something worse, if you need it." He pulled her closer into him. "Stop trying to recreate the past and just start over. But do it with him. Just ... try."

She stared hard at him for a long second. He held his breath as he watched all the reasons for her just to give in or run farther away crossed her face en masse.

"Okay," she said. "I have a rental car to return. Give me a lift to Washington. I mean, you'll go with me, right?"

Thank you, God. "Need an entourage?"

"I think I might need a navigator since I seem to get lost a lot."

He grasped the handles of the duffel bag. "I've got this."

And he did, right up until he crossed the threshold and saw Alexander's eyes light up with all the love in the world ... for Rebecca.

47

Alexander rolled to his back and stared at the ceiling. His hand possessively gripped Rebecca's, unwilling to have at least one part of him touching her at all times. He'd spent half the night buried inside her. They'd not spoken more than six words to each other all night, instead, they unleashed all the desperation they'd harbored and let their bodies talk to one another, as if they needed to feel the corporeal being first to make sure they weren't hallucinating each other's presence.

Rebecca snuggled closer, and he lifted his arm so she could settle into his shoulder. "Thank you for coming back."

"It was inevitable."

He laughed. "Oh?" It sure as hell hadn't felt that way to him.

"I'm not sure I could have stayed away for much longer. You're my kryptonite, drug, and lifeline."

"Is that why you stayed away for nearly forty years?" He made sure no anger or upset colored his voice.

"Yes." She pulled up to her elbow. "I thought I was doing

you a favor. Let you have your life. Make sure no one hurt you."

"I know, mo rúnsearc." He eased up and touched the moonstone necklace around her neck.

"Do you? Because it's the truth." Her fingers covered his. "I'll never take it off again."

"I know." He dropped his hand. "I should have tried harder to find you. This whole time I thought I'd been trying to best the Wynter family when really I think I was trying to be good enough for you—to have you want me again." That truth had bubbled up sometime in the night and was a bitter pill. Time to cough it up.

"You were always good enough. I hate that the Wynters made us both feel like we weren't."

"I told Eric not to go looking for you. No one should be here or be with me if they don't want to be, but I'm glad he did."

"He's another great man."

Alexander murmured an acknowledgment. "Where is Eric, anyway?"

"I think he wanted to give us space. Time to talk."

Alexander's lips twitched up. "We've not done a lot of that."

"True." She smiled. "But I need to. I mean, that is if it's okay?"

He turned his face to her, the pillowcase catching some of his hair, making it askew and adorable if one could ever consider someone with the presence of Alexander Rock-ingham adorable. "Of course. Always. Talking is mandatory."

"I don't know how to fit in here." Eight words that summed up everything, but to date had been hard to say. Why? Why had she waited to voice that she'd been over-whelmed? She hadn't wanted to disappoint him, that's why. Sarah had been right.

He sat up as if waiting for a shoe to drop, and now that she thought about it, those words had been tinged with cynicism.

"I love you, and I'm not going to leave you," she added quickly.

"I'd never force you to do anything you don't want to do." The intensity in his voice made her sit up and join him against the headboard.

"I know that."

"The limo ride. I scared you."

"No. I love it when you take command, dominate, control our sexual dynamic. Honestly, the things we do together when it's just us are … magic. It's everything else. This huge estate. The parties. The one hundred and fourteen people. The jet. The wardrobe consultant. The haute couture." She ran her hands down the pure silk camisole she didn't recall putting on last night. "I missed just talking to you. It seemed you were always working."

"Perhaps I've been in my own world for too long."

"And I've been everywhere else for too long."

He smiled at her. "How about this? Less haute couture. More of me."

"And, you and Eric." She bumped up against his arm. "I like the three of us together."

"Three." He repeated the word. "Yes. Eric. You like him."

"I think I love him. Don't get me wrong. Nothing will dim what I feel for you, but it hit me as he was bringing me back. He's selfless. He loves you so much, he brought me back to you without hesitation. Who does that?"

Alexander just nodded.

"It feels weird in here, doesn't it? Without Eric?" Rebecca glanced around.

"It does." Alexander eased himself from the bed. "Care to go get some breakfast? Just the two of us? Or three, if we can find him." His gaze caught something on the floor. He strode over and picked up a folded piece of paper, pushed under the door at some point in the night.

Sorry to reunite and dash, but the Marietta estate needs me. I need to get back to London. What can I say? I'm a genius.

Hang on to each other, okay? You being together reminds me there is magic in the world.

Yours always, Eric

P.S. Sorry I didn't hide this behind a painting.

He'd left? Alexander scrubbed his chin. He was really starting to hate notes.

"What is it?" Rebecca hopped from the bed and took his side. She lifted on tiptoes and peered down at the writing. She pointed at the simple drawing at the bottom. "Is that a—"

"Bird." He lowered the note. "Eric's left."

"But why?" She grasped the paper and yanked it closer to her face. "I'm not loving this sign." She moved quickly to the closet in the corner room. She swung open the doors. She turned to Alexander. "He's *really* left." She swept her arm over the space where he'd hung his few things.

"Because that's what he does. He helps people settle their affairs, and moves on."

She still clutched the note in her hand. She swallowed. "Who settles his?"

A long minute passed as if neither wanted to speak the obvious truth. He had been callous with the man, taking what he offered and believing the little he returned would be enough for Eric. He always figured Eric would be fine. He'd seemed fine—even loving an arrangement that had no strings, no commitments.

"We're good together, just the two of us," she said. "But …
"

"Better when it's three? You may be right there. He is rather good at gluing us together."

She grew excited. "Then, let's go get him. You're the master of the universe, right? Unleash your … minions to find him."

He laughed heartily. "Your wish is my command." He could do that because the truth was, he'd missed the guy. How hard could it be to find him? Not hard at all.

48

Alexander slapped the table. "I bring this meeting of the Tribunal to order. The Grand Arbiter has the floor." He cleared his throat. "Eric Morrison is missing. I can't find him." Eric was as good at disappearing as Rebecca had been. Nearly two weeks had gone by and not a single estate sale had his name on it.

No one said a word. Jonathan, Carson, Mark, Derek, and Sarah—none of them appeared concerned, which irritated.

"Alexander, what would you like us to do?" Leave it to Jonathan to ask the right question.

"Find him. Call in every marker I have."

That one got their attention. Eric's absence had grown like a toothache, leaving a gaping hole he had not been prepared for.

"He have family?" Jonathan asked.

"None that I know of." Why didn't he know that?

"Rebecca?"

"Hasn't heard from him either. Texts, calls, go unanswered. His office simply said he told them he was going on vacation. Someplace off the grid." Misplaced anger filled him.

He scrubbed his growing beard. He was merely frustrated because finding people was generally easy. Digital footprints coupled with a small art world meant finding Eric Morrison shouldn't be that fucking hard.

"His work doesn't know where?" Ryan asked. "Not like Eric. I mean, to abandon things in mid-auction."

"Why not? Nearly everything is going up for private sale, correct?" Sarah cocked her head. "I mean, he'd done his job. Gotten inventory to the next step and now—"

She stopped when Alexander's hands fell to the table in two tight fists. He was so done with people running from him. No number of private investigators—even Stan Tocatto who could find a coconut floating in the ocean—had been able to ferret out anything. Eric had landed in London, and the last time anyone had seen him, he'd been getting into a taxi at Heathrow Airport. *Shit.* That city had more cameras per square foot than a movie set and still nothing.

Carson tapped his pen back and forth between two fingers. "Sounds like he doesn't want to be found."

Could that be right?

"Find him anyway." Alexander straightened. "Use every marker this Council has amassed. Every one until he's found."

Glances darted around the room as if the Council members didn't believe what they'd heard.

Carson rose first. "Consider it done. We won't need to cash them all in. No need to spend a million chits when only a few might be necessary."

"But do it if necessary."

Carson went still, his eyes assessing. He didn't believe him? Finally, Carson lifted his chin. "Understood." He turned to Ryan. "You still have the list of the Wynter estate items that are at each auction house?"

"Of course."

"I'll call them." Carson leveled his gaze at Alexander. "I'll tell them Alexander's attorney is calling with some discrepancies. That should rattle a few cages — enough for the directors to put out feelers. It'll make its way to Eric. As you've said, the art world is small, and he won't want his reputation dinged."

Smart, but cruel. "No, don't do that." Another idea formed. "I believe the Danube Brothers in Boston have the Klimt paintings. Call them. Tell them I'm taking the sale public. No more private sale. I want to be there when they go up for auction—and publicize that fact. Put my name up as seller." To date, he'd been anonymous. If Eric wanted to see him, he might show. If not, then Alexander knew they'd lost him for good.

"And there's one other thing you all need to know before we adjourn," Alexander said. "I'm retiring as Grand Arbiter."

All six bodies around the table sat back in their chairs. Shock registered in various forms around the room. Sarah's face flickered the least surprise, as they'd had this conversation in the past—how she should be the one to take over. Derek showed the most with his slumped shoulders and wrinkled forehead. He had been the man closest to him as a son though they shared no blood. The thought he hadn't even been granted the courtesy to mourn the biological son he'd lost so long ago ran circles in his brain. He'd never been as pissed at himself as he was right now. Leaving Rebecca to the tender mercies of the Wynters and then raging at her for not telling him? Yeah, not his smartest play. She'd been trying to protect him. It was so ass backward. He should have played that role for her. She might forgive him—someday—but he'd never forgive himself for his prideful actions, or lack of action.

This retirement move was right.

In the last few years, Alexander hadn't participated much

in the world outside of Accendos. It was time to end that behavior. He'd gotten too insular while trying to keep everything out and everyone he loved in.

Time to change it up, starting with finding a man who'd crept in unnoticed and become necessary to him, a man he hadn't realized he'd miss so much.

49

Snow flurries danced around Alexander's coat as he took the two steps into the Danube Brothers gallery in one leap, not giving the old brownstone façade on Chestnut Street a single glance. He blew hot breath on his hands as soon as he was through the door.

"Mr. Rockingham." A balding man scurried forward, hand extended. "You made it. Come in, come in. I apologize for the snow." He waved his hand toward the long glass panes framing the door. "You know, Boston. Are you sure you don't want to postpone—"

"No."

The man stopped his vigorous handshaking of Alexander's hands in shock at his bark.

Alexander inclined his head. "It's important to me that we do this before Christmas."

"Whatever you wish." The man's face stretched into a smile. "We may not have as many visitors—" he lowered his voice to a whisper "—but I made some calls."

"I appreciate it. You let the regulars know about the Klimt?" Alexander shrugged off his coat and handed it to a waiting attendant.

"Of course. And I fielded a few interested parties who heard about the sale. You know how the art world is. Things get around. Wine? Or perhaps something stronger?" The man swept his arm toward a young woman holding a tray of champagne flutes and wine glasses filled to the brim.

Alexander raised his hand in a 'no.' "Thank you, but I'm going to take a look around." He was already scanning the area for any sign of blond hair, hands stuffed in pockets like Eric always did. Just a few couples milled about looking as bored as he'd expected.

Alexander took a few minutes to nod politely as he passed them, predictable whispers beginning. He rarely showed up to these auctions anymore. Collecting things had lost their appeal long ago.

It took less than ten minutes to walk the entire perimeter of the three room gallery. He paused before a sculpture, a young boy holding a book, his hand on a puppy peering up at him. It would look nice in his gardens. Hopeful and sunny and bright and all the things he didn't feel at this moment.

He turned the corner and came face to face with the Klimt, a portrait of a woman with her hand cocked on her hip as if she hadn't a care in the world. A couple stood before it, hands linked, gazing up at it. The woman turned her face to her male companion. "Buy it for me?"

The man inclined his head down to the small white square with SOLD tacked on to the etched plate under it. "Seems someone else got here first."

Alexander could only hope whoever did appreciated the piece and didn't store it away in some crate in a warehouse.

"Was it you?" she bumped against him playfully. He dropped his grip on her hand and circled his arm around her. "I'll buy you one. Someday."

She set her head against his shoulder. "I know you will."

Such trust was reserved for the young. He didn't know why, but he sent up a little prayer that everything would work out for this unknown couple.

He should go. The gallery was small, and he'd circled the three rooms twice. Eric wasn't coming. He'd promised Rebecca a dinner at Amelie's that had a small table before a fireplace reserved just for him. Three people would fit nicely there—if there had been three.

Tonight, there would just be two.

It would be enough. He had Rebecca, and his blessings could circle the earth ten times. Like a cat who landed on both feet, Eric would be fine without Alexander Rockingham. *"But you won't be fine without him,"* a small voice whispered in the back of his mind. Regrets—all the things that could have been, all the things he should have done for the man—would live inside him forever.

"Wonder who bought it?" a male voice asked behind him.

Alexander's heart seized and his chin dropped to his chest for a long moment. His eyes stupidly pricked. All was not lost—yet.

Eric could have pinpointed Alexander in Time Square on New Year's Eve. In a half-empty gallery showing, identifying that expensive black cashmere jacket over those broad shoulders and that salt and pepper hair? Easy.

The man slowly raised his head and turned to face Eric.

"Word on the street says it's some sentimental fool." His mouth inched up into a smirk, because why not? He was a sentimental fool—for buying the Klimt, for coming to see the man he knew would be here, for venturing out in a goddamned blizzard and walking four blocks to get here because the taxi pussies wouldn't come down this side street in a storm.

Alexander took two steps forward. "Sentimentality has its place."

"Now that is a surprise." He flicked his eyes up to the painting and circled Alexander to stand before it. "Tell me you didn't fly up in this snowstorm. The commercial flights have all been cancelled."

Alexander moved to stand next to him. "Benefits of having your own jet. Can fly into a nearby regional airport."

"Yes, I guess so." He stared hard at the painting. "You here to buy back the Klimt?"

"No. I came here for you." Alexander cleared his throat. "To thank you."

His eyebrows shifted. "For?"

"For bringing Rebecca back to me. For reminding me who I am."

He squared himself to the man, searched his face for any hint of humor or, worse, pity.

"Rebecca told me you were interested in me. A while back. When we were at the Wynters."

"Interest doesn't begin to cover how I feel about you." What the hell. Truth was better than hiding the obvious—or should he say the obvious to everyone but Alexander.

"Good. You always bring things back to me, Eric. Now it's my turn."

"Going to make me an offer for the painting?"

"I told you. I'm not here for the Klimt. I'm here for you. I never chase after people." He blew out a sharp breath. "But you? Well, obviously, I should never say never because here I am. Coming for you. Care to come back to Accendos? Permanently?"

Fuck him. The-man-who-doesn't-chase-after-anyone *came* for him. Alexander hadn't pursued even

Rebecca, but he'd come after *him*. A long minute stretched. Jittery nerves threatened to slip his control, but he subdued them with one long breath.

Alexander finally dropped his hand. Those icy blue eyes made him want to drop to his knees, grab the man in a hug, and run like hell, all at once. Fuck him, indeed. This couldn't be happening. He crossed his arms over his chest. "Give up my fabulous single life? All those men beating down my door every night? I don't know, Alexander."

"You use humor when you're nervous."

Yeah, well, Alexander used force. Which was worse? How about being used? That was worse. "I won't be a replacement for Charles."

"Charles is dead." The words hurt Alexander. A sliver of pain had run across his eyes, but then it was gone. "He was a long time ago and now ... I've missed you. I care for you."

Eric swallowed.

"I see you don't believe me. I more than care for you." Alexander's breath drew in. "You and Rebecca ... you're my last loves."

Eric turned back to look at the painting because he needed a moment. Hell, he needed a full day to understand those words—words he'd have killed to hear a month ago. "I don't usually buy things. I travel light. Paintings, in particular, don't fit well in suitcases."

"No. They don't, but it would fit on my plane."

Eric let out a half laugh. He shook his head slowly from side to side and studied his shoes. He ran his hand down his chin and then squared himself to Alexander. "Okay. I'll go." His voice cracked some strange heaviness in the air. "But only because you brought the jet."

Alexander snorted a laugh. "Prima donna."

"Look who's talking. Needing Rebecca and me."

Alexander eyed him. "You may be the only person willing to talk to me like that."

"Willing to take the punishment."

Alexander held out his hand, which Eric took. Alexander yanked him into his chest. "And you will be punished," he said into his ear. "You know what I can do on a plane."

Eric's head pulled back. "Promise?"

"I always keep my promises."

"I know." They stepped back and eyed one another for a long minute.

"You ready to go?" Alexander asked. "I have reservations for dinner. I made them for three."

"So sure of me?"

He shrugged. "No ... but it's Christmas, traditionally a time for hope. Or so Rebecca reminds me."

"She's here, too?"

"Outside in the limo."

Eric chuffed. "Of course she's in a limo."

Alexander circled his shoulder and led him to the doorway. Outside, snow flurries swirled all around them, and a vehicle that resembled more tank than limo. In the doorway, under the enormous pendant lantern, Alexander roughly turned him. His lips came down on him, hard, forcing his mouth open. As soon as tongues touched, flamed licked up Eric's skin as if they'd been dropped into the middle of the Sahara. For several long seconds, he lost himself in that strong mouth, the calloused hands on each side of his neck.

When Alexander broke the kiss, he kept one hand around Eric's neck. Those eyes as bright and blue as a summer sky bored into him.

Eric licked his bottom lip. "If that's your idea of punishment ... "

Alexander dropped his hand, laughed, and swung open the tank-slash-limo door himself. "Get in."

Inside, a smiling Rebecca sat with legs crossed, a tea mug in her hand, not the expected champagne.

She smiled at him. "Runner."

"Elf Queen."

As soon as he was settled on the seat, she nestled her tea mug in a drink holder and straddled his lap. She flattened her hands on both sides of his face. "I love you, Eric Morrison. So, next time, you're taking us with you."

"Next time?"

"That you disappear. It's a new deal I've struck with Alexander." She turned and smiled at the man. "If any of us wants to run, we can, but only if we take the other two with us."

"Interesting." Guess his days of traveling light were over. Settling down? Hell, yes.

50

Alexander swung her in a wide arc across the Library floor. Somehow he managed to avoid crashing them into the other dancing couples under the strings of fairy lights hung in graceful crescents from beam to beam.

Her breath caught in her lungs from excitement. The string music from the small orchestra players on the gallery above showered sounds down on them, and the smaller crowd—just seventy-five people over Accendos' usual three hundred for Christmas Eve—smiled and laughed as they raised wine glasses to their lips or swished across the floor in a waltz.

His blue eyes fixed on her. "Was I right?"

"You were. It is better." The gown's gossamer fabric did feel amazing against her bare ass. His one request tonight— at least the only one she'd heard so far—was she wear no panties under her custom gown of midnight blue tulle and silk. And it felt amazing.

She let her back arch, and Alexander's arm cradled her as he swung her again. She wanted to see the thousands of tiny lights mimicking stars on the ceiling. She may not see stars in the night sky, but Alexander ensured she'd see them anyway. He'd had the turreted ceiling painted a deep indigo with glow-in-the-dark constellations scattered across its surface.

"As good as the stars in West Virginia?" he asked.

She lifted her head. "I don't know. I was never there." The truth now spilled from her lips as natural as breath.

"I know."

Her mouth dropped open. "You knew." Oh, God, was he angry?

"I did." He drew her into him tighter, his lips inching up into a smile. "You think I'd let you disappear again?"

"No. And, thank you for that."

"Thank Eric. Ultimately, he was the one who found you."

Her gaze landed on Eric. Even behind the black mask, she'd never mistake him. He really knew how to wear that tux, almost as well as Alexander. Eric, as usual, fended off two or three of the ball's other female guests. *That one's mine*, her inner voice called. As was the man currently spinning her in another arc. Now, she'd only say it silently, as the jealous green monster, while not entirely gone, had little sway over her. Who could feel anything but happiness under such stars, even ones made of glow-in-the-dark paint?

She let herself get lost in the rhythm, the cinnamon and clove scents, and lights—and Alexander's arms holding her.

"Mind if I cut in?" Eric's lips lifted into a half smirk. The man would not eradicate that facial expression despite Alexander's persistent attempts to make him do so—something Eric had confided in her. No matter, as she wouldn't change a hair on his head, just so long as he stayed.

Alexander's lips tugged up into a half smile. "Only if you give her back."

"I always do." Eric swept her into his arms, earning a small titter from her throat.

"There's enough of me to go around."

"We know." Eric's eyebrows waggled. "Of course, we're going to make you prove that."

"My pleasure."

A glance Alexander's way showed he lacked no company after being let go. Carina Rose grasped his arm. He bowed and took her into a chaste, dancing embrace.

Okay, so perhaps the jealousy would never be too far from her heart. She'd spent far too long without these men. She wasn't about to lose them again—or herself.

Tony's voice drifted to her ears. "Sir, someone is here. Someone not on the guest list."

She had the curious sensation Alexander had stilled, letting go of Carina. Eric stopped dancing at the same time. They glanced at one another, and as if possessing a sixth sense, the two of them joined Alexander.

"Carina, may I interest you in a dance?" Eric bowed to her, and her smile was worth every diamond in the place. And there were a lot of jewels tonight. Eric crooked his elbow toward Carina and nodded at Alexander—a secret message passing between them. That was another thing Rebecca hadn't expected. Eric and Alexander had fallen into a rhythm as if they were two instruments meant to duet. She, as well, found she could spend time with either of them, alone or together. Regardless, whatever form they took felt *right*.

"Everything okay?" she asked Alexander.

His lips pursed as Tony whispered in his ear.

"Rebecca, why don't you get us some champagne? I have something to attend to."

"If you're going to work—"

"No, Marston is here."

Again? "I want to see him." She wasn't sure where those words came from, but they slipped over her tongue, leaving a curious taste, not bitter but not welcoming. Rather, she was curious. Why would he sacrifice his own Christmas Eve to continue to needle them?

Oh. How had she not put the pieces together before now? She grasped Alexander's arm. "Please. It's the Christmas holiday. I think I need to see him."

"He tried to take down this club. I can't let him inside it."

"He has nowhere else to go." It seems this truth thing also had a mind of its own because the idea that perhaps Marston was alone arose so fast her brain couldn't keep up with her mouth.

He took her arm and led her off the dance floor and into the hallway. By the blue blaze of his eyes, he wasn't going to yield easily on this one. "This man tried to blackmail me. This club. And you."

The angry, whispered words only raised more sympathy for Marston, which was ridiculous because why would it? "No, he didn't. He made an offer that I'd have been foolish to refuse back then, despite the fact that it turned out to be wrong. Can you imagine what it was like for him? Having those people as parents? Being gay and seeing what they'd done to Charles? I was his way out."

His brows furrowed. "What?"

"You know his parents … "

"No, I mean being gay."

"I thought you knew. I mean, it was so obvious. In fact, I think he was in love with you. I've always suspected it. I mean, why keep after you all these years except he was frustrated and trying to get your attention?" She shrugged. "I can tell you from experience you're not an easy man to get over."

He shook his head a little as if disbelieving her. "He's not in love with me. He hates me."

"Love and hate are a fine line. Let's go find out." She turned to head down the hallway toward the entranceway, the likeliest place Marston would be.

Alexander's large palm stopped her. "No. I won't let that man near you again."

"It's not me he wants. Never was." The more she talked about it, the more she knew she was right.

A long second passed, his blue eyes assessing her face but not seeing her. He was thinking. "Stay here. Tony." He jerked his chin toward the man who'd hovered behind them. "See she gets back inside." He looked down at her. "Yes, mo rúnsearc. Remember, you're not a prisoner here, but I want you safe when he's in the area. "

Okay, she'd give him that one, but only if he considered her idea that maybe, just maybe, Marston had been attempting to get Alexander's attention all this year, and not to destroy him.

"And you'll consider what I said?" She clasped her hands together at her chest.

He didn't answer. He turned on his heel and headed to the front of the Club.

She inhaled deeply and took Tony's outstretched arm. She'd tried.

∽

As Alexander approached, he noted that Marston stood in the same place he had the last time he'd breached this entranceway, hands in pockets, staring up at the DaVinci line drawing that had once hung in his parent's house.

He didn't turn when Alexander strode in, and he had made no effort to be quiet.

"I've always hated this rendering. Black and white scratchings."

"My gain then."

Marston finally turned. "Oh? Huh." The man swayed a tad. He'd been drinking.

"Not an art fan?" Why was he asking this man anything? Perhaps because Rebecca's words unexpectedly rattled him. "Why are you here, Marston?"

The man shrugged. "Thought I'd wish my ex-wife a Merry Christmas, that's all."

"You have a cell phone."

"Not sure you'd let her talk to me."

Oh, yes, he'd been drinking.

"I don't monitor her calls." Alexander strode forward more. "Rebecca has some strange ideas about you and me."

His brows inched up, and his face reddened a little. "Oh?"

Marston wasn't angry. He was embarrassed. This was beyond peculiar, and suspicion grew. "She thinks you have nowhere else to go." Alexander began to walk a wide circle around the room. "Strange, given you have $200 million to work with. Surely you have friends." He stopped and stared at the man. "Lovers." No way would he let this man go out into the D.C. streets, drunk and unstable. He'd make him walk it off.

"I'm … between things right now."

"What did you expect? You'd come here and find me also 'between things' and needing comfort?" Why not push it a little, take a page out of Eric's playbook. Getting Marston's adrenaline flowing would burn off some liquor. Then he'd throw him out.

Marston scoffed and that red stain across his cheeks blurred to a fire. "I don't need you."

"But you want me?"

The man swallowed too hard for Alexander to discount

what Rebecca had said. She'd been at least half right. Which half, he didn't know.

"Like I said, I don't need you," the man gritted out.

"Wasn't my question."

Marston seemed to regain his ground quickly because a smile spread across his face. "You know, when you first arrived at our house in Connecticut, I knew you were arrogant, but this idea … this … " The man seemed to grasp for words, so why not help him out. It was Christmas after all.

"This idea is true?"

Marston cleared his throat and his face fell into a frustrated scowl. "Do you have any idea what it was like for me after Charles died? Left alone with those two?"

The man didn't need to elaborate on which "two" he referenced. He began to pace, and Alexander found himself in an odd walk about with the man—he on one side of the round portico stepping slowly, Marston on the other, mirroring his movements.

Marston seemed to be in a mood to talk. "The night he died, we had a terrible fight. Mother going on and on about how Charles wouldn't have died if he'd never met you."

"He didn't get sick because of me."

"I know. He'd always been a free spirit. Brave. I knew what he did when he snuck out, starting at age fifteen. Then when he went to school, the constant fights and threats of expulsion. Someone in this family had to balance out his entrenched need to be a black sheep."

His need? "How about he was just being himself?"

"Yeah, well I never got to be that."

Okay, Rebecca's thoughts could be true.

"Being non-normative in this culture hasn't been easy for anyone. Gay, bi, trans or whatever. It's never been easy, Marston. But you like easy, don't you?"

The man stopped. "When is it my turn?"

He was stunned. Rebecca was one hundred percent right. How had he gotten this wrong? "Turn for what?"

The man made a motion like he was going to launch himself at Alexander, and his inner fight mechanism reacted. It was at that moment, Tony stepped inside and grasped Marston's arm before he could get any closer.

"Get off me. It's not you I'm here for."

And, there it was.

"Tony, leave us alone."

The man looked aghast. "Sir?"

"I've got this."

Marston sighed and slumped into a chair. Tony, seeing Marston was drunk and likely harmless, turned away. He wasn't in any danger from Marston. Knowing Tony, he'd frisked the man, seeking weapons, before letting him step foot inside.

He took the chair opposite him. This was beyond strange. "Marston, why don't you just come out with it?"

Was he really going to take this man's confession? He'd reformed people in the past, but a Wynter? Some part of him —likely the part fueled by the goodness of spending so much time with Rebecca and Eric—trumped the part that wanted to throw his ass outside and down the stone steps into the snow.

"Charles wasn't Alice and Raymond's only gay son." Marston's head hit the wall behind him.

"I know." Because now he did know. He rose, and he had no idea why he was about to do what he was about to do. Then again, he did. He didn't throw people out on the street who had nowhere to go, the dead opposite of the Wynter family protocol.

Alexander pinched the bridge of his nose. "Tony is going to come back in here. He's going to show you to a room where you're going to sleep this off. Christmas lunch is at noon."

Alexander got out of there as fast as he could. He had better things to do on Christmas Eve than spend another second in Marston Wynter's presence. But he wasn't cruel. He would never, ever be like them, and he'd prove it.

51

Alexander delivered the news that Marston was spending the night at Accendos to Rebecca and Eric. Her acknowledging smile was worth the strange turn in events. Eric was less enthusiastic but wisely didn't question the why behind his sudden change of heart. He wasn't sure himself, though he supposed the holidays were making him sentimental. They would discuss this latest Marston development later—much later. He had other ideas for tonight.

He held out his elbow. "Ready for your Christmas present?"

"Oh, goody, presents."

Eric took her other arm and laughed. "You are such a princess."

"But I'm *your* princess." She hung on to both men as they made their way to the circular stairway leading up to the gallery. "I rather like two men vying for my attention."

Alexander winked at her. "Of course you do."

As they climbed the stairs, Eric held her long train, the midnight blue fabric embroidered with tiny gold stars. Alexander kept a hold of her hand. With each slow step, he let his gaze occasionally drift over the scene below. People milled about or swung each other on the dance floor. He made a point of picking out the Tribunal Council members, the people closest to him of all the friends wandering about.

Sarah laughed at something Laurent said, as Steffan rested his head on her shoulder, eyes alight on his best friend. Jonathan, with Christiana's back banded to his front, swayed back and forth in time with the music. Derek and Samantha swept over the dance floor, earning applause and exclamations at their dance moves. In the farthest, darkest corner, he could make out Marcos cupping Isabella's chin, whispering to her, earning a shy smile. Carson had London on his lap on a couch. Ryan and Yvette clinked champagne flutes. The man's eyes couldn't have been torn away from his wife's face. Alexander had built this place for them, and it was his greatest privilege that they shared it with him. If he thought about it, his life's work was embodied not by the splendid architecture and award-winning gardens of his estate but by the people who inhabited it and considered it a place of refuge, a safe haven.

His nostalgia broke when Rebecca giggled at getting her dress caught for the tenth time on the railing support.

"Gah. Such a princess," Eric laughed.

Once freed, he tugged Rebecca by the hand across the gallery, and the three of them stepped through the low door into the Master's Private Library.

Rebecca gasped and clapped her hands. A fire already crackled in the fireplace, two leather chairs pointed toward the flames with a small footstool placed between them.

A small Christmas tree stood in the corner lit with tiny white lights that illuminated the old-fashioned tinsel, candy canes and hand-crafted ornaments Rebecca had admired at a Christmas fair they'd visited the other day. It was the damndest thing, but walking around the crowded street fair watching Rebecca squeal over crocheted snowflakes and wax-dipped pine cones had been the best moment of his week.

Her gown whispered over the hardwood floor as she skipped to the tree. She fingered a tiny nutcracker made of hand-carved wood. "You bought them." Her gray eyes beamed love at him.

His heart pressed against his ribs, and he had to take a long inhale before sentimentality overtook him and prevented speech. "For you? Anything."

Rebecca threw her arms around him. "Thank you."

"I'm trying to … simplify."

"It's—" she glanced around "—perfect." And, understated when compared to his previous Christmas décor. Hell, not like him at all.

"Smells like a pine forest in here." Eric laughed.

Alexander had asked his decorating team to string only natural garlands of pine, holly, and juniper along the mantle, windows, and paintings, in this room. Rebecca wanted simple, well, this was as close as he could get. His decorating team had eyed him like he'd been replaced by an alien, but they eventually understood and appeared quite relieved when they'd been given freer rein in other parts of the house.

He gestured for Eric to take a seat in one of the chairs. Rebecca lowered herself to the embroidered footstool, her dress pooling around her, creating a lake of blue and gold between them. He had to chuckle at their faces. Like kids on Christmas morning.

Alexander retrieved two boxes from under the tree. "I decided we needed privacy for this." He handed Rebecca and Eric a long white box tied with a green ribbon.

She took hers, hesitantly. "Hey, did you go over the fifty dollars we agreed upon?" Her eyebrows lifted.

"I did." He settled himself into the chair.

"Good, because so did I." She freed the ribbon and lifted the box top. After cracking open the long, black velvet box inside, her lips parted and her cheeks pinkened. Yes, that's exactly the face he'd been going for with this gift.

"Oh, Alexander. I … " Her lashes, wet with the threat of tears, lifted to reveal her pale gray eyes. Even better, she'd lost her words.

His ego inflated a little at her awe at the piece he'd had designed. A crescent moon of moonstones hung from a platinum chain, and intermittent, diamond-encrusted stars linked every inch of its length.

"So you'll never have to search for the stars." His description was a tad theatrical, but it was Christmas Eve, a time for over-the-top emotions.

She rose up on her knees and crushed her lips to his. "Thank you," she said into his mouth.

"I think she likes it," Eric said.

She eased back down and grasped the Eric's hand, as well as his. "I love it." She then quickly twisted at the waist and lifted her hair. "Put it on me?"

After fastening the necklace on her, her fingers touched the pendant. Still speechless. *Good.*

He watched as Eric open his gift—a bracelet of heavy, flat, platinum links and black diamonds. It was masculine, subdued, and perfect for a man who didn't need flash but required something substantial and as valuable as he was. Opposite the catch, a brushed platinum plate held a message, OURS, bordered in twenty carats of black diamond baguettes. Alexander had considered the word carefully. He'd gone so wrong with this man in so many ways. He wouldn't hurt Eric again, and if Eric had any doubts on that front, he merely had to glance down at his wrist.

Eric examined the links, ran his finger over the engraving in what could be considered a caress and cleared his throat.

His lashes glistened with wet. "Thanks. It's … perfect." He began to return the item to the black velvet box when Alexander stopped him.

"It belongs on you where you can be reminded every day." He held out his hand indicating the bracelet, and Eric placed it in his palm. "Your arm, please." Eric held his left arm out and watched solemnly as Alexander fastened the bracelet around his wrist.

"Let me see," Rebecca murmured. Eric held up his wrist and let her examine Alexander's gift. She applauded softly and giggled. "There. Now you have something to show all those encroaching women—"

"And all those men beating down your door every night," Alexander interjected flatly, letting his lips twitch into a smile.

Eric surprised him by pulling out gifts from a black bag. He handed him a large, heavy, rectangular package. Alexander stripped off the brown paper to reveal an original publication of Audubon's "Birds of America." He blinked, staggered at the beauty and rarity of the book sitting on his lap. He found it difficult to stop petting the Moroccan leather binding. "This was more than fifty dollars, Eric. There are only a few of these in existence. I … thank you."

Eric shrugged. "It came up for auction at Christies. All the proceeds go to a wildlife conservation charity. I thought you'd like that … plus, you know … the bird pictures."

Alexander let his head fall back and laughed softly. "Yes, the bird pictures. I know this had to have sold in the tens of millions. Please let me help."

Eric smirked. "Absolutely not. I'm not left penniless if that's what concerns you. I had a few old paintings moldering away. Their sale easily covered the bird book. And, it seemed fitting that Charles be represented in the room."

Alexander laid his hand on the priceless "bird book" and slowly nodded.

Eric straightened with a broad smile. "Excellent. Now … "

He presented Rebecca with a "magic wand," encrusted with real diamonds, Alexander noted.

Rebecca, not to be outdone, announced she'd booked a trip for the three of them to the Grand Canyon with a promise to show them the star constellations. June, she declared, when they could see something, particularly the star clusters, Cygnus Dark Rift, the Northern Coal Sack, and something called "Prancing Horse." He'd do it, just to see her eyes light up again like they had when describing them.

There wasn't a single place he wanted to be other than here, right now. His body was weightless, his breath even, his mind calm, but most of all, nothing was wrong anywhere in the world—not at that exact moment.

Eric cleared his throat and stood. He strode to a far wall and pulled out a large rectangle in brown paper from behind the curtain.

"Another for Alexander," he explained. "This one was hard to hide from you."

Alexander rose and accepted the package. After tearing off the brown paper, his breath stalled. It was the Gustav Klimt painting he failed to win in Paris seven years ago. He set it against the chair and scrubbed his chin while he studied the rich golds that seemed lit from unseen light. "It's the real deal, isn't it?"

"Yep."

His gaze moved to Eric.

Eric's lips quirked in a half smile. "Because you should always win. You are invincible."

Eric's smirks were growing on him. "It's … " Remarkable? Priceless? Not as much as the man who'd gifted it to him. Eric's green eyes danced with delight in the firelight, and it dawned on him that he had won something far more precious than exquisite art or rare books. He had been chosen. He was loved and he loved in return. The words had to be spoken. "I love you, Eric Morrison."

The man's expression displayed shock. His green eyes blinked, and his head cocked as if not understanding.

"You got it wrong." Alexander half-smiled at Eric's puzzlement. "I did win that Paris auction. I ultimately got you—far more valuable to me than any painting could ever be." The two of them stood there for a long minute.

It was Rebecca who broke the stalemate. "Well, kiss him. Do I have to orchestrate this? Because you'll only accuse me of topping and … "

Somehow Eric's mouth was on his, and the man kissed—hard. He probably should stop the topping move, but, fuck, the man could use his tongue.

Eric pulled back. "Willing. Always."

Willing to take the punishment? Or his love?

Eric answered his silent question. "Love you. Since the first day." His eyes went to the painting and then back to him.

Alexander straightened and nodded. He had more to do. "I have one more present for you both." He reached into his suit jacket pocket and pulled out a piece of paper. He handed it to Rebecca. "Read it. Aloud."

She took it, her fingers sliding into the tri-folded paper. "I, Alexander Rockingham, hereby resign my—" Her eyes darted up to him. "Alexander, you … "

"Keep reading."

She cleared her throat. "Resign my position as Grand Arbiter of the Tribunal Council. Sarah Claire Marillioux will replace … " She stopped, her throat clogged. She peered up at him. "But you can't. I mean, retirement?"

He laid his hand on hers. "No. I can and I will. I've spent my life making sure people are taken care of. It's time to take care of those who matter the most." He lifted his eyes to take in Eric, eyes shining, his blond good looks paling in comparison to his selfless heart.

Alexander took Rebecca's hand. "It has taken me forty years to realize something. People say a broken heart can kill, but I know it's the secrets that will take you down. I've held more people's confidences, pain, and regrets, than I care to know. It's time to start building something new." He drew in a long breath and sat back. "Of course, I'm going to suck at retirement."

Eric's laughter cracked the shock off her face. "Did Alexander just say suck?"

"Careful, or I'll make you do it."

He cocked his head. "With pleasure." He stared directly into Alexander's eyes, daring him, or perhaps waiting for permission.

"Eric, help Rebecca off with her gown."

Her eyes grew as round as the moonstones around her neck, alight in the firelight, but her smile—the one he'd spend his life ensuring she always wore—lifted her cheeks.

Eric rose from his chair and held out his hand to her. "A queen deserves attendants."

As does a king. "Slowly, Eric." Alexander leaned back in his chair. "I want to watch you both."

And watch he would. He would watch, and enjoy, and protect them both for the rest of his days under a shared, new purpose—loving.

EPILOGUE

Alexander lifted his face into the bright early spring. Alice's grave was now a barely visible mound under a sheen of green sprouting up from recent rains. He lifted the sledgehammer, rested an end in each palm. He assessed the trumpet over Alice's grave. One strike and it'd be dust.

He didn't have the time—or inclination.

"So, Alice." He sighed heavily into the air ripe with the promise of another spring rain. He sent his gaze upward, as suddenly words seemed to be lost in his brain.

Rebecca would know what to say. Eric, too, but the two of them were inside the house greeting the new residents, youth who had nowhere else to go, at least until now.

He resettled his gaze on Alice Wynter's headstone. "Once, you gave me a life purpose spawned in hatred. I have a different purpose now, one inspired by love. Here. You keep this … " He dropped the sledgehammer on her grave. "Consider yourself erased." At least from his life.

The wet stone pathway was slick, and he stepped carefully toward Charles' new headstone, a bright, blue-gray, granite with his full name carved in large letters.

CHARLES DURHAM WYNTER
BELOVED PARTNER AND FRIEND
JULY 12, 1959 - JUNE 8, 1981

He brushed debris off the ledge with his hand. "Hello, Charles." Damned emotion clogged his throat. Would he ever be through with it? For long minutes, he drank in each letter while a brown thrasher sang its song in a nearby tree.

He coughed, an attempt to dislodge the words he knew he needed to say. "You may not see me for a while. I'll stop by when I can, but you won't be lonely. I promise you. This estate is a half-way house now—for anyone who needs it. People like you, me, Rebecca ... and Eric. You'd love him. In fact, I'm not sure I'd trust you two together." He laughed a little at that thought. "Check that. I know I wouldn't."

A flash of red caught his eye. A cardinal flitted from stone to stone, cocking its head right and then left. A sign, perhaps? He'd leave those to Rebecca.

"They have strict instructions to keep the bird feeders stocked." Alexander scrubbed his neck. "And, you'll never be forgotten. Not ever." Fucking tears. "I promise. And I always, always keep my promises. You'll never be far from me. Not ever."

His whole life had been designed around one thing—to never again feel the kind of loss he'd once been forced to endure. But a great loss can never be overcome, one can only learn to live with it. He'd live with Charles' memory, poignant and treasured.

Time was his most precious resource, and while he was proud of his life, he'd still squandered too much of it trying to shoehorn justice into something that, quite frankly, would never change—the past.

No more.

He felt his jacket pocket for the photograph of him,

Rebecca and Charles from so long ago. He'd had half a mind to leave it here. He couldn't bear the thought. He was keeping it, a memento of a time that, while no more, would remain cherished.

He then placed his hand on the granite, and after one, long, last read of the headstone, turned away.

Somewhere between Charles' grave and the stone archway leading out, the past released its hold on him. It was the damndest feeling, as if the hooks within uncurled and slid right out.

It felt like peace.

∾

If you loved INVINCIBLE, you'll love all the Elite Doms' books.
Visit your favorite online retailer or visit Elizabeth's Web site at www.ElizabethSaFleur to view them all.

~~~

Get ready for Elizabeth's latest books, the **Shakedown Series** where ex-cons and ex-gangsters find love, redemption and justice at the high-end burlesque club, Shakedown.

The introductory novella, **SHAKEDOWN**, is available today at all major online retailers.

Rachel's lying, embezzling ex-fiancé Trick Masters shows up three years after stealing all her money. How dare he show his face. How dare he spit out all those accusations at her about being set up. How dare he show up looking so … so *hot*.